A Little Bit of Hellion

Ladies Who Dare
Book Four

Tanya Wilde

ARE YOU SIGNED UP FOR DRAGONBLADE'S BLOG?

You'll get the latest news and information on exclusive giveaways, exclusive excerpts, coming releases, sales, free books, cover reveals and more.

Check out our complete list of authors, too!

No spam, no junk. That's a promise!

Sign Up Here

www.dragonbladepublishing.com

Dearest Reader;

Thank you for your support of a small press. At Dragonblade Publishing, we strive to bring you the highest quality Historical Romance from some of the best authors in the business. Without your support, there is no 'us', so we sincerely hope you adore these stories and find some new favorite authors along the way.

Happy Reading!

CEO, Dragonblade Publishing

Additional Dragonblade books by
Author Tanya Wilde

Ladies Who Dare Series
Almost a Scoundrel (Book 1)
By No Means a Gentleman (Book 2)
A Knave By Any Other Name (Book 3)
A Little Bit of Hellion (Book 4)

Chapter One

THEODOSIA KING, SISTER of the current Marquess of Kingsley, stared at the man before her and studied the pearls of sweat that dotted the line of his brow, one drop trickling down the side of his cheek. The man's nervous laughter as he dabbed his handkerchief along his face reminded her of a timorous actor who forgot his lines in a Shakespearean play.

The Earl of Saville was to blame for this. Her once unperturbed life was in shambles.

Because of him.

And his friends, it must be said, but most of all him. *He* was the reason her mother had started hosting what she disturbingly called "blind matchups." Every morning—unless she escaped before her mother seized hold of her—she would be stationed in the blue drawing room while her mother and Aunt Rose, her father's only sister, selected King-approved suitors from the receiving room, allowing them each fifteen minutes in which the men could display their peacock feathers and do a little social dance in the hope of attracting her interest—chaperoned by her trusted maid, Nancy, of course.

She loathed *every* second of *every* matchup.

She resented her mother's strange mind.

And she hated the Earl of Saville.

Most especially today.

Even if the earl hadn't been directly responsible for these matchups, he'd still poked at the sorest of the sore spots when he'd claimed, on that horrid heiress list—the one that listed each woman's assets and drawbacks—that she had Satan's eyes. To make matters even more dreadful, he and his friends had given the whole of White's good entertainment when they'd lost the list and it had found its way into the club's betting book. The result had been predictable. Wagers about the heiresses and how quickly each one would be successfully wooed spilled over the book's pages, luring all sorts of wretched creatures to her drawing room.

All in all, an unpleasant reminder of her place in the world. She hadn't liked the Earl of Saville to begin with. Not since the first time they had been introduced in her first season, and he'd visibly flinched when their eyes met. The man was arrogant, pompous, and *rude*. And now he, *they* believed to be her biggest flaw . . .

Theodosia had thought she'd gotten over the incident from her childhood, but that man had brought everything back to the surface with that one comment. Reminding her—no, *taunting* her—that she could never escape the judgment of others. What was it that her governess had once said?

Ah, yes.

How unfortunate. With eyes like that, you must be cursed, girl. Best lower your gaze when suitors come calling one day.

Theodosia inwardly scoffed. In truth, she couldn't quite recall the woman's exact wording, but it had been something to that effect. Lower her gaze, she'd been advised.

What nonsense. It had never been in Theodosia's nature to lower her gaze. Instead, she made a point to look a man dead in the eyes—like she had done with the Earl of Saville—and their discomfort be damned.

The result? Nine times out of ten brought about the flustering, sweaty mess before her. Lord Chance. Would that this had been the only count against him.

He'd also been late. How long did it take to walk from one drawing room to another? In his case, an entire cup of tea. That had been the first count against him.

The second point against had come in the form of kissing the back of her hand upon their greeting. His mouth hovered not one, not two, but three moments too long. Must the man cling to her hand?

"Do you like tea, Lady Theodosia?"

Ah, small chatter. Smallest of the small. Irrelevant. Unnecessary. A waste of her breath. Another mark against.

What sort of question was that anyway? Did she like tea? Would she be drinking tea if she did not like it? Does anyone in England not like tea? She didn't bother to reply, merely took a sip from her cup in answer.

A small but purposeful belch slipped from her lips, and she bit the inside of her lip to keep from laughing when his eyes widened. "Oh, my apologies. The gasses in my body oftentimes demand release in the most inconvenient moments."

He stared at her without blinking.

She tilted her head back, matching his stare.

"You . . . that . . ." He cleared his throat. "Inconvenient gasses should be left for more convenient settings."

Is that so?

And *this* was the man Mama selected as a possible match. She loved her mother, but she sometimes wondered if the marchioness had any sense in her head. Her mother ought to have been able to tell with one glance this man would never do. He even wore the colors of a peacock. A green waistcoat adorned with a striking blue tailcoat.

Theodosia considered the man across from her, deciding to conclude this meeting ahead of the fifteen-minute mark. "Do you wish to marry me, my lord?"

Lord Chance sputtered on air. A true feat. "M-Marriage? N-no, I wouldn't say that. I mean that is too early to speak of such m-matters."

"Why is it too early to speak of such matters?" Theodosia arched a not-so-subtle brow. "You are calling on me, are you not? If you do not know if you wish to marry me because it's still too early to decide, may I then help facilitate this decision?"

"I beg your pardon?"

"Lord Chance." She set her cup down and leaned forward in her seat. "Would you enjoy a wife who is outspoken, stubborn to the bone, has a temper, hates dancing, loves bickering, and has no problem when it comes to insulting the opposite sex?"

His eyes had turned to saucers that grew with each trait she listed. By the time she said "loves bickering" the man had already jumped to his feet. "Quite right, quite right. I cannot see myself with such a . . . such an unconventional wife."

Theodosia dipped her head. A resolute nod meant to encourage him to scamper away. She fell back onto the divan even before he'd cleared the room, shooting him a sweet smile when he glanced over his shoulder before hurrying off. How many more? She'd already entertained five lords today.

Five!

Her mother breezed into the room. "What did you say to that poor man? He rushed out of the house as though the devil was on his heels."

Theodosia gave her mother a deadpan look. "Perhaps the devil *was* on his heels."

"Oh, bah, if you are referring to that dreadful reference to your eyes, please stop. Your eyes are beautiful. It's your temperament that needs working on."

"I quite like my temperament as it is."

Her mother scoffed. "That is no reason to frighten your suitors away."

"That 'poor' man sweat all over the sofa," Theodosia said without lifting her head. "Plus, we both agreed, we are not suited for each other."

"Was no one to your liking then?" her mother asked. "You must marry, Theodosia. If your brothers return and you have not so much as a suitor—"

"I have many suitors."

"An active suitor," the marchioness corrected, "one that you are genuinely considering, then they will find one for you. You know how they are."

Theodosia sat up. "Mama, if that is the case then there is only one other option left for me."

The countess cut her a curious look. "What is it now?"

"I wish to retire to Brighton for the season."

"Brighton? Why?"

A myriad of reasons. These blinds matchups, for one. For another, Theodosia had the stolen betting book in her bedchamber, hidden amongst all her bonnets. She also had an annoying tail—Saville. She wanted to escape him most. He'd been following her all over town, showing up at events she attended, and generally getting in her way. And then there were her brothers. Lord knew what they would do when they discovered all that had been happening in London while they were away on business.

And then there were the men of the *ton* as a group. Their faces annoyed her. Their smiles. Their gestures. Urgh! Nothing seemed sincere anymore this season. The sea air sounded like just the thing she needed. The country life. Peace. Calm. She didn't want to deal with the men of London anymore. Not this season.

But she couldn't confess all *that* to her mother.

"Aunt Crystal is there, is she not? After everything that has transpired—"

"You mean making copies of the betting book of White's and distributing it at the Stewart Ball in a spectacular fashion and causing a scandal? Those events?"

Well, her mother never was one to mince words. "Yes, exactly that," Theodosia admitted. And so much more. "Have you not wanted me to retire since the list of heiresses appeared?"

"Yes, after the scandal of the copies being spread by your hand, when it seemed you were skirting the edges of ruin. Now, with the blind matchup meetings, I believe you'll be sure to find a husband in no time and secure your spot in society before any more scandals erupt."

"Mama, if Lord Chance is any indication of my prospects this season, then I'm afraid the next scandal will blossom in this very drawing room in the form of some truly magnificent rumors as I scare each lord witless with my strong-willed temperament that would make me a most inconvenient wife."

Her mother gave her a flat look. "You do make an exceedingly exasperating, yet valid point."

"See, it is best to retire to Brighton, Mama. And those hellion brothers of mine are going to raise hell when they return. I'd rather not bear the brunt of their rage."

"There is that . . ." her mother murmured, tapping her chin. The marchioness suddenly lifted a brow. "Are you sure you are not running away from a certain earl?"

Theodosia shot upright. She . . . "You know about him?"

"Of course," the marchioness said. "I am your mother. I know much more than you imagine."

Theodosia cocked her head to the side. She wasn't sure if she should be more amused or afraid. "What exactly do you know, Mama?"

Her mother shrugged. "I've heard some birds chirp that this certain earl feels guilty for his part in the list and that he and the others responsible have chosen to protect the heiresses as much as they can."

Just who *was* her mother's source? "Well, that is quite impressive."

Her mother's smile turned sweet as sugar. "I am impressive, dear. And perhaps you are right. Retiring to Brighton might not be the worst idea while the dust of the season settles here. Especially for Seth's sake. Once he learns about this season's events, I believe he shall require a moment to cool his temper. You know how protective he has been since your father's death."

Protective? More like infuriating. However, it was true that

Seth had been under immense pressure the past year as he took over and began managing the full duties of their estates. He'd even decided to forgo the season and tour all of their properties. In fact, all of her older brothers had decided to attend estate matters rather high-handedly all over England—much to the vexation of her mother. At least some of them were still at school most of the time.

But they would all return home—sooner rather than later—and she would prefer not to be here when they did. As her mother said, it was best to allow their tempers to cool once they discovered the events of the season. "Then it's settled," Theodosia rose. "I won't entertain callers anymore today, Mama. I'm done with them since they are a moot point now. I will go pack for my trip."

Her mother sighed. "Very well. I shall not stop you. After all, there was a time I ran away from your father, as well."

What? Where did *that* come from? "I have so many questions, Mama, but first and foremost, our situations are different, do you not think?"

"You are running away, are you not?"

"Even if I call this running away—which I am not—it's not from a man." It was from several.

If she were running away. But this was simply a tactical retreat. For peace. Period.

The marchioness arched a brow. "If you say so, dear."

"I do say so, Mama."

Her mother chuckled. "Do not be vexed with me, Theodosia. I have your best interest at heart, after all."

Theodosia eyed her mother thoughtfully. "Why *did* you run away from father?"

"All women run away," she smiled. "Whether they realize it or not."

"How cryptic."

"You shall understand one day, dear. I do so look forward to that day."

"We shall see," Theodosia murmured, not quite certain how to respond to that. "About your sons . . ."

"Leave your brothers to me. I have worked hard enough to keep them in the dark about their sister dressing up as a man and distributing copies of the betting book, not to mention that Turkish trousers parade."

"Mama." Theodosia sent her mother A Look. "Do not think I don't know about *your* Turkish trousers."

The marchioness let out a small chuckle. "Ah, well, they are comfortable, are they not? Your brothers will absolutely hate them."

"All the more reason for me to make haste for Brighton."

She would leave first thing tomorrow.

⇻⇺

"FIELD!"

Field Savage, the Earl of Saville, flinched as his sister slammed into his study, causing his ears to ring.

Christ, what now?

"What's the problem? I'm leaving within the hour. I don't have time for theatrics." He had a minx to catch up with.

Selena came to a halt, startled, and then exploded, "Theatrics! You will see theatrics in a moment if you don't get beneath your desk!"

Beneath his desk? Was this another trick to inflict misery on him? Had destroying his waistcoats and his portrait not been enough? His eyes caught on her robe. "Why are you flaunting Warrick's robe in broad daylight again?"

"It's comfortable."

"Well, it's deuced uncomfortable for me. You are betrothed, yet you act like damn newlyweds." He tried to ignore their displays of affection as much as possible, but his eyes hurt whenever he saw them flaunting convention.

"In our hearts we *are* newlyweds." She flashed him a grin before it once more disappeared. "But that is not the issue at hand. You need to hide!"

Field cast her a suspicious look. "Why?"

"The King brothers are here. Well, four of them." She came around his desk. "There is no time—get under the desk."

The King brothers? Why the hell would he hide from them? "Let them come."

"Do you want to die today?"

Why would he die? "I'm not afraid of them, and they have no reason to kill me."

"Are you sure? And do you think reason matters at a time like this? Warrick is leading them over as we speak."

Just whose house was this anyway? "How do you even know this?"

"We happened to be on our way to the dining room when they crowded into the foyer, demanding an audience. Warrick went to save your hide."

"And you rushed here?"

"Of course, the moment it became clear they wouldn't leave. You are after all, my dearest brother."

"Why not bundle them into a drawing room?" Field grumbled.

"Don't look at me like that. They were being difficult. The last thing I overhead was the marquess insisting that the study is the only place where men should talk business."

"I am *not* hiding!"

"And what if they make it difficult for you to leave London?" Selena asked. "What if they follow you? There is no telling how a meeting might end if you lose your temper."

"Fine, damn it." He would do it, but only because he wanted a seamless departure and had no wish to be delayed. He hunched down and crawled under his desk, a big solid mahogany desk that would shield him from the view of anyone who entered. Selena crawled in after him.

What are you doing, he mouthed.

I'm hiding, too, she mouthed back.

The pad of footsteps followed seconds later, "Make yourselves comfortable," the Earl of Warrick said as they entered the room.

Field imagined the Kings piling into his study, their eyes ablaze with the fire of whatever they wish to confront him on. He cursed them in his head. Even if they were out for blood, why should he hide in his own damn house?

"We're fine," one of the brothers said, Seth King, the Marquess of Kingsley. The man had a low drawl, a cadence that could only belong to the one in charge of the group. "I'll be brief. Where is Saville? We have questions for him."

"I'm afraid he is out. You can direct any questions to me."

"Do you always speak for your friend?" the marquess asked.

"As his brother-in-law, yes, I can speak in his stead."

"I see," the man said. "You married Lady Selena. Congratulations." More soft, almost reluctant murmurs of congratulations filled the air.

"Thank you."

Field snorted. *You haven't married her yet, you damn blackguard.* He shot his sister a hot look. She smiled back at him.

"Now let's get to the point, shall we?" Warrick continued. "What questions do you have?"

Yes, let's get to the point so I can leave.

"I've heard rumors. Rumors I don't like."

"You will have to be more specific than that, Kingsley," Warrick said. "There are hundreds of rumors going around town these days."

"Your brother-in-law has been pestering my sister."

Field took offense at that word. Pestering? What rubbish was this? He'd been keeping an eye on her to protect her. Granted, from a mess he had a hand in causing, but that was him taking responsibility for his mistake.

"Pestering? Are you sure? I haven't heard such a rumor,"

Warrick responded. "Saville may be many things, but he is not a pest."

Thank you very much.

"What would you call following her around like a lost puppy—"

Lost puppy? More offense!

"—and showing up at our house uninvited, giving my sister gifts?"

"Fair point," Warrick said. "I can't answer to that."

Field furrowed his brows. Were they griping about a simple birthday gift? They hadn't said anything about the heiress list or the wagers, but he didn't believe these brothers hadn't already ferreted out the truth. Perhaps they were testing the waters before they made their move. And why the hell was he hiding beneath his desk again? The space was cramped, especially with Selena hunkering with him.

Deuced embarrassing.

"I'll be frank," Warrick said. "What is it you hope to gain from calling on Saville today? A few rumors are hardly something to get riled up over."

Good, redirect the conversation.

"There are enough rumors for us to want his head," another voice snapped.

There was a short pause, then Field's ears perked up once more. "We want to confirm whether he has designs on our sister." The marquess again.

He did not. But what did it matter to them anyway?

"What happens if he has designs on your sister?" Warrick asked, an unmistakable hint of curiosity woven within his question.

Why would this blackguard even ask this?

"Then I will politely warn him to lose them."

Field pulled a face. *Politely my arse.* But he did lose something then and there, his damn patience. A hand clamped down on his arm. His sister shook her head. Only then did Field realize he had moved to crawl out from under the desk.

A silent curse rattled in his head as he settled back with a scowl.

"And what if he doesn't?" Warrick pressed. "Does your sister not have a say in this? She might even enjoy his designs."

"I'd still caution him to keep his distance. We know about the book, and we don't want our sister to get caught up with a man with no scruples. We shall protect her in any way possible."

Field inwardly scoffed. No scruples? He had many scruples.

"Your sister might not share your view or welcome your meddling. I speak from experience."

Field shot a glare at Warrick through the wooden furniture separating them. While his meddling in Selena and Warrick's "courtship" hadn't been accepted with a smile in any shape or form, Lady Theodosia might just bask in her brother's. After all, she had helped his sister cut up his waistcoats and turn his portrait into a devil. And hadn't Selena said Lady Theodosia had called him a weed? A. Weed. He'd certainly been called worse in his life, but nothing had ever stung like that one word.

How did I sire a son like you? What a waste you are.

Field dragged a hand through his hair.

Those taunting words had bothered him for a long while now. However, it was hard to dismiss them while he was hiding beneath his own desk. He'd damn well failed. He'd failed his sister. He'd failed the women on the list. He'd failed himself.

A horrid feeling if he'd ever felt one.

He wanted to rid himself of it.

"Our sister will follow the directive of her family, so tell Saville to stay from any and all Kings."

"This is bullshit," another brother said. "She has already been caught up with him. I say we put a hole in his heart and be done with it. I demand satisfaction."

"Then why not demand it from me, too?" Warrick asked. "I, Deerhurst, and Avondale are just as responsible for what happened as Saville is."

"Then you are openly admitting you are the cause of this chaos?"

"We had a hand in it," Warrick admitted. "However, we did not draft the list."

"There are other rumors, too," the marquess announced.

Fields frowned deepened. It seemed they were finally getting to the true point.

"Ah, and what rumors are those?" Warrick echoed his thoughts.

"Rumors about my sister and Saville," Kingsley said. "Rumors that they are engaged. Our sister might have fled London because of this."

Come again? Rumors about *what*?

What utter drivel! This was the first time he had heard anything about any such rumors!

Field paused. Though if true, this might very well be a part of why she suddenly decided to leave.

"That rumor can be cleared up by asking your sister," Warrick said. "I suggest you do that."

"And we will ask her, but first we want to ask with Saville directly."

A light scoff. "That's why we want his head."

"Warrick," the marquess said, "you know as well as I do that one rumor is all it takes to damn a woman as spoiled goods. There are several whispers of our sister about town. All with a thread back to Saville."

"Then you want him to take responsibility?" Warrick asked, and Field could just imagine him crossing his arms over his chest. "I cannot see what else you hope to gain from this."

"Clarity," the marquess replied. "While, our family connections are strong, and many would not dare speak ill of Theodosia, they have their limits. And I cannot control the narrative from a place of darkness. I also have a duty as the head of this family to make sure she's not been hurt or used in any way, but this engagement rumor needs to be addressed as soon as possible."

Well, they agreed on that score.

"Very well then, do you want me to inform Saville of your grievances, or will you wait for his return?"

Field bared his teeth in Warrick's direction. Why give them the bloody choice? *Chase them off!*

"Neither, but he can expect another visit soon."

"Of course."

The light thud of the men's footsteps leaving faded from the room, and Field motioned for Selena to crawl out from under the desk the moment they cleared his study. He followed her, muttering, "Damn Kings," as he stretched out his limbs.

Selena brushed a tendril of hair from her face. "Thank goodness they didn't suspect us. Lord, I have newfound sympathy for Theodosia." She turned to him. "They warned you to stay away from their sister. Are you going to listen?"

Listen? Field scoffed. "Who the hell are they to tell me what to do?" His gaze fell on the large portrait of himself leaning against the wall off to left. He had moved the painting from the drawing room to his study after it had been mutilated by his sister and her friend. Lady Theodosia was apparently responsible for the rouge on his cheeks and coloring his eyes black. They turned him into a damn she-devil!

Warrick strode over. "Cavendish is the best art restorer in London."

He scowled. Best or not, could it even be repaired at this point? What remarkable feat that the King pups hadn't commented on the masterpiece. But then, perhaps they couldn't see much else except their own anger. They were looking for answers. Well, so was he. He was going to hunt that little minx down and demand restitution.

"I'm leaving on the hour," Field announced.

"I don't think that is a wise choice," Warrick murmured, arching a brow.

Field glanced at his friend, his scowl deepening. "Are you warning me away too?"

"That's not what Warrick meant," Selena spoke up. "I have the same concern as well. Perhaps it is best to keep your distance from Lady Theodosia."

"Why?" Field demanded. "What concern, pray tell, do you have?"

She shrugged. "I'm just afraid this time you might really die."

Field's face contorted. "Are you referring to the time you failed to kill me in a duel?"

"You know I am a perfect shot," Selena said.

"So, you keep saying," Field muttered.

"And so are her brothers," Selena said pointedly. "Why are you so dead set on chasing Theodosia down?" she asked.

"Retribution." Field sent his sister a heated look. "You should know all about that, should you not?"

"*That* is your reason?"

Field never claimed to be perfect. Or forgiving.

"We are just worried," Warrick said, settling an arm over Selena's shoulder and pulling her close. "Are you sure retribution is the only reason you are giving chase? The Kings won't hold back if you make a mistake."

Mistake?

Everything leading up to this damn point had been mistake after mistake. He couldn't go back in time and change the list of heiresses back to its original form, though he had tried to make amends, atone for his mistakes by having them protect as many heiresses as they could. But it seemed that was just another deuced mistake. In the grand scheme, he couldn't see that following her now could even make his list of mistakes.

"The chit cut up my waistcoats and helped you turn me into a devil. Would you not demand payment? And what is this engagement rumor? I don't agree with King on many things, but I must address this rumor." And he couldn't do that without her.

His friend's arched brow inched a fraction higher, but Field refused to read into what that slight lift might mean.

He simply wanted answers.

There was no other reason he was chasing that minx across the country.

No other reason at all. Definitely not proving to her, or himself, that he was not the weed she claimed him to be.

Chapter Two

H ER BROTHERS OUGHT *to have returned to London by now.*
Well, most of them.

Theodosia slapped the book in her lap shut and wondered whether Seth would chase after her. If he was already home, hopefully her mother was keeping him in London in some way or other.

The marchioness was good at that.

Of all her brothers, he was the most difficult one to anticipate. Unpredictable in most ways, yet still entirely predictable in others. But it was still hard to guess what he would do when he learned of the list, the wagers, and everything else. In any event, she'd taken a different route from usual, just in case, and had stayed in a quaint little village for a night with her lady's maid, Nancy, and the driver, Thomas. And wouldn't you know, just the act of leaving London had washed away the tension that had been building in her body this entire season.

Ah, bliss.

No blind matchups.

No talk about wagers and fortune hunters.

No Saville.

And certainly, no addition of six demanding brothers who could only find satisfaction through constantly badgering her. She loved those big ruffians, but they could be a touch much at times.

Especially when so many of them were home at the same time.

"Whoa!"

Theodosia scrunched her brows at the sudden call of the driver. She glanced at Nancy, who lifted her shoulders in a small shrug.

The carriage drew to a slow halt, and Theodosia peered through the window, but couldn't see anything out of the ordinary.

"Why on earth did we stop?"

"Perhaps there is an obstruction barring the road, my lady," Nancy said.

The gallop of hooves approached, and she rapped on the roof, calling to the Thomas, "What's the matter?"

"Ah," he murmured, shortly pausing before hesitation filled his voice, "it seems the Earl of Saville hailed us down."

The *who* did *what*? "Keep going," Theodosia commanded. Why in Heaven's name had he followed her? And how had that devil even found her?

"My lady?"

"Keep on going, Thomas." Just because he had followed her—and even found her—didn't mean she had to accommodate him. "That man has no business with me."

"Now that is not a very nice thing to say," a low, raspy voice came from outside.

Theodosia grit her teeth. She rapped on the roof again. "Ignore him and leave."

The door wrenched open, and a disheveled head popped in. The head glanced at her maid. "Can I have moment with your lady?"

"No, you may not," Theodosia said with a lift of her chin. "Stay put, Nancy."

"If Nancy stays put, then—"

"Then what?" Theodosia interrupted, wanting to roll her eyes to the carriage ceiling. "Will you carry me out of the carriage to get your way?"

"I . . ." He blinked. "What do you take me for? A mongrel?"

"Well? What should you say, then?" She sent him an arch look.

His clenched, but he still bit out, *"Please."*

A small bud of interest began to form. In truth, she was a bit curious and still rather shocked that the earl had chased her all this way. Theodosia nodded to her maid. Best to find out his motives and get this over with so the man could be on his way. Saville stepped aside for Nancy to pass, then took her place and shut the door with a resounding slam.

"So," Theodosia crossed her arms over her chest, "what are you doing here? I cannot believe you followed me from London."

"Believe it, my lady." His eyes bore into her. "For I am here."

"How did you even know—" She suddenly cut off. "Selena."

He didn't deny it.

"And just how did you find me on this route?" She matched his stare. "Don't tell me you had someone spy on me? Or is it just that you can't seem to stay away from me? I must have some great power of attraction for you to cling to me like this."

"Spy? What am I—a scorned husband? A lovelorn lord?"

Theodosia arched a brow.

He pulled a face. "I followed you, yes, but it's quite by accident I caught up to you on this road."

"You expect me to believe that?"

That already intense stare intensified further. "Upon my honor, it is true."

She studied him, and then sighed. "What do you want, my lord? Speak up so that I can get this unpleasant interruption of my journey behind me."

He didn't hold back. "You missed quite a lot happening in England over the last few days. Selena and Warrick are betrothed."

Theodosia started. *"What?* How on earth did that happen?"

"How could it not?" Saville retorted. He sounded thoroughly put out. "They've been having an affair behind my back." He rubbed his temple "Then we got kidnapped and she and Mortimer saved us."

What on earth? "Selena saved you? And Mortimer, the duke? Why didn't she tell me anything?" She had missed all that?

"Knowing my sister, she probably didn't wish to bother you since you decided to leave London."

How aggravating! "I have so many questions."

His eyes narrowed, his complete focus directed at her. "I also have several."

"Is that why you followed me? Because you have questions?" Theodosia had to hand it to the man, he had gall.

"I've followed you for less reason than that."

A pertinent instance. "How chivalrous of you to remind me. Then go on, what is your first question?" The sooner she answered them the sooner she could remove him from her sight.

His gaze burned into her. This should be good.

"Did you call me a weed?"

Her mouth threatened to drop open. Of all the things . . . Selena must have told him so in another of their bickering matches. But just how much *had* her friend blurted out?

"Nothing to say?" He settled back into the cushions. "Am I to take that as a yes, you *did* call me a weed?"

Confounding man. "It's not that I have nothing to say." And it wasn't that she hadn't called him a weed—she just couldn't recall. Had she called him a weed? She had called him lots of things over the season. A weed might very well have been one of them.

She shrugged. "So, what if I did? Is it not a compliment? Weeds do not perish easily."

"Weeds tarnish all the other plant growth."

She grinned at him. "So you do understand. Next question."

A vein in his jaw flared up. "Why did you snip up my waist-coats?"

Well. "To be fair, I did not snip up all of them. Only some. Your sister took scissors to the rest. But to answer your question,

Selena said it would feel rewarding, so I wanted to try." And it was a most rewarding memory. "I must admit, it did feel like heaven."

The corner of his lip lifted in a sneer. "What about the rouge you used to color my cheeks on a damn expensive painting of me?" He clenched and unclenched a hand. "And you made my eyes black."

"Pure revenge," Theodosia admitted. "Did you not call me Satan? I was curious to see how Satan's eyes would look on you."

His face contorted. "Damn it, I never called you Satan."

"Was that not implied when you said I have Satan's eyes?" Theodosia cast a venomous look his way. "And do not even think to deny it. Avondale told Ophelia, and Ophelia told me."

"Very well, I deserved the eyes. Did I deserve the pink cheeks?"

"That was for my own satisfaction."

"And cutting up my waistcoats? What would you call that?"

"Double the pleasure?" Theodosia couldn't help but taunt. "Would you like an apology? Because I can apologize, but I'm sure I will not mean it."

"Did I ask for a bloody apology?"

"Do you have any more questions," she countered, "or are you done? If you are done, please make haste back to London."

"I'm not done." He crossed his arms over his chest. "I demand restitution."

Theodosia stared at the man in disbelief. "Who do you think you are to demand restitution from me? Have you lost all your senses? Shall I help you search for them?"

"Don't be tart, Lady Theodosia." He leaned a bit forward. "But while we are on the subject, who am I to you?"

What sort of question was this? "Who you are to me does not matter as much as how you make me feel."

"And how do I make you feel?"

"You make my skin crawl."

That vein in his jaw flared up again. "In a good way or a bad way?"

"Is there a good way for such a thing to occur? My skin crawls when I see you. My skin is crawling right now. I assure you, it's not a pleasant feeling."

"It can be." He rested his elbows on his knees. "If it's really anticipation."

Shivers raced over the bumps of her arms. *Not* shivers of anticipation. She drew back to gain some distance between them. "Your signals must be getting tangled, Saville. It's called repulsion, not anticipation."

"Your eyes say otherwise."

"My Satan eyes? Are you even sure you can read them?"

"I'll ignore the first, but I will say I've never been wrong about these things before. You do not find me repulsive."

Fine. She didn't. No exactly. But she still didn't like him. That should be clear. So, what exactly did this man want from her? "You are making my head spin."

"In a—"

"*Not* in a good way," Theodosia snapped. Her palms stung from her fingernails digging into them. "You, my lord, are a hellion. Hellions belong in London. You should promptly return to your habitat."

"Harsh," he shot back with a scowl.

"But the truth."

"Is this what you think of me? That I'm a weed. A rogue? A weedlike scoundrel?"

"A said hellion."

"Are they not the damn same?"

"Yes, but hellion as the word hell in it, which is what my life has turned into since you entered the fray."

The furrow between his brow deepened. Two lines that always seemed to split his face when with her. He tugged at his cravat. "You certainly have a knack for ruining the mood."

"I don't know what mood *you* are in, but I doubt we have been on the same page at any point. No, we aren't even in the same book. So please, I beg you, get out of my carriage before I do or say something we both might regret."

"There are tons of regrets already," he muttered, almost too low for her to hear. "Well, this is certainly the first time I've been kicked out of a woman's carriage so boldly."

"If it's payment you want . . ." She pulled a smaller pouch from her reticule filled with coins and tossed it at him. "There you go. It should be enough to cover the cost to your waistcoats and your portrait."

"I don't want your blunt." He tossed the pouch back to her with a foul expression. "There is something else we must discuss."

"Oh?"

"Your brothers paid me a visit."

That caught her attention. "Which brothers? And why would they call on you?"

"The marquess and three others. As to the why, they wanted to warn me away from you, of course."

Her head tilted to the side. Well, it didn't surprise her all that much. "And you didn't even think to heed their warning?"

"Never crossed my mind." He gave a remorseless shrug. "They also want my head."

"I've wanted your head plenty of times. You still have it."

"This is different. This is about a new rumor circulating about town."

Theodosia paused. "That doesn't sound good."

"It's not," he admitted. "It's horrific."

"Well, tell me what it is!"

"It's . . ."—he dragged a hand through his hair—"that we are secretly engaged."

"*What?*"

"That was my same sentiment," Saville said bitterly.

Theodosia blinked that the man, then burst out laughing. "You are right, that *is* horrific." She clutched at her belly. "Who on earth would start a rumor such as this?"

"How the hell should I know?" He eyed her askance. "It's not *that* funny."

Theodosia took several deep breaths to calm herself. "Ah, well, I'm sure the rumor will die down shortly."

"Your brothers also seem to believe that this rumor is the cause of you running off to Brighton. I want you to pen them a note telling them that I am innocent of all their claims and they have nothing to worry about. I want them off my arse."

"And what if I don't?" She crossed her arms.

"Then I shall follow you until you do, as I am reluctant to return home under the threat of multiple Kings wanting my head without clarification on matters."

Hah! "Do you want me to give clarification on *all* matters?"

"No need." He picked at the seams of his sleeves. "Just about the rumors of an engagement and that I am the reason you are taking to the waters in Brighton." His eyes bore into hers. "Or *am* I the reason?"

Oh, wouldn't you love to be the reason, you rogue? She'd rather gnaw on a piece of bone than give him the satisfaction of ever answering in the affirmative. "Rest assured, you didn't even make the list of reasons. As you must know by now, my brothers are a rowdy bunch, hotheaded, and annoying as hot summer sun glowing on your skin."

"An apt description. Be sure to put that in the note as well." He paused, considering her. "But that's hardly a reason to leave London."

"Those hellions live to provoke my temper," Theodosia said. *Much like you.* "I'm afraid my brothers will push me to choose a husband, and given this absurd new rumor, who knows what they might do now?" She'd made a good decision by leaving town.

He inclined his head. "I can understand why they would."

"Oh, you can now, can you?"

"I have a sister, too."

"And how did attempting to marry her off to Warrick work

out for you?"

"To be fair, they are engaged now, so it worked."

"If they are engaged, they are so because your sister chose Warrick as a partner and they must have feelings for each other, not because of anything you did, I assure you."

"Such a harsh tongue you have, Lady Theodosia."

She was about to answer when they were interrupted by a deep voice coming from outside.

"This is the Black Knight. And you are hereby being held up."

FIELD'S LAST WEEK had been hell. Hell on a scale he had never experienced before in his life. Not even his childhood memories of his father topped this, and that had been true fire and brimstone.

In no particular order, he'd been held captive in a damn brothel, had to watch his best friend and his sister flirt right in front of his eyes, *and* his own sister shot him in a duel. Not even to mention being called a weed, having all his waistcoats cut up, and his painting being turned into a devil.

And now highwaymen?

"God, this is not happening right now."

Of all the near-death experiences he'd navigated so far, was this one to be his end? On a dirt road in the middle of nowhere? He glanced at Lady Theodosia. And with her, the one woman who drove him damn near to insanity? They had never been on good terms to begin with, and he couldn't say their relationship had improved since they were first introduced. Not that he had tried. And not that his recent deeds had helped.

It wasn't that he didn't like Lady Theodosia. This had nothing to do with like or dislike and everything to do with the fire that exploded in his chest whenever their gazes locked. If he could, he wished to avoid that feeling, and yet every step, every decision seemed only to bring him face to face with it—with her—again. But surely even Heaven had been mocking him these past weeks.

Perhaps he should have heeded Kingsley's warning.

But bloody hell, he couldn't accept that she found him repulsive. He just couldn't.

"Are we being robbed?" she hissed softly.

He placed a finger on his lips to indicate that she should remain quiet. Would it be possible to convince the highwaymen he was alone? Well, he could try.

"Who the hell are you?" Field called out. "Away with you. I'm not in the mood to be robbed today."

Lady Theodosia pinched his leg, her eyes filling with question marks. Field shot her a warning look. *Don't fuss.*

She returned a warning look of her own. *Then don't say anything idiotic.*

Outside, a bark of laughter met his statement. "That's the attitude you take before the most infamous highwayman in England. How interesting. This has never happened to me before."

"Well, then," Field shot back, "we have something in common. This has never happened to me, either. What highwayman announces himself in such a fashion? The Black Knight, you said? I've never heard of you. How bloody famous can you be?"

"You've not been held up by many highwaymen before, have you?" The Black Knight's voice held a hint of edge. "Or else you would know arrogance has no place in in those being robbed."

"Fair point," Field begrudgingly muttered through clenched teeth.

"And, you cannot dispute," the highwayman went on, "you've heard about me now."

Was the man in a romantic relationship with his image? Field pulled his lip upward.

"I shall be gracious today and give you three seconds to exit your carriage," came the condescending voice.

Field's lip pulled up in a sneer. "Gracious my arse."

"One."

"Saville!" Lady Theodosia hissed in a barely audible whisper, though her eyes bellowed obscenities at him.

Hell and damnation.

"Two."

She stomped on his foot.

"Fine, I'm coming, I'm coming," he muttered, reaching for the door. *Stay here*, he mouthed to Lady Theodosia. It was wild hope, but a chance he would take if it meant her safety.

She cut him a look designed to peel his hide before whispering, "You think I'm just going to sit here and await my fate?"

"The lady, too," the man called as if reading his mind.

Field cursed.

Confound it! All his wild hope dashed.

He wrenched open the door and stepped from the carriage, turning to help Lady Theodosia down. She refused his hand. He didn't bother to insist but kept her shielded from the highwaymen's greedy eyes as much as possible.

Before them stood a man on horse flanked by six riders. Tension crackled the air. *Danger*, his head bellowed at all the nerves in his limbs. All but his eyebrows and mouth, which remained arched and loose.

They cut seven imposing figures, and yet none of the men moved from atop their horses. He instantly noticed Dream, his thoroughbred—now in their hands—and inwardly cursed. That was his best horse.

"Nancy!" Lady Theodosia suddenly called out and motioned her lady's maid over to them.

Nancy glanced at the highwayman, who shook his head, and she retreated a few steps farther away from her mistress, making her stance clear.

"*Nancy?*" Lady Theodosia sounded just as shocked as Field felt. "What are you doing?"

Nancy averted her gaze, saying nothing. The driver was also not looking at them, his back straight as he looked ahead.

Field sighed.

So that's how it is.

"I believe they are betraying you," Field said, his pure loathing directed at the two servants. "Is this the part where we hand over our baubles?" Field said with a dry calm he was not feeling.

"No need."

No need? He didn't need to wait long to find out what the man meant.

"I hear that the lady doesn't wear bits and baubles, but she does carry hefty money pouches. If you can toss them over, I'd be much obliged. No one has to get hurt today."

Lady Theodosia tossed a pouch over without protest.

The Black Knight didn't so much as glance at the pouch, only arched a brow. "I heard the lady travels with more than one pouch."

An elbow nudged Field, followed by a low whisper, "Should we run?"

"I'd love to," Field tossed back, "but can we *out*run?"

"So pessimistic" She rummaged through her netted purse, which she'd brought along outside, and three more money pounces flew over while a sharp glare was flung to the maid.

The Black Knight grinned. "Much obliged." His gaze turned to Field. "You too, my lord."

Field gritted his teeth and tossed over all the coin he had on him, then motioned to Dream. "You already have the rest."

The highwayman tipped his hat.

Field scowled while Nancy scampered to collect the money pouches before retreating into the carriage. The driver flicked the reins and all they could do was watch it drive away. Usually, he could find even a slight silver lining in any nightmarish event, yet he could not locate even the slightest of slightly silver threads as he watched the man in question send them a parting smile.

The Black Knight tipped his hat. "A good day to you."

Was leaving them in the middle of the road *not* harming them? Damn blackguard. "Forgive me if we don't say the same."

A chuckle.

One by one they turned to follow the carriage. Not one of the men looked back at them has they followed the carriage, but each did tip their hat.

Field clenched his fists.

Were they mocking them?

"What the hell just happened?" he muttered to himself. Were all hold ups so structured? He turned to Lady Theodosia, half expecting her to collapse in fright. Instead, two black coals shot fire at him. "Are you . . . all right?"

"This is your fault."

Field started. "How is this my fault?"

She jabbed a finger at him. "You brought those highwaymen here with your twisted luck."

"How am I responsible for this? *Your* servants betrayed you. Just how did you come to hire such poor candidates for servants?"

"*I* did not hire them," she shot back.

"But you did end up traveling with two betrayers. Could you not have chosen your traveling partners better? Why blame me?"

"No one expects to be betrayed like this."

Field swallowed his biting retort. Arguing over the matter solved nothing even though he wanted to shout and rage. What if she had been alone today? Would the outcome still have been the same?

He balled his hands into fists before slowly unclenching them. He didn't even want to think about what might have happened. "Fine. Let's not argue over this."

They both averted their gazes.

"Those dratted traitors. How could they be involved in such a plot?" She gave him a reluctant glance and sighed. "I'm sorry. This was not your fault."

"No need to apologize. We both had a shock."

She nodded. "What do we do now? We have no money and no carriage. All my belongings. My—" Her head snapped back. "*The book.*"

A bad feeling formed in the pit of Field's stomach. "What book?"

Her head swung to him. "The *betting* book."

"You mean the betting of White's is in the carriage the highwaymen absconded with?"

"Yes!"

Of all the things . . . why was this happening to him? "Mortimer is going to kill me."

"Why? Did something else happen that I don't know about?"

Field shut his eyes.

Yes, something had happened.

Something that told him their shared sojourn through hell had only just started.

Chapter Three

THEODOSIA HAD NEVER been so flabbergasted and, quite frankly, so penniless in her life. And now not only was she caught off guard and pauperized, but she was also stuck and stranded with this man—her eyes flicked over him—the waistcoatless Earl of Saville. A man she despised above all.

Selena Savage! I should never have let you plant the seed of leaving London.

But she couldn't blame her friend—not really. She had willingly allowed that seedling to grow, driven by all the reasons that escaping the season was a good idea. And it would have been, had everything gone to plan.

"Let me see if I have this right. The secret women's club your sister wished to join with all her heart and soul is a suspected criminal mob, and the betting book of White's, the one we heiresses nabbed, the very book that is stowed in my carriage, the very carriage that those ruffians absconded with, is part of the *evidence* that is needed to bring this suspected mob crew to justice?"

"A succinct way of putting it, but yes. That is correct, yes."

"And you are only telling me this *now*?" Could he not have started with this instead of lamenting over weeds and nonsense?

"Was there a better time than this? It's not like we could have hidden the book in our pockets. Also, it was not the first thing that came to mind when we met."

She curled her lip. "No, I suppose it wasn't."

"We should send for Mortimer as soon as possible."

"Send for the duke? No! We need to get that book back!" She refused to be the one responsible for such a tragic event as losing that precious evidence.

"That is why we need to send for the duke."

"And what is he going to do? Hunt the highwaymen down? The book was entrusted to me. No heiress has lost it yet, and I shall not be the first!"

"Strictly speaking, the book has already been lost."

She shook her head. "No, if we do nothing it will be lost. We can't waste time waiting for help." Then the book might well and truly never be found again.

Theodosia surveyed her surroundings, struggling to distinguish their location. The dirt path stretched on endlessly with no village in sight on the horizon. Nothing looked familiar. Not the fields surrounding them. Not the trees scattered across the landscape.

Drat. She should never have altered her route.

The sound of birds chirping overhead drew Theodosia's gaze to the sky. Darkened clouds gathered overhead.

Double drat. Their rotten luck continued.

"What exactly do you propose we do?"

"What else? We need to get the book back ourselves."

"You want *us* to hunt down those bandits?" Saville asked incredulously. "A lady and an earl? We are not equipped for this sort of adventure."

Theodosia cast him a bitter look. "I can't tell if you are being self-aware or self-depreciating."

"I am stating a damn fact, you vexing woman. They are outlaws. Dangerous. Armed. It would be tantamount to suicide to confront them."

"Unless we *don't* confront them. And now that you mention it, they weren't pointing pistols at us." She looked at him, suddenly aghast. "Dear Lord, did we just get robbed by unarmed highwaymen?"

"Unarmed or not, we were still outnumbered. And just because they weren't waving pistols at us doesn't mean they don't have them."

"Fine, you are right," Theodosia conceded. No good came from arguing with the devil. But she wouldn't have lost evidence on her conscience. "You do what you want. I shall do what I need." She started to march in the direction of the highwaymen had left, the same direction she had been heading initially, but down a lane that branched off the man road a few steps ahead.

"Where the hell are you going?"

Theodosia kept her eyes firmly fixed on the path. "Why should I respond when you already know the answer?"

A foul curse was followed by the crunch of footsteps gaining on her.

"Tell me this," he said. "What will you do when you find them? Negotiate for the book? You have nothing to negotiate with."

"I have the promise of more blunt."

"And what if they don't want more blunt? What if they want *you*?"

"Must you be so dramatic?" Though, the man had a point. The Black Knight seemed like an opportunistic fellow, yes, but also a complicated one. "Who says I plan to negotiate with them?"

"If not, what?"

She arched a brow, and he read it accurately, matching her look with an expressionless one of his own.

"You plan steal it back."

"Is that not the best course of action? They stole from us, so we shall steal from them."

"We must find them first."

"Them or the carriage. The book is in a hidden compartment behind the seat. Nancy doesn't know about that, neither does she know she know about the book. All we need to do is find my carriage."

"They are probably going to pick it apart."

"Which is why we must hurry."

"Damn it, I don't know about this. What if we are caught?"

"Don't be such a pessimist, Saville. Do you want your horse back or not?"

He hesitated, just as she thought he might.

"We can escape on your horse," Theodosia went on. "As plans go, I won't deny it's a bit vague—find highwaymen, retrieve book, escape on horseback—but a plan is a plan. It is better than doing nothing at all."

"Fine," Saville grumbled. "We will try it your way. But if any danger presents itself, we abort the plan and alert the authorities. We should alert them anyway."

"You can send word to the local watchmen and the duke once we arrive at a village. Waiting for help is not an option. As you said, the highwaymen could pick apart the carriage at any time. Or sell it, and then the book might be as good as dust." Theodosia started walking again. She hadn't taken three steps before a voice boomed.

"Bloody hell! What the devil are you wearing?"

"You're only noticing my fabulous Turkish trousers *now*?" Theodosia shot over her shoulder.

"Fabulous is *not* what I would call them, and I had other things on my mind."

"What would you call them, then?"

"A damn nuisance to society."

Well, then mission accomplished, she supposed. She didn't bother asking what else was on this mind. Since the moment he'd caught up with her today, all he'd wanted was answers to silly questions, and she wasn't about to invite more.

Foolish man.

"A nuisance for you or not, I for one am rather glad I wore them," Theodosia remarked. "They do come in handy at times like these. Dresses restrain our movement too much."

"You are not supposed to move much, are you? You should leave all the moving to us men."

Theodosia favored him with a particularly annoyed look. "Speak for yourself, not for someone else, especially if that someone else is a woman." She pointed at the field to her left. "Do you even know where we are?"

"I'm not overly familiar with these parts, but there should be a town about an hour away if I am not mistaken."

"An hour's walk or an hour on horseback?"

Another expressionless look. "Horseback."

All right then.

They would walk until their feet bled if that was what it took, or they could hail down passersby if they were lucky. However, the highwaymen were still on horseback. "Do you think the villagers know who the bandits are? Will they point us in their direction if they do?"

"Would you if you were a villager?"

Fair question. "We don't have many options."

"We can certainly probe, but don't get your hopes up. Folk in the country won't speak if they are afraid of the Black Knight's retribution. If he even is as infamous as he claims."

Theodosia bit back a smile as the last of his sentence turned into a grumble. To be fair, the bandit had been exceedingly arrogant, and she hadn't heard of him, either. But whether he was known or simply boastful, it didn't alter her determination.

"I shan't stop until I find that blasted ruffian," she declared, her face set. She didn't care about the coin. Heiress or not, money could always be earned back. But his cocky grin? She wanted to wipe it off his criminal face.

"There is a reason why these brigands are hard to catch."

"Well, they haven't been hunted by me yet."

"I have nothing to say to that. I don't want to say anything to that. I'm just going to pretend I never heard that."

"That's well and good. I enjoy walking in silence, anyway."

Theodosia didn't have to look at him to know his lip was curling up in a sneer. There was no denying this simple fact: she and Saville did not get along. They never would. But as loath as she was to admit it, she needed to get the book back and perhaps some of her belongings, if possible. And she needed his help to do it.

Because her knees were a bit wobbly. Though she might probably appear unaffected in the earl's eyes, she only pretended to be untouched. Those men and the betrayal of her servants had given her a fright. And that feeling had yet to leave her body.

She peeked at Saville. His face resembled a thundercloud, almost like the ones gathering overhead. Yet two faint lines of concern gathered between his brows, as well. One could easily mistake them for a scowl, but for this man, and having experienced all sorts of scowls from him, they were too shallow to be mistaken for that.

He'd been rattled, too.

She almost laughed out loud but was grateful she was able to stifle the urge, certain it would come out in hysterical peals. Well, weren't they two peas in a pod? Neither of them wanting to reveal just how shaken they were by the ordeal. Perhaps they were more alike than she had first thought. And even though the man was mostly infuriating, he had tried his best to protect her.

What am I to do with you, Saville?

But for the first time since she met the earl, she was glad he was by her side.

Three hours later

HIS FEET HURT. His belly growled. And his annoyance stirred more with each silent second. They'd been walking for what felt like days and days. As much as Field wanted to throttle Lady Theodosia for being stubborn and insisting on traipsing after those brigands, he had gone along with her plan to steal the book back simply because, yes, they did need to get the book back.

That much they agreed on.

It was perhaps the only thing they agreed on. The method . . . *that* he didn't agree on. Let Mortimer and his watchmen hunt the highwaymen down. The duke, at least, had the determination and the people to do it. They were just a lady and an earl. He inwardly scoffed. Again. Self-awareness was a good thing. However, if there was one woman in England that might match Mortimer's determination, it was Lady Theodosia. Each step spoke to her sense of purpose, and she had known just which of his weak spots to jab.

Dream.

His horse was the true reason he had put one foot before the other for the past three hours. Nevertheless, no matter how much he went along with her plan, no matter how much he wanted the book back, too, their own safety, their *lives*, were the most important. The Black Knight might try to seem like an honorable criminal, but that was just a mask he wore. A criminal was a criminal.

"What if we took the wrong path?" Lady Theodosia asked as she gestured toward the ground. "I can't see the imprints of carriage wheels anymore."

Ah yes. Earlier they had come to a crossroads and followed the tracks of the carriage—the only tracks he could see—down another road that led away from the town he'd had in his mind to stop at.

But a certain lady had insisted.

And those trousers?

His eyes kept being drawn to the soft flow of the material as she walked, as though they were beckoning him with their gentle allure. *A nuisance, I tell you! A nuisance!* There was a reason woman ought not to wear trousers. Field supposed he was lucky that they weren't tightly fit, like the trousers the women had worn the night of the Stewart ball. That would have driven him crazy.

"Wait, I see something." She gestured to a spot off in the distance. He followed her line of sight. "See? Houses. This must be a village." Her footsteps picked up the pace. "Come, let us hurry."

Field didn't complain. He could do with a bath, a good pot of stew, and a few hours of sleep. His gaze dropped to her slippers. Her heels were dragging more than they had earlier. "You should pick up your feet."

"What do you think I'm doing?" came her mocking retort. "Would I be moving forward were I not?"

"You are dragging them too much."

"Would I even be walking if I dragged them?" she shot back. A moment later, one of her legs wobbled as she stepped into a wheel rut.

"Ah!"

Field cursed and reached to catch her around the waist. "I told you, you are dragging your feet too much. Are you all right?"

She gripped his arm. "Damn it."

He arched a brow. "Such words coming from a lady's mouth."

"And what words should come out of my mouth? You swear all the time." Her face contorted, and she patted his arm. "Let me sit. I think I hurt my ankle."

Field helped her lower down, hunkering before her, as she inspected her ankle.

"It's not swelling."

Field sighed in relief. "These slippers aren't ideal for walking the distance we've covered."

"What else should I have worn? It's not like I woke up knowing today was the day I'd be held up by highwaymen and then walk hours on end so I'd better put on boots."

Field almost rolled his eyes heavenward. For a moment, he had forgotten what a viper she could be when she opened her mouth. Why was he even worried about the woman? *Don't react. She's hurt.* "The village off yonder isn't far. I'll carry you."

"I'd rather perish."

His temper sparked. "You think I wouldn't also rather perish than carry a minx like you?"

"Then why offer in the first place?" she snapped.

"I was just trying to do what any *gentleman* would do for a damsel." Christ. He was forever trying to do what was right and forever getting it wrong.

"I am *not* a damsel."

"Says the damsel damseling on the ground."

"You are so infuriating." She scrambled to her feet, a slight flinch the only evidence she might still feel any pain. Field slowly rose with her, ready to act should she stumble on something. But he needn't have worried. Stubbornness could heal even the sorest of ankles, it seemed.

They continued to the village, and he also very stubbornly, if a bit reluctantly, ignored the limp in her gait. What should he care? She'd rather die than be carried by him anyway. And he'd rather . . . damn woman. Making him say things he didn't mean.

One step. Two steps. Three steps.

One limp. Two limps. Three limps.

Field cursed.

He couldn't take it anymore. He stepped into her path without looking at her and lowered to his haunches before her. "Get on."

"What are you doing?"

"Get on my back. I'll carry you."

"Didn't I say that I—"

"Yes, yes, you'd rather perish than be carried by me." He glanced over his shoulder with a challenge in his eyes. "But I'd not be carrying you. You'd be clinging to my back. There is a difference."

"And you think *those* words will change my mind?"

He rested one hand on the ground for balance, half turning to her. "Would you rather die than cling to my back as well?"

"Are you purposely trying to provoke me?"

"Yes," he snapped back. "But also, I've changed my mind. I'd much rather perish than watch you limp a moment longer. By the time you hobble into the village, darkness will have already descended."

"Then it seems we are at an impasse. You would rather die than see me limp and I'd rather die than touch you in any sort of way."

"Is that so? And what about your ankle? Do you have no care for your poor limb? It needs rest or it will swell."

"It shall survive, as shall I."

"I daresay it will. But what if it hinders your great, vague plan of stealing back the book? What if your ankle is the reason we can't execute that plan and lose Mortimer's evidence to bring a band of criminals to justice? Would you rather perish than risk all of that? Just because you'd rather die than accept help?"

She glared at him. "I've never met a man more infuriating and animated in his responses than you."

"Are you getting on or not?" Field asked. His legs were starting to burn. "You can let me carry you or limp your way to the village, but if you choose the latter and anything goes wrong, don't you dare cast the blame at me."

Field glimpsed the struggle within her.

A muscle ticked in her jaw. A sight rarely beheld in a lady. But then, Lady Theodosia had never been an ordinary one. The way she looked now, the trousers, the shirt, the jacket, the long cascading hair, she could easily be mistaken for many things other than a lady. Only the poise of her shoulders, that haughty lift of her chin, and the firmness in her gaze spoke of a goddess born into the upper ranks of society.

And just why did it feel as though he was holding his breath? He purposefully exhaled a puff of air. Yet for some reason, her choice—would she agree or not?—seemed to carry the destiny of the world in the balance.

What in the blazes are you thinking now, Field?

"Fine," she stepped up to him, albeit a bit grudgingly. "I

might still die, but I shall take the chance. For the sake of my ankle and for the sake of our plan."

Field gave a curt nod, slowly letting out his breath. "For the sake of your ankle and the plan," he agreed.

Her hands circled his neck as she climbed onto his back, and he hooked his arms around her legs, rising to his feet. Ah, Christ, his feet. They pricked and burned from being hunkered down for so long.

No matter, they'd arrive at the village soon.

"You were right," Field said as started toward the village again. "These trousers are good for something." A dress would not have worked, and he was sure she would have allowed him to carry her no other way.

"See, I told you," her voice came at his ear. Ripples, shivers, and all sorts of chills swept down to his toes.

Field held back a grunt, trying not to focus on the soft body on his back. The scent of sweet flowers cloaked him.

"I am not too heavy, am I?"

"Light as a feather."

"Liar."

He chuckled. She wasn't heavy and she wasn't light as a feather, but he knew better than to make a comment on a woman's weight.

By the time they reached the village, sweat beaded his brow, steady drops trickling down his jawline with each step. However, every drop carried with it the satisfaction of a hero saving a damsel in need.

"You can put me down now," her soft voice tickled into his ear. "Before you collapse with me on your back."

Field slowly lowered her to her feet. "How is it?"

"Much better, thank you." She stretched out her limbs, testing her ankle as she surveyed the landscape. "Why is this town so. . . empty? There is not a soul outside. Are they all inside?"

Field agreed that something did seem odd here. He studied the decrepit buildings as they ventured down the main street. Not one building had a window. They weren't even stone houses, but wooden structures that spoke of a life that had already passed on to the next. "There is no one here."

"How can that be?"

"This place is deserted, and by the looks of it, it has been for a long time."

They had just stumbled upon an abandoned village.

Chapter Four

THEODOSIA NEVER THOUGHT her pride could throb more than her ankle while being carried like a monkey on this man's back. How mortifying. The only reason she'd allowed that travesty was because her ankle stung. That was all. Her ankle hurt and it was welcome relief from pain.

But her head spun with questions. How could things have gone so horribly wrong? How could there not be a person in sight? How could there be a forsaken village? Were there more servants like Nancy and the driver in their household? If her mother decided to travel to Brighton tomorrow, would she also fall prey to the Black Knight? All these worries churned in her mind, transferring the throb of pain from her ankle to her temples.

She plopped down on a patch of grass and inspected her foot again. Still no swelling. A relief.

Her gaze shifted to Saville, stretching out his limbs.

Would she *ever* be free of this man?

Strangely, he cut a rather dashing figure with his jacket flung aside, wearing nothing but a shirt, beeches, and dust-covered pair of Hessian boots. How maddening. She wanted him gone, yet her eyes quite enjoyed the sight.

It made no sense, these feelings mired in opposition. It made even less sense that she could still feel her front pressed against his hard back. Carrying her all this way had been a truly impressive feat.

The man infuriated her like no other. And she'd already had her fair share of infuriation with all the blind matchups her mother had subjected her to over the past weeks. Yet she couldn't help but be glad—a *tiny*, extremely small bit glad—that she hadn't been alone when robbed by her own servants. Once again, she had been used for others' benefit and disregarded when she had nothing to offer anymore. She absolutely loathed the feeling.

Only this fool hadn't left her.

He turned to her, and their gazes locked. A little shock shot through her spine, and she promptly averted her gaze. The crunch of boots on the ground made her ears twitch. A moment later, he dropped down beside her.

Well, for better or worse, there was no escaping him now. She had done her best in London—she had left London. Yet here he was, in all his rogue glory, and she was *stuck* with him. The fact settled into her bones.

The Earl of Saville.

A man that kept popping back up near her no matter how many times she tried to root him out. Weedy indeed. *Should I just stop plucking already?*

A shadow suddenly cast over her as he leaned toward her, closer, too close. He gestured to her foot. "Does it still hurt?"

Theodosia wiggled her ankle. "Just a little bit. The pain has almost subsided."

"That's good. I don't think it's sprained." He reached for her ankle, and Theodosia swatted his hand away.

"Don't you dare poke my foot."

His hand snapped back, and he cleared his throat. "My apologies."

"It was just a slight misstep—of course it's not sprained." She inched her trouser leg down. "The brief respite from walking helped." *Thank you*, she silently sent his way, though there was no way she would voice those two words aloud.

"So long as I don't have to carry you anymore."

Her gaze swung to his. "What *exactly* are you implying with such a disgruntled tone?"

"You are mistaken if you take offense. I am merely saying my feet hurt." He peeked her way. "And I'd hate to see you perish, after all."

Theodosia snorted and pulled a face at him. The man must always have the last word. However vexing it was, though, it didn't irk her like, say, the bumble and bluster of all her blind matches. A sudden thought occurred to her, and she raked him with her gaze from head to boot. How would he compare in other ways?

She held out her arm. "Kiss my hand, Saville."

He eyed darted at her with shock and suspicion. "Whatever for?"

She shook her wrist impatiently. "I want to test something."

"Do I really have to?"

She stared at him.

"Fine," he muttered, clasping her hand in his with great reluctance. "If I must."

"Yes, you must."

He said nothing, just raising them to her mouth, placing his lips against her gloved hand. Softly. Gently. Barely.

Then he dropped her hand like a hot iron poker.

"There. Done."

She shook her hand. Rude man. However, the kiss hadn't annoyed her as Lord Chance's lingering touch had.

Odd.

Theodosia scrunched her brows and rose to her feet, dusting off her backside. She surveyed the old houses. None looked occupied, and none looked fit to be occupied, quite frankly. "What should we do now? Should we continue on? I doubt those brigands would be hiding here."

"No," he agreed, then angled his head to the sky and cursed. "It's going to rain soon."

"I suppose we could shelter here. An abandoned roof is better than no roof at all." The temperature would drop as well. "We can make a fire."

"Yes," he drawled with a razor-sharp edge to his tone. Theodosia tensed. *Here comes a blurt of sarcasm.* "We can make a fire in a half-crumbled fireplace. And burn what's left of this village down to the ground."

Urgh. "It will be raining."

"And yet I'm not confident it could rain hard enough or long enough to prevent such a fire from setting the town aflame."

Must he always be so snippy? It was merely a suggestion. "I'm happy with that if you burn along with it."

"I'm sure you would love to see me burn." He plucked at an odd-looking plant. "Like the weed I am."

She huffed out a breath. This again.

A raindrop landed on her cheek. Theodosia followed its trail up to the sky. "Well, we must find shelter anyhow. Perhaps we can ferret out something to eat as well." She rubbed her belly. "Can you go hunt us a rabbit?"

He rose as well. "With what exactly do you want me to hunt a rabbit?"

Her gaze dropped to his hands.

"Do I look like I grew up on rural farmland?"

She arched a brow. "At the moment, you do sort of resemble a farmhand." At his stormy look, she lifted her hands in surrender. "I know, I know. No fire and no cooked rabbit."

"Can you even roast a rabbit?" he shot back. "I certainly can't."

Before she could retort, a shout drew their attention to a distant field. Theodosia was pulled by a strong urge and she hurried as quickly as she could go to the nearest dwelling to hide. Saville followed her.

"The highwaymen?" Theodosia asked in a low whisper once they'd rounded the house. Her heart started to pound in her breast.

"I'm not sure." He peeked around the corner. A soft curse. "Not highwaymen, thank God. There seems to be a farm over yonder."

"So farmers?"

"They don't look like any farmers I've ever met."

"Really?" Theodosia murmured, suddenly interested. "Then what do they look like?"

"Suspicious." He cut her a look "And don't sound so damn intrigued."

"Why shouldn't I be?"

"These people could be dangerous. They may not be highwaymen, but the Black Knight and his gang seemed quite comfortable around here. These people could easily be in league with them. And your intrigue sets my teeth on edge."

She peeked over his shoulder to get a look of the group of men in the field a short distance away from a simple farmhouse. To the side of it, there was a stable, too. True, it all appeared big and somewhat rough looking—structures and people alike—but nothing that unusual. There was even an older man and woman among them. "How can you say they look suspicious? They look like ordinary people of the countryside to me."

He shook his head. "Then why did I catch a glimpse of a pistol tucked into one of the men's trousers?"

"Given that there is an infamous band of brigands in the area, is that truly so shocking?"

"Then if this is a normal farm, where are the livestock? I don't see any. It's suspect."

"Dear Lord, have you always been this suspicious of people? Perhaps they don't farm with animals."

"Then where are the crops?" Stormy eyes met hers. "And when there is a female in the mix, then yes, I'm careful."

It was clear he wasn't referring to the gray-haired woman in the field. So he was being cautious because of her? It shouldn't have set her pulse aflutter, but it did. "Oh, well, even if they are suspicious characters, we don't have anything to steal. Perhaps they can even offer us—"

"Don't even think about approaching them," he cut off her sentence. "We don't know who they are, which makes the entire situation too unpredictable, which makes it dangerous."

"Because they seem suspicious?"

"No," Saville said. "Because I can't protect you if they are not good people. I'd much rather we keep you out of sight lest *you* get stolen."

"That will never—"

A finger pressed on her lips. "Do you really wish to take the chance, Lady Theodosia? What will happen if you are harmed in any way? How am I going to explain that to your brothers? They might as well kill me."

It's true they had been remarkably lucky with the highway-men. "What about food? They have food."

"Short bursts of hunger are a good thing for the body."

"Speak for yourself," Theodosia grumbled. As her belly emptied, her annoyance levels rose. And her belly was now very empty indeed. Her gaze caught on a tree in the near distance. She stabbed a finger toward it. "That's an apple tree, is it not?"

His gaze flicked between the farmhouse, the people busy on the property, and the tree. "No."

"It's going to rain soon, and we need to eat. Who knows how long we will be stuck here." She looked at him. "We can't make fire, and we won't be eating rabbit. Apples seem to be our only option. If you get us some apples, I shall obediently wait for you inside this house." She patted the wooden wall.

He cast her a look that was rife with suspicion. "Why don't I believe you?"

She fluttered her lashes at him. "I promise."

He clenched his jaw while his eyes lit up with one unspoken curse after the other. "Fine, I'll go pick apples." He motioned to the door. "*After* you go inside and stay out of sight."

"Very well. And get a few, all right?" Theodosia didn't tarry any longer, and entered the house.

Dust covered every surface, and the smell of dirt tickled her nose, but there was a roof that would provide a shield from the rain. She padded over to the window—really just a hole in the wall—and peeked through. She immediately found Saville's tall figure and he strode, upright and confident, to the tree.

The people on the farm had noticed him, but for a few brief glances, paid him no mind.

See, they don't seem to be rabble-rousers.

Not dangerous at all.

Her gaze returned to Saville. He had his jacket laid out on the ground and dropped apples onto it one by one. Something fluttered in her heart, and her eyes narrowed on the broad-shouldered man.

He was the true danger.

SAVILLE DIDN'T KNOW what had possessed him to leave London, a vague thought that now exploded to the surface with a vengeance. He'd never picked a damn apple in his life. Now he was picking apples for a chit who would probably bemoan that he hadn't picked more, or that he hadn't picked fast enough Or, God forbid, that he hadn't plucked each one gently enough.

Where to even put all the apples?

He tossed his jacket on the grass and dropped the apples there. Six should be enough, shouldn't they? He wouldn't eat more than two. Even though his stomach clamored for food, there were only so many apples a man could eat.

He nodded at his handiwork.

Gathering the jacket-wrapped apples into his arms, he cast a glance at the farmland. It made him uneasy. He hadn't been exaggerating when he said they didn't look like any farmers or farmhands he'd ever seen. It looked more like they were patrolling the property than anything else, and given what fate had already tossed at them as well as the proximity of the house, it would be best if they made their way quickly to the next town. The only problem with that was that Field didn't know where the hell they were. Was there even a next town? Unless they returned the way they came, he had lost all sense of direction.

He angled his face to the clouds as scattered drops of rain finally turned to a soft drizzle.

No, leaving was not an option.

This was what he got for trying to be helpful. Trying to do the *right* thing.

Come on man, following the woman was not *the* right *thing.*

Fine. He was just a man with flaws. Deep flaws. He couldn't make sense of it either.

Field had, by all reason and by all madness, been questioning his choices ever since this season had begun all the way up to now where he found himself alone and defenseless with Lady Theodosia on the road somewhere between London and Brighton. He couldn't deny the pettiness of some of his actions. And others had been driven by pure selfishness. Though most had been out of a sense of duty and protection.

But following Lady Theodosia to demand she tell him why she'd helped his sister cut up his waistcoats and color his eyes black? Was that duty and protection?

No.

If he had to reflect on the *why* of his choices—why he had to hunt her down to demand answers—the first thought, his first defense, was that he had nothing else to do and he could not take watching his best friend and his sister flaunt their improper relationship.

Yes, that was right.

It had nothing to do with Lady Theodosia herself. She served as a mere excuse to escape his household which had turned into a den of scandal. An excuse, he was well aware, that lacked in substance, since he himself failed to fully understand his profound urge to question her about her little deeds. He could only describe it as madness.

Unexplainable madness.

Not a pleasant thing. It made frustration wrap around him like vines twisting up the rail of a balcony. Though he supposed *that* was nothing new. The emotion had settled into his life like property tax. He could not rid himself of it. He could only manage it and hope he managed it effectively.

With one last glance at the farm, he hurried back to the dwelling, relieved to see the minx had stayed true to her word. Yet this same compliance made him suspicious. "Since when are you this obedient?"

She glanced over to him. "What you mistake for obedience is preservation of energy while waiting for my food."

He placed the jacket with apples before her feet, retrieving one for himself. "Apples are not food."

"They are better than nothing."

His belly agreed. Field bit into his apple and promptly made a face.

Sour.

He curled his lip. But like she said, an apple was better than nothing, so a sour apple was better than no apple at all. And she didn't complain either as she bit into hers. She also didn't comment on his reaction.

Very suspicious.

And Saints preserve him! Did all women look so enticing biting into an apple? Her tongue darted out to lap up the juice of the apple. Field grimaced and wrenched his gaze away from her. He moved his eyes over the walls, the ceiling, inspecting each corner of the room to escape that disturbing sight.

Then he caught on another sight that brought him up short.

The window.

With a clear view of the farm.

He pulled up the corner of his lip, but didn't comment, because the window and farm weren't exactly what had caught his attention.

It was a highwayman.

A particularly familiar one.

The Black Knight. Alone. On a horse. *His* horse. Dream. Speaking to one of the farmhands.

Before Field could block Lady Theodosia's view, the crunch of her apple signaled that she had drawn nearer, and she peeked out the window to the scene outside. Her eyes flew to him. "So, we are on the right trail! This is wonderful! Wait, is this our chance?"

Field summoned a deep breath, holding it in for three seconds before slowly exhaling. Chasing after highwaymen was already too dangerous in his book. Now they had found them, and suddenly he wanted to do the opposite. He wanted to alert the Duke of Mortimer about the book and be done with it. "I don't think this band is part of his gang. But they are clearly friendly."

"What do you think they are doing?"

"He is selling his horse by the looks of it." Field snarled at the second horse the bandit had brought along. He instantly recognized it as the one the man had been on when they were robbed.

A crunch of apple. "Why would he sell his horse?"

"Because he"—that blackguard—"is on mine."

Her chewing paused. She said nothing, but Field could *feel* her stare. As though she sensed that one word, one small thing would be enough for his temper to erupt.

It was.

He speared her with a glare as her chewing continued. "Are you chewing on glass and bone?" Field snapped, clenching his own apple in his hand.

A layer of frost covered her face instantly, and she skewered him with an unflinching look as she took another deliberate bite from her apple.

I deserved that.

He looked away, trying to block her out. Christ, even in this moment, vengefully piercing her apple, his faculties scattered into a thousand pieces.

Field should have kept his mouth shut.

She jabbed a finger into his ribs. "We will get your horse back, so don't yell at me."

"I'm sorry." In the grand scheme, Field wasn't so attached to his horse that he would give his life for the thoroughbred. However, the thought of Dream in that arrogant man's possession set his teeth on edge.

He couldn't accept it. *Refused* to accept it.

"Apology accepted," Lady Theodosia said. "The rain shouldn't last long. It's barely a drizzle."

Field nodded. They couldn't keep traveling on foot. Not while it appeared they were stuck between a suspicious farm—growing more suspect with each passing second—and a group of bandits. He glared at the Black Knight, and a newfound resolution stiffened his spine. The highwayman handed the reins of his horse over to the man he spoke to and left, his direction pointing them in the way they would need to travel to find him and his gang.

"Why are you not saying anything?" The minx jabbed at his ribs again. Mistrust outlined her tone. "It's unlike you not to bellow, grunt, or snap."

"What? Is my silence that unnerving?"

"Quite frankly, yes."

"If you must know, I'm considering a plan."

She tossed her apple core out the window. Finally. The tension in his shoulders partly relaxed. Not all of it, but some. Enough to have a bit of blood flow to his head, clearing some of the fog in his brain.

"For food?"

"To follow that highwayman."

"I thought we *were* following him."

"Not fast enough." Another quick glance at the sky. It should darken soon. And once evening set upon them, *that* would be their chance.

"What are you thinking?" The complete distrust in that one question made the corner of his lips quirk.

"I'm scheming."

"Scheming what exactly? Since we are a duo, you must let me in on each and every one of your ploys."

Field stilled. "Since when have we been a duo?"

"Since the moment you poked your head in my carriage and we became stuck together without a penny to our names."

"I wish I could argue that point, but I can't."

Her eyes widened. "Now that is something truly miraculous!"

"That I can't argue with you? Is that so bloody astonishing?"

"That you have no argument, yes. How lovely!"

Field sneered. "I have plenty of arguments, my lady, just none I wish to voice."

"Why? I welcome you to voice them all."

If he voiced them all, they would not sleep tonight, neither would they accomplish anything. They'd be bickering back and forth, too distracted with the other's next retort to worry about anything else. *This*, he had become clear about. They needed to focus if they were going to succeed with the half-cocked plan that was currently forming in his mind.

"So?" she pressed.

"No arguments, only plans" Field said, the corner of his mouth lifting. "We are going to borrow," he motioned to the horse they were securing on a branch of a nearby tree, "that horse."

"Borrow?"

Yes. But not just that. "It's our way out of hell."

Chapter Five

BORROW A HORSE?

Theodosia had never thought that the Earl of Saville would ever steal anything in his life. He might bluster and bellow, and cause trouble left and right, but he had always come across as rather righteous. Quite frankly, the man was a conundrum. One moment he snapped, the next moment he carried her on his back and picked apples for her. Then he snapped again. Was there actually enough good in him to balance out all the ways he'd prickled her anger bone? She couldn't say. Yet. Her opinion of the man oscillated like a pendulum, swinging between *Thank Heaven I have you* and *I want to throttle you.*

"You mean steal a horse?"

"No," he denied. "I mean to borrow their horse. It's only stealing if we are running off their property with no intention of returning it."

Lord. "It's only borrowing if you ask for permission to help yourself to someone else's property. Besides, how are we going to return the horse? Are we going to set it loose with a thank you note tucked into the saddle?"

"We can if you want."

"Ridiculous."

"Since we cannot come to an agreement about the correct term to use, let's not squabble over it. We need a horse. They have a horse. Simple as that."

"And you are certain we shall return it once we are done? It doesn't sit well with me, stealing from the less unfortunate. Plus, you picked apples in full view of them. They will suspect you as the thief."

"That is why I am considering leaving the horse with the highwaymen."

"Why ever would you do that?" Theodosia suddenly caught on. "That way when the farmer and his boys find the horse with the Black Knight, the very Black Knight who sold them the horse, they will suspect the highwayman swindled them and they will be the ones squabbling. How diabolical."

"Correct. While we make off with the book on the back of *my* horse."

"Aren't you afraid these people might get hurt by the Black Knight and his band?"

"Forgive me, but I doubt it very much. He didn't hide his face from us, he claims he is infamous, and something tells me it's not the first time he has done business with those *farmers*."

"Very well." Theodosia nodded thoughtfully. "That is not the worst plan I've ever heard. Rather ruthless, but brilliant."

His expression turned turbulent. "Those blackguards brought this on themselves."

"Another thing we agree on. So, do we steal the horse under the cover of darkness?"

"No, *I* will set out to borrow the horse under the cover of darkness. You will wait for me here."

Theodosia's eyes narrowed. "I won't be left behind."

"You aren't being left behind, Lady Theodosia. You are merely waiting for me."

"And who made you the leader of our little group?"

"I'm bigger than you are."

Hah! "What does size have to with anything?"

"Everything." He smirked. "Some might even argue," he leaned in closer, "that size is everything."

"Are you sure about that?" Theodosia, who had grown up with six brothers, had a canny idea she knew what he spoke of, so her gaze shifted to his crotch, then lifted back to his face just in time to witness his smile drop. "If you are referencing your pride, I will agree it is quite large. Anything else remains up for debate. However, size has nothing to do with what's happening here."

"Provoking minx. My size is just the right size."

"Such arrogance." She curled her lip. "I don't know if I should applaud it or scoff at it. Perhaps wipe it off you with a slap? Which I might very well do if I'm made to wait in this rickety building in the black of night. I *hate* waiting, Saville." Especially waiting for a man. It made her feel too much like she was waiting *on* him rather than for him. She'd already waited while he'd picked apples, she didn't want to wait for this. "Plus, what if something happens and I'm stuck here in the house? It's better to go together so that we can escape together."

A sigh. "Very well, you can accompany me to get the horse. But you must do everything I say."

"I can do that." *Try* to do that.

"Good. I suggest we get some rest. This is going to be a long night."

Theodosia motioned to the room. The only furniture in the dwelling was an overturned chair and a table with only three legs. "This might be stating the obvious, but there is no bed. Only a cold, hard, dusty floor."

"You can spread my coat on the ground and sleep on that."

"What about you?"

"I'm already dirty. More dust won't affect me."

More dust won't affect me? This from a man with a waistcoat obsession? A man who always looked pristine? Though come to think about it, since he hailed her carriage down, he hadn't looked all that put together.

Had calling him a weed, cutting up his waistcoats, and drawing on his portrait bothered him that much? Theodosia still couldn't quite understand why anything about *her* would bother *him.*

But then, that was the conundrum that was Saville. As simple as he seemed on the surface, his complexities apparently ran deep. In that regard, he reminded her of her brother Seth. He also had a hot temper, but beneath all that lava, deep emotions churned. The weight of all his responsibilities lay heavy.

And he was a thorn. A thorn that loved to sting!

"I'm not sure I believe you, but I won't fight your suggestion." She spread his coat on the floor, setting the apples aside. One sour apple had certainly been enough.

She dropped down on his coat, thankful for the thin barrier it provided between her and the floor. There would be no comfortable sleep, but nothing about her life since the moment *he* had entered it had been comfortable. She peeked at Saville, who had settled across from her. No thin barrier to shield him from the dust and dirt.

In a way, he was a thin barrier himself—at least right now. A light shield firmly standing between her and the harsh elements of the outside world. This version of him was much more handsome and appealing—to a degree—than the version of him she'd seen in London. The man in London grated her nerves so that she'd had almost none left.

The man here had a more rawness about him. More appeal. Once the waistcoat came off, another side of him appeared it would seem.

"What color is your hair, anyway?"

He turned his head to her. "My hair color? Can't you tell?"

"Well, your sister's hair is light, fair, sandy. Yours . . ."

"I'm blond."

"No, you are not."

"Sandy, then, like Selena. We have the same hair color."

"No, you have not. Your hair is darker than hers."

He tugged at the tufts of his hair. "Then a dark sandy."

She glanced at the tendrils once again sticking upward. "Your hair has quite the temper, just like its owner."

A grunt. "What does my hair have to do with anything, any-way?"

"I'm merely curious. Making an observation. Filling the si-lence." Making normal, boring conversation. Lord knows, it had been a struggle up till now.

"There are other, more relevant subjects to fill the void, if we must."

"Such as?"

"Did you leave London because of me?"

Ah well, the moment of normal was fun while it lasted. "You already asked me this and I already told you. No."

"Yes, but I never know whether you are being truthful or whether you are mocking me with impertinence."

Fair enough. "Would it matter if it were the truth?"

His eyes probed hers before he averted his gaze and stared at the ceiling. "Maybe, maybe not. I don't know. That's why I am curious. I'm reflecting a great deal on my actions these days."

"Very well, if you must know, partly yes and partly no."

"I see."

A silence stretched between them at her answer, one where they were both occupied with their own thoughts.

Not uncomfortable.

Not comfortable either.

Theodosia mimicked his posture, placing her hands behind her head and staring at the cracked beams overhead. So much had happened in such a short span of time. Exhaustion started to overtake her mind.

Her mind wanted to race over many things, but she didn't have much mental energy to focus on any one of them in depth. Her brothers, well some of them, were back in London—her timing had been on point in that regard. And by now, they ought to know everything. That ridiculous rumor circling about town would have them turning over every stone looking for her once they discovered Saville had left London, too.

Seth would be too suspicious to think it a coincidence.

Just how on earth could anyone believe that she and Saville, of all men, could ever form a union? They were both too stubborn, hot tempered, and refused to back down from their stance whatever the subject. There was hardly any capacity to compromise between them. They were really far too much alike for it ever to be a happy marriage. No, theirs was an exact recipe for an unhappy one.

Not that happiness had ever been a requirement between the business arrangements of the *ton*. It all came down to benefits when deciding to marry. If a party couldn't benefit, why enter into it in the first place? And at the very least, if it were not a love match, there ought to be mutual respect. That didn't exist between them either. Not on the things that mattered most.

Who could have formed such rumors?

The men? The women? An acquaintance?

Sleepiness claimed her eyelids, making them heavier. It didn't matter who started the rumors, she supposed. Rumors didn't even need much of a spark to create a wildfire. All that was required was one whispered thought leaving the lips to spread.

No matter.

They would all soon all see there was no basis to these rumors. They'd all soon see that she, Theodosia King, was the master of her own fate.

FIELD STARED AT Lady Theodosia's sleeping face. He couldn't see much, since darkness had descended upon them a while ago. Earlier, he could scarcely see his hand before him, but the moment the moon broke through the clouds along with a stretch of stars, soft light filtered into the dwelling, allowing him to draw his gaze over the outline of her face. There was something to be said about the moonlight in the country versus the moonlight in the city. It was much softer here.

The minx was pretty when she slept.

No glares.

No viperous tongue.

No chasing after her.

Field didn't know why he'd pressed the question of whether he had been the reason she'd fled London. He only knew that it mattered. He'd suspected he was, now he had confirmation—at least partially. He sighed. Now that he knew he wished he'd never asked.

What to do with this information?

Apologize?

Make it right?

He didn't want to be the reason, even partially, that she'd fled London. He'd always wanted to do the right thing, even amidst all the things he got wrong. But why try to fix a problem that doesn't want to be fixed? Much like him.

A problem . . .

All his life, he'd been just that for his father. The late Earl of Saville had ruled his house with an iron fist. He'd been a ruthless man, both inside and out, and he had tried to cultivate that same ruthlessness in Field. He'd believed that was the only way to stay at the top. People were only pawns to be used. Women should be seen and not heard.

Blackguard.

Only Field's nature had rejected all his father's attempts.

His father, according to the late earl himself, had only ever made one mistake: not beating his son harder into submission. Everything else was a calculated decision, a deliberate choice. Which was why when Field did make mistakes, he tried his best to act opposite to what his father would have done and take responsibility for his actions. His father had been a master at shifting the blame onto others. He was never wrong.

And Saville's greatest mistake had been his participation in that damn list. He rolled onto his side, his gaze refusing to leave the woman that slept an arm's length away. He had never thought he'd be the cause of a woman fleeing the season.

Certainly not *this* woman.

With the glares.

The viperous tongue.

Who always made him give chase.

Honestly, if he were her, he'd have fled much sooner. He admired Kingsley. All her brothers, really. They weren't the sort of men to suffer characters like his father, and they would not suffer bad behavior from him. They protected their family as best they could.

He reached out to poke her cheek gently. "Lady Theodosia. It's time to go."

Silence.

Should he let her rest and go retrieve the horse by himself?

He grimaced.

If she woke to find him gone, he would surely be the recipient of her wrath. He poked again. "Lady Theodosia." Two seconds. "Theodosia. It's time to clear out."

A soft snore.

"If you don't wake up now, I'll leave you behind. Do you not believe me? Try me, then."

Her lashes fluttered, and her eyes opened and she groaned. "My back hurts."

"The princess isn't used to hard floors."

She sat up, rubbing her eyes. "Help this princess to her feet."

Field stood and clasped her outstretched hand in his, pulling her up in one swift woosh. "Have the residents of the farm settled in for the night?" she asked.

"Yes, a while ago. It should be safe to approach the barn." He bloody hoped. The farm seemed to be a simple dwelling. If they were silent, very silent, and a bit lucky, they might get the horse without being discovered.

She nodded. "Then let's go."

Damn it. He didn't like this. He wanted her where it was safe. There was something very wrong with him for allowing her to hold him in thrall like this.

He scowled. In thrall?

I meant allowing her to lead me by the nose, confound it!

Every single one of Field's senses went on alert as they padded from the dwelling. The rain had stopped, but there was still a fresh crispness in the air. A layer of fog clung to the meadow. This was the best possible situation. It would provide coverage for them when they left.

Field stealthily made his way across the grass to where he'd picked apples before, Lady Theodosia traipsing cautiously behind. Not a sound could be heard except for the creatures round about—crickets and frogs and the occasional snort of a horse. In the distance, an owl made his presence known.

When no further sounds came, he made his way directly to the small barn, motioning to her to tread carefully. "Be my lookout," he whispered to Lady Theodosia over his shoulder.

"My eyes are peeled," she whispered back.

They were indeed lucky. The barn didn't have much in the way of stalls, and the highwayman's horse was tied to a beam in the far corner. No humans were present. It seemed they all slept in the main building. Other than that, there were several other beasts, but Field didn't pay them any heed. He wanted the Black Knight's steed.

The horse was black as his infamous master's title, but a bit on the older side. Field ran a hand over the horse's neck, whispering soothing words.

"That's a good boy. We are going visit your previous owner, all right?" The horse accepted Field's touch. "That's a good boy."

He undid the reins from the beam to which the beast was tethered and as quietly as possible and led the horse from the barn. He didn't stop until he reached the apple tree.

A heavy cough echoed in the foggy night.

Field froze. So did Lady Theodosia. He inched closer to her as his gaze tracked over the farmhouse.

"Come." He motioned her over when after a few seconds no further noise or movement could be detected. The horse had no saddle or stirrups. Not an issue for him, but for a lady . . . "Can you get on by yourself or should I lift you?" he whispered.

A soft snort of derision answered him. "Of course, I can"— she stopped when she reached the horse—"not. There is no saddle."

"You're only noticing this *now?*" He rather enjoyed using her own words from before to mock her just a bit now.

"I was keeping watch," she hissed back.

"Right you are, right you are. Come here, I'll lift you." Then he couldn't help adding, "I suppose weeds are useful after all."

"They do have a way of prevailing."

Field gave a little snort of his own. "Brace yourself." He gripped her waist and lifted her onto the horse in one smooth go. "Again, those godawful trousers come in handy."

"How big of you to admit," she whispered down from her perch.

Field pulled himself onto the horse behind her and shifted her a bit forward with his thighs. Big enough to admit, yes, but not big enough to ignore.

Her head whipped back. "Should *I* be sitting at the back?"

"Why would you be sitting at my back? The front is much more secure."

"That's the problem," she muttered. "It's too secure."

He might agree on that. He was becoming all too aware of his legs enveloping hers. But . . . "You aren't used to riding astride a horse. It's for the best if you sit in front for now."

Just don't think about it, Field.

He nudged the horse into a walk, and at a pace akin to a snail, he guided them from the field. Finally, they could leave this place.

"Shouldn't we explode from here as though the devil is on our heels?"

"The devil is not on our heels. Yet. And hopefully won't be. We do not want to alert the people that we have stolen their horse."

"Very well, I concur. Silence is precious."

"We have been agreeing a lot lately, don't you think, my lady? If I hadn't been with you the entire time, I might think you are plotting something against me."

Her hair feathered across his chin when she turned her head to cast him a pointed sidelong look. He couldn't be certain, but he thought he also caught the slight lift of the corner of her mouth. An infinitesimal twitch in her lips that told him she shared his sentiments.

He smirked, but his amusement didn't last long. A shout filled the air. Then another. And another.

Field cursed.

"Hell's bells. We've been found out."

A soft cheek touched against his as Lady Theodosia shifted again to look over his shoulder, leaving a distracting prickling sensation all along his spine. *Hold fast.*

"I can't see anything through the fog," her breath tickled his ear.

Keep your wits about you, Field. "If we can't, they can't either."

"Yes, but they'll be watching the ground for the hooves' imprints."

His mind cleared. She was right. They were leaving a trail of hoofprints on the grass for anyone to follow. They had to get to the road as soon as possible. Damn it. They also needed to move as stealthily as possible. Distance and the absence of a trail to follow were the things that would save them now.

"It's fine, we will be fine," Field said for himself more than for her. They still had the fog as their advantage. "We have a lead on them."

"We might not for long." A soft, dry-as-the-desert voice returned. "What if we get caught? Do you think they will accept your explanation of borrowing their horse? I think they will act first and ask questions later, if they ask questions at all."

"So you finally believe they are not your average welcoming farmer family?"

A hand pressed on his thigh. "Saville . . . I don't want to get caught."

Field's chest constricted. His arms tightened around her. Just ever so slightly. A means to provide the smallest bit of comfort. They had entered an extremely dangerous situation by taking the horse from these strangers. The woman in his arms came across as so strong that he hadn't even paused to think how she might feel if things didn't go according to *his* half-arsed plan.

"Don't worry, Lady Theodosia. I won't allow you to get caught. Ever."

"Can you even promise that?"

"I can. I am. Can you trust me just this once?"

"Fine. I shall trust you. But do you see why I wanted to follow you, now? Imagine if I were still stuck in that house."

Field didn't want to imagine it at all, quite frankly.

"To hell with it." Field nudged the horse to a trot, and then to a full out run—as quickly as he dared in the fog—heading in what he hoped was the direction the Black Knight had left earlier. There must be a road or path up here soon. And if they were lucky and found the highwaymen quickly, they could get their business settled tonight. If not . . .

They would have to wait and see where this path would take them.

Chapter Six

THEODOSIA'S HEART POUNDED. She was tightly caged in Saville's embrace as they raced across the dirt road. No. In his arms. One could not call this an embrace. Embrace implied affection, gentleness, and even comfort. This hold was hard, muscled, and all the things that alerted her to the raw strength of this man, stretching from his thighs clamping around hers, to his chest supporting her back, to his arms circling her. She couldn't even tell anymore whether the erratic beat in her heart was because of the fear of being chased or the man at her back.

Collect yourself, Theo.

Now was not the time to notice things like raw strength! Not while they were being chased down by angry people whose horse had just been stolen! Not at all, in fact. Not with *this* man.

Had she been swayed by that one little—yet undeniably grand—question. *Can you just trust me this once?* She had no other choice *but* to trust him. And in having no other choice but to trust him, Theodosia had a rather shocking revelation.

She *did* trust him.

She trusted him to be himself. And while the infuriating Earl of Saville might be many things, and while he might go about doing things in an unorthodox way, he had always operated as a protector.

Even the primitive scent of dirt and sweat wasn't half as annoying as it might have been yesterday, or the day before that. Though in truth, she could very well just be smelling herself!

But then it wouldn't have smelled as good.

Urgh, Theodosia!

Apply your focus to the matter at hand!

She glanced over their shoulders, still unable to detect any riders because of the fog. But she could hear them. Hooves of several horses hitting the ground. Whether they were gaining on them or not, Theodosia couldn't tell.

"Hold on." A rough voice tickled her ear, sending sharp shivers down the base of her spine.

"Hold on?" Theodosia exclaimed, rather rattled. "Hold on to what?" Just as the words flew from her mouth, Saville drew the horse to a sharp halt and yanked on the reins. Her fingers dug into his upper legs, and she braced her back against his chest as he maneuvered the protesting beast into a patch of bushes.

Note to self: Riding a horse astride without a saddle is not fun. Never do so again after this!

Saville's legs clamped tighter around hers, holding her secure on the beast.

Another note to self: Weeds are more than useful.

That term must have truly stung for him to be going on about it still. And perhaps *weed* was too much. He had gone to pick her apples, after all. A small gesture, but given how hungry she had been at the time, that sour apple had meant everything.

He also insulted your chewing. Rogue.

Half of her sympathy evaporated at the memory. But the half that remained advanced him from a weed to a seed. What the seed would sprout into remained uncertain. He may very well sprout as a weed again, but she would remain hopeful for now.

"Where are we going?" Theodosia asked when he brought the horse to a halt.

"We're hiding."

"What if they catch us?" She didn't want to say it out loud, but the thought terrified her. Saville may very well have been right about those farm residents.

"We have to take a chance. They are gaining on us too fast. We have to use the advantage of the fog while we still have it."

"How can they be this fast? Were we not outrunning them at all?"

"Their horses are younger, and we are two people atop ours," Saville answered. "And even if we did outrun them, what would happen if we blindly dashed straight into the highwaymen? That would be a disaster. No. It's better to hide and regain our stealth and slower pace."

Theodosia begrudgingly admitted he made sense.

Saville had had a point earlier. They were agreeing with each other so much that in some ways, it was rather disconcerting. They went from one extreme to the other, giving her an unsettling feeling or being yanked back and forth. But they had no choice but to rely on each other for the time being.

I suppose it's not all bad.

Well, except for being chased.

A breathless silence fell between them as the hooves of horses drew nearer and nearer until they were just about on them.

Theodosia swore her heart stopped for several beats as she waited for them to be discovered. But that didn't happen. The hoofbeats passed right by. One horse. Two horses. Three. *Four* riders.

She let out a shaky breath.

We weren't caught.

Theodosia almost couldn't believe it. With everything that had gone wrong lately, it seemed rather refreshing for something to go right for a change.

"I told you, you can trust me."

"There are some things that aren't in even *your* control, Earl."

He chuckled. "You can let go now, *my lady.*"

"Let go?" She glanced at him questioningly.

"Your hands." A finger gently tapped one of the hands still digging into his legs. "At this rate I might lose all feeling in my legs if you don't."

Oh! She snatched her hands away. How mortifying, clutching onto him like that! "My apologies. I don't know what I was thinking."

"No need to apologize."

Her cheeks flushed as she surveyed their hiding spot. "How long must we wait?"

"I'm not sure myself."

Theodosia's gaze arrested on a particular spot on the bushes. "Saville, look."

He followed her gaze. "Is that . . .?"

"A path," she finished for him. "It seems so. I wonder where it leads. Should we follow it?"

"The path has been hidden behind these bushes."

"You mean it's not a good idea to follow it, correct?"

He didn't look happy at the discovery. "From my experience, if something is hidden, it is hidden for a reason."

"It could also just be due to the overgrowth of the bushes, and no one saw fit to trim them," she countered.

"If they didn't see fit, they didn't see fit for a reason."

"What else, then? We can't go back that way. What if they catch on that we've hidden? We'll definitely be caught if they start searching the verge."

His body tensed against her. She could feel the reluctance vibrating through him. He did not want to take that path. His whole being resisted. Honestly, she had her reservations as well. But hope outweighed them.

Her desire not to get caught with a stolen horse was greater than her fear of whatever they might find venturing into the unknown.

"I believe the risk is worth it," Theodosia cajoled. "How much time do we have left before they realize we aren't ahead of them anymore? What if they know about this path, too? That means we need all the head start we can get."

A curse flew past her ear.

This man. "You have a foul mouth. Has anyone told you that before?"

"Constantly," he said. "Damn it, I don't know what the right choice is here."

Theodosia suddenly understood. Of course, he would be hesitant. It wasn't the hot-tempered earl protesting, it was the protector earl.

"Think about it this way," Theodosia said frankly. "I am the one pressing us to take the path. I made the choice."

"I'm steering the horse."

"See?" She sent him a smile over her shoulder. "A team effort. That is the best we can do in this circumstance. Work together."

"A team effort . . ." He let out a long-suffering sigh. "Very well. We shall do it your way. But you better not blame me if what we find at the end of this path is worse than being chased by a posse."

What could be worse? Theodosia wanted to ask, but she held back. Nothing ever good came from tempting fate with such a glib question. Fate might just decide to show exactly *how* much worse it could get.

"Do not worry. If what we find is worse, then I shall be sure to not allow you to get caught."

"Words I shall take to heart," Saville said a bit mockingly. But he still directed the horse to the hidden path, the muscles in his thighs flexing as he nudged the animal into a trot. Again, Theodosia questioned her life choices. She should have insisted on sitting at his back this time.

"I can't wait to get off this dratted horse," she muttered.

"What's wrong?"

"Nothing."

"Clearly, it's not nothing. Nothing doesn't sound like *I can't wait to get off this dratted horse.*"

"Why are you so tactless? Did they not teach you in school not to provoke ladies?"

His shoulders shrugged against hers. "We don't receive that

sort of instruction."

"Of course, I suppose there are no finishing schools for boys to teach them basic etiquette. They should incorporate this in your studies."

"Aren't there books for these things?"

"Have you read them?"

"Are you one to speak? It doesn't seem as though you went to any finishing school, either, or read any books."

She hadn't.

"Why would I attend finishing school when I had a governess?"

"Forget I asked. There is no winning against you."

"Not even your sister attended finishing school."

"An oversight on my part. Perhaps she would not be so rebellious had I sent her."

A snort. "You are such a man. It's most annoying." It was a true accomplishment the degree to which this man had set her teeth on edge in the past with this sort of nonsense.

"What else am I supposed to be then, a woman? I'm rather happy to be a man."

"I just bet you are. Very well, you *man*, just get us to those dratted highwaymen so that we can retrieve the book." Then they would be done with this adventure. Done with each other.

"Will I be less annoying if I do?"

"Of course." Her voice turned syrupy. "I'd be *so* happy."

"Then who am I to keep you from such happiness?"

Happiness . . .

The sooner they could get out of each other's hair, the better. Yes, that would be happiness.

SAVILLE DIDN'T KNOW the last time he had felt so damn powerless as he nudged their horse further down the overgrown path. He shared her sentiment—he wanted to get off this horse post haste, as well. However, he was certain their reasons weren't the same. He couldn't feel anything but her, and he was ready to be done with that. He wasn't even spared her breath. The movement of every inhale and exhaled played against his chest.

Distracting.

Lord, what he wouldn't do for a hot meal. And a bath. A river, a brook, or anything to wash the sweat from his skin would do right about now. A soft bed.

Anything but this torture.

Admittedly, this "torture" was still better than hiding beneath a desk from her brothers in London. Hell if he knew why. He just knew that it was.

The body between his arms squirmed.

Not bad, this feeling.

He stiffened. Where the hell had that thought come from? Not bad? Very, very bad!

Theodosia King didn't like him. In fact, there were moments when he might even say she loathed him. He had known this much to be true from the start. They didn't get along, and he understood why. He'd made too many mistakes, plus he had a bad personality. Not brooding, yet not that cheerful either. An in-between mess with a hot temper.

Field had no illusions about himself. He'd been called a waste too many times in his life for that. While he didn't believe he was an actual a waste—for that meant his father would be right—his character was not the sort that mamas and their daughters flocked to.

Women didn't like him. They found him the exact opposite of charming.

He leaned closer and sniffed. Even having gone through all they'd gone through, she still smelled of spring. Her soft body against his also. . .

No, Field. Stop there.

It must be because this was the first time he had ever ridden on a horse with a woman. Honestly, it was the first time a woman had remained locked between his arms with their clothes still on. A sobering thought.

This was much more intimate.

A moment he didn't hate.

"What's wrong?" came her voice.

He jolted. "Nothing is wrong. Why do you ask?"

"Then why did you go stiff as a stick?"

Field wanted to laugh. They were having nearly the same conversation over again, only with roles reversed.

"You caught that?"

"How can I not? We are cramped with each other on the back of a horse."

Cramped? That would be one way of putting it. He cleared his throat. "I thought I saw a snake slithering in the underbrush." A lame excuse, but the only one he could come up with.

"In the pitch-black dark?" she asked skeptically. Rightly so. He couldn't see a deuced thing. "Wouldn't the horse have skittered?"

He glanced up at the moonlit sky. The fog had already cleared here. "It's not pitch-black dark."

"Fine, don't tell me."

It's not like he could. *I sniffed your hair, and I liked it.* That would earn him no points.

They fell back into silence, and Field wisely directed his attention to the road. Lady Theodosia was far too sharp for his tired and fog-filled brain at the moment. Then again, the minx always had been. Though she must also be tired—why else refrain from raking him with a cutting remark?

As the horse plodded onward, Field reflected on his recent decisions. This hidden road would not have been his first choice. But the only other he could think of was to abort all plans and head back in the direction they came. Field didn't need to be a prophet to know about how well that suggestion would have been received.

As they rounded a bend in the path, however, their new

prospect came as a surprise. A small town spread before them. This one was not abandoned. A few men stumbled about, and the drone of enthusiastic laughter in the distance grew louder and louder as they approached. Even though it was night, the town still bustled with activity.

Saville had a bad feeling.

From an abandoned village to a secret road leading into another village. No, he didn't feel good about this at all. Was this road simply a shortcut? But used by whom? And for what purpose?

Not a good feeling at all.

Because the only answer Field could come up with was that of a certain highwayman and his gang. He dismounted and held out his hand to help Lady Theodosia down.

She didn't protest his assistance and, looking around the town, merely commented, "Well, this is quite the rapid change."

Field nodded absentmindedly. "That, we are in an agreement about."

"More agreements. I declare," she said, a grin in her tone. "Our tides are changing."

Don't speak too soon, sweetheart.

Field hailed a man who was passing them.

"Is there an inn in town? One where we can get a good meal and a hot bath?"

The man didn't even look at them, just pointed to a building in the distance.

"Much obliged."

A few minutes later, Field retracted his sentiment. They stood before the door of a three-story building, their hopes dashed with the shake of the innkeeper's head.

"We don't have any more rooms available tonight."

"Is there another place that can grant us a bed and a meal?" Lady Theodosia asked.

The man pointed to an establishment opposite them. "But I don't know whether they will have rooms for you, either. Prickly hosts, too."

Well, they didn't have much of a choice but to ask, did they? "Let's go," Field said, casting a parting glance at the potbellied man. Who was calling who prickly?

"It's rather strange to have two inns in such a small village?" Theodosia murmured as they walked away.

It was. Though the town was active enough that it might be larger or more popular than it seemed at a nighttime glance. Even if it was off a hidden path. In the middle of nowhere. "While it's odd, nothing can surprise me any longer. The world is tipping on its axis already. This is a mere drop in the ocean of strangeness."

"Well, don't despair," Lady Theodosia chirped with a brightness Field didn't share. "This inn should have rooms for us."

"I would say let's hope, but hope does not spring eternal, as one might be inspired to believe."

"Oh pish, do not be such a bore," she chastised. "Hope with me for just one minute more."

Field wanted to say *no*, but one look at her face, and all that came out was, "Fine, one minute. I'll hope."

One minute later, Field once again retracted this damnable sentiment of hope. Disappointment shall forever rule eternal.

"We only have one room."

Field and Lady Theodosia stared at each other. "See? Hope has proven fruitful." An undeniable sparkle lit her eyes.

Fruitful? This was *fruitful*? They would need to *share*. Anything else would require him to be a man with *luck*. He lowered his voice to a mutter, "You do realize we'd be sleeping in the same room."

Her head turned to him, her voice dropping even lower, "What are you so fussy about? Didn't we sleep in the same room before?"

"Calling that dwelling a 'room' is a bit farfetched, don't you think?"

The innkeeper of this establishment was an older woman, tall, resolute. She jabbed her chin toward Field. "He is not welcome."

Field's head snapped back to her. "Excuse me?"

"Only women allowed."

Mentally, his jaw dropped. "I'm not sure I take your meaning, madam."

"No? Then allow me to make it clear. This is a women-*only* establishment. No men allowed."

No, Field was not a man with luck. What the bloody hell were the chances that of the two inns in this town, the only one— with only one bed left—was a female only business? He pinched the bridge of his nose, resisting the urge to glower. Just glower— at anything. He drew in a deep breath, exhaling slowly. "Then what about your stables?"

"They are women only stables, as well."

God above. "Do you have only mares in there, too?" *Give me strength.*

"That's right. We only have female horses, too."

Christ, calm him. "Do you have women standing guard at the stables too? Stablewomen?"

"No." A flat look accompanied the next statement. "But we do have girls patrolling the property at night."

Could his world turn more upside down?

"How grand," Theodosia murmured softly, sending him a louder smirk. "Women on patrol."

"This is madness." He could only go back to the other inn and ask if they were willing to open their stables to him. But that meant being separated from a minx who reveled in snapping rules in half. Who could say what trouble she'd start in his absence in this strange, boisterous town?

Everlasting damnation.

The minx stepped forward. "It is not at all possible? We are in a bit of a pickle, you see, and would rather not be separated."

The woman did not move an inch. Not even her facial muscles twitched. "The rules are the rules."

"Are there no inches between these rules?" Field asked.

"Room for a man in trouble?"

"That is not our establishment's problem. We will take the girl, not the man." The flat look never wavered. "No men allowed."

"I see," Theodosia murmured, peeking up at him. "I suppose then it cannot be helped."

Cannot be helped?

Cannot be *helped*? What the hell did she mean by *that*? And what the hell was wrong with this town? "Am I allowed to ask why there are no men allowed?"

The woman said simply, "Our guests prefer a setting with no men."

What in the blazes did he just hear? He stared at the woman. "That is rather fascinating."

"We adapt to the fashions of our guests."

Field's eyes turned to Theodosia, who was glowing with delight. "I see." *Fashions*. Meaning the current little rebellions of the ladies, he suspected. "News must travel fast from London."

"We do keep up with the papers."

Of course.

"Well, that is fabulous," Theodosia declared.

"Fabulous?" Field bit out between teeth that wanted to remain clenched. The minx and her heiresses had caused half of England's female population to revolt! However, he was not foolish enough to think he could fight this. And quite frankly, he didn't have the bloody strength to even try.

Theodosia ignored him, asking the innkeeper, "Is there room for negotiation? We were robbed by a highwayman, you see, but I am Lady Theodosia King, and I always pay my accounts."

The innkeeper's eyes softened a fraction of a bit. "I am not opposed to discussing arrangements."

Well, that was something, at least, Field supposed. At least Theodosia would be able to negotiate for her own stay at this inn and pay later.

His temples were starting to throb.

I need sleep.

But he also needed peace of mind. Perhaps he could try to sneak into the stable without them knowing and stay as close as possible to Theodosia. He could sidestep a few women on patrol, could he not?

He cast a quick glance at their noble companion. A mare. Thank God. The horse would also have a place to sleep tonight. Fortunately, while the smell of horses would be unpleasant, he actually *liked* them. Given the state of his body after sharing a horse with the lady in question, sharing a barn with the mare wouldn't be all that bad. And he'd be close.

He leveled a look at the innkeeper before grasping Theodosia's arm. He pulled her a few feet away, lowering his voice to a whisper, "You and the horse stay here. I shall make another plan."

She blinked a few times. "No."

"Yes. This is the only way. Get some sleep."

"What about you?"

Field squared his shoulders. "I shall find a spot to rest, don't worry." Even if he couldn't manage to sneak into the stable, there had to be a soft patch of ground somewhere nearby he could occupy for a few hours.

The stare directed at him lasted three seconds too long for his comfort. A sparkle suddenly entered her gaze, and she said, "Take the horse to the stable. I'll meet you there."

"What are you going to do?" Field couldn't keep outright suspicion from his tone. "No silly business."

Her lips quirked. "Trust me."

"No need for tricks and schemes. I'll be fine. If that woman is willing to negotiate payment, take the room."

"And what if any one of the people we're currently avoiding finds you being fine in whatever spot you chose to rest? They all know your face, and I'd rather not have your blood on my hands."

"Then what do you propose?"

"Let me talk to the innkeeper, I shall make an arrangement for us both. I have a marvelous suggestion for her. One I think she will take pleasure in."

Why did that sound like it wouldn't bode well for him? "That woman won't move an inch."

"Not with you grumbling about, no. Take the horse to the stable," the minx urged again. "I'll meet you there. Trust *me* for once, if you can."

Theodosia stepped up to the inn again and addressed the innkeeper directly. "Will it be all right if he settles our mare in the stables?"

The woman looked between the two of them before nodding.

I'll be damned.

Field didn't wait around; he led the horse around the side of the building to the inn's stable. He'd do as she asked. Because God help him, he did trust her.

He didn't catch sight of any women on patrol, and entered the stable without being stopped, choosing the first empty stall on his right. "There you go. You ought to be safe here for the night." His gaze flicked over the other stalls. Were they really all mares in here? And just what arrangements was Theodosia trying to negotiate for *them*?

He scrunched his eyes shut.

If they were very lucky, he supposed the innkeeper might soften a bit more and allow him to sleep on a patch of hay. Then tomorrow, they would continue their search for lawless highwaymen while also trying to evade a bunch of farm folk hunting for them. Could this country trip get any worse?

"We are in luck!"

Field nearly jumped from his skin at the sudden sound of Lady Theodosia's voice at his back. He placed a hand over his heart, applying pressure to settle the beat. How much time had passed? A minute? An hour? He turned to find her flouncing into the stables with a big grin.

He had another bad feeling.

"Christ, woman. Can you not sneak up on a man like that?"

"Did you not hear me? I said we are in luck!"

"I heard you. I'm just not sure you and I define luck the same way."

She tossed a bundle of clothes at him.

"What's this?"

"Your way into the all-women inn."

What was this now? Field lifted the garments to inspect them. His mood promptly turned from suspicious to outright bitter. "You want me to wear a dress?"

She nodded. "It should all fit, I believe."

"And just *where* did you find these clothes?"

"I borrowed them from the innkeeper."

"*This* is your grand plan? Have me dress in women's clothes to get into a women's inn?

She plopped her hands on her waist. "Why not?" She waved a hand over the stables. "Or do you want to sleep where danger lurks around every corner?"

"I won't be in danger," Field denied.

"We don't know that. I'd rather not spend the entire night worrying about whether you are well or not."

"Why, Lady Theodosia, you are that worried about me?"

"Oh, pish. Stop wasting time and get dressed so we can go inside and rest."

"Fine, you win," he muttered. "But did the innkeeper actually say I could enter if I don a dress?"

A slight pause. "Not exactly. But she also didn't say no. However, I do believe her lips pursed with a moment's worth amusement when I brought up the suggestion."

He glared at the clothing in his hand. "This is never going to work, you know." That woman would surely only amuse herself at his expense and then send him off.

Her grin brightened. "I think you'll be surprised."

Christ, at this point, nothing could surprise him anymore.

Chapter Seven

"How are you doing?" Theodosia asked, and she stifled the urge to laugh at the grumble that followed. Ah, she'd needed this.

Entertainment.

When last had she been this amused? When her brother, Broden, had tripped over his own feet and fallen into a pile of horse manure? Was it really that long ago? Certainly it was before the mess with the wagers when she'd been labeled as having eyes as black as Satan's. Strangely, the label that usually sent good humor fleeing from her had at least momentarily lost its power in the face of the anticipation that brewed inside her.

Saville.

The *Earl* of Saville

Field Savage.

In a dress.

A curse drew her attention to the stall. "No one is ever going to believe I am a woman." His head appeared above the door of the stall, and he pointed at his jaw. "Not with this stubble." He glared at her in a menacing way—as menacing as he could manage at least.

"Would they believe it if your face was shaven clean?"

"No," he grumbled, reminding Theodosia of a small child. "I have a very masculine jawline."

"I'd be surprised if you didn't." She was having trouble keeping a straight face. "Since you are a man."

"Is that laughter I detect?"

"Of course, not. Who could laugh at such a wretched tragedy as you having to put on a dress?"

"How the hell do women wear this every day?"

She glanced at the Turkish trousers she wore. "How indeed?"

"What's this?" A sudden curse. "Must I wear the bonnet, too?"

"Why of course. It completes the look. And we must hide your hair. Plus, there are lots of women with masculine jawlines and even some with facial hair."

"Hogwash."

"No, it's true."

She heard a rustle, and then the stall opened and Saville stepped out in all his humble, maid-like glory.

Theodosia's hand flew to her mouth.

He was tall, and broad shouldered, but the dress still fit him. However, it stopped a several inches above his ankles, drawing one's eye to the Hessian boots he still wore.

Oh, well, that cannot be helped.

"Look at you, bonnet man."

"Don't call me that."

She laughed.

His hands plopped on his hips. "Tell me, who the devil is going to believe I'm a woman? Stubble aside, there is still my build."

"I mean . . . there are plenty of woman who are tall and also have wide shoulders. Otherwise the dress wouldn't fit you."

"You have an argument for everything, don't you?" He rubbed a hand over his jawline. "Do they also *shave* their faces?"

"Anything is possible in this world."

"Anything is possible my arse. You did this on purpose, didn't you? Damn it, couldn't you have borrowed a better color? Why is everything purple?"

"Don't you prefer purple?" She handed him a pair of stockings. "Here. Stuff them into your bosom."

"Hell. No."

"Come on, we need the full effect of what it means to be a woman."

"What it means to be a woman?" He stuffed the stockings into his dress. "This does *not* make me feel like a woman."

Theodosia almost laughed at the accusatory glare he leveled at her. "You know only woman are allowed in the inn. If you wish for an opportunity to enter, we need to turn you into a woman. It's all about illusion." And to show a certain innkeeper their determination and sincerity. She motioned for him to turn around. "Let me see."

"We are not fooling anyone."

Theodosia's gaze caught on the gaping material at his back. "It won't entirely close." She handed him the shawl. "I wasn't sure, so I grabbed this as well. Wear this to cover your back. It might still be a bit chilly, though." She forgot to snatch a jacket.

He draped the shawl over his shoulders. "Tell me the truth. You are doing this to punish me for chasing you down?"

Theodosia grinned. "I am not."

She really wasn't.

But she did draw endless enjoyment from the sight.

Luckily she had piqued the interest of the mistress of the establishment with her idea. They would never have fooled her otherwise. Not only did he not look like a woman, but the innkeeper had already glimpsed his face. Even if he covered the lower half of his face with a mask, the glowing intensity of his eyes would be recognized in an instant.

But this seemed the only way to remain together.

Something she never thought she'd ever want. And yet, she truly didn't want to separate from the earl—not yet—which was why she had implored the innkeeper to accept her outrageous idea.

Honestly, her plan could have gone either way. The older

woman had proved a force not to be trifled with, and yet she had given them a chance, and also provided clothes because, in her own words, *You remind me of my daughter. She, too, loved to help stray dogs.*

A look of fondness had broken through the woman's stern features. Theodosia laughed in her heart. Even though the comparison thoroughly amused her, she certainly wasn't about to tell this prickly hedgehog that he'd been compared to a stray dog.

Poor Saville.

This hot-tempered rogue would probably explode in ire.

"I don't know whether to believe you or not," the man muttered sulkily, "but I shall give you the benefit of the doubt."

"Let's not tarry any longer."

He nodded. "Lead the way."

Theodosia was profoundly aware of the man as he followed her back to the main entrance of the inn. Even in such hilarious attire, his presence was powerful. No, with a presence like that, he could never be mistaken for other than he was.

She knocked on the door of the inn, and her accomplice to Saville's transformation appeared before them once more. Theodosia lifted her chin a notch, deciding to act the part as well. "My maid and I would like a room, please. I believe you still have one available."

The woman glanced from her to Saville and back to her again before once more settling on Saville, her sharp gaze flicking over the bonnet and wandering down over every inch of him. The corner of the woman's eye twitched.

Please, please, please, don't laugh.

"This is your maid?" the woman asked with an arch of her brow.

"Yes, this is"—she thought for a name—"Gertrude. I, as you recall, am Lady Theodosia King."

"I see. Well . . ." The innkeeper pursed her lips and then with a shake of her head, then stepped aside. "The room is still available if you want it. You and your *maid* will have to share."

Inwardly, Theodosia did a little dance.

"We don't mind." She glanced at Saville, who sported a deep scowl on his face. He could at least try to act the part. Rotten man. "We shall only be staying for the night."

"Very well," the woman said. "My name is Margaret Latch. I'm the owner of this establishment." She retrieved a key from the cupboard and handed it to Theodosia. "You can call me Mrs. Latch. The room is on the third floor, second door to the left. "Can I send up food and drink?"

"God, yes," Saville burst out, and promptly recovered after a look from Theodosia. *"Please."*

Theodosia nodded. "We shall be sure to keep to our room."

"I think that is for the best," Mrs. Latch confirmed. "I'll have Shelly bring up your meal and some ale."

A throat cleared. "Do you have anything stronger than ale?" Gertrude-Saville asked.

The woman stared at them for half a beat before she announced, "Gin."

"That will do." Saville said.

Gin?

Theodosia had never heard of this drink before, but it seemed Saville had. "Send us a cup of gin, then."

"A bottle," a low voice intoned behind her.

Theodosia cast him another glance. "And some ale, please."

Mrs. Latch nodded and led them to the stairwell, after which she disappeared through another door.

"I cannot believe that woman went along with this little scheme of yours." A grumble followed Theodosia up the narrow flight of stairs.

"Oh shush. She let you in, did she not? That makes her a saint. And mind your voice lest you alert everyone that there is a man masquerading as a woman amongst them."

Saville grunted but dropped his voice to a whisper. "She must not have believed I'd ever agree to such nonsense."

They reached their room and Theodosia turned the key in

the lock. "Well, you did agree to such nonsense." And created a memory she would never forget!

The door swung open, and Theodosia stepped into the room, her gaze flicking over a small writing desk, the chair in the corner, and finally over the rather narrow bed pushed up against the wall. "It's not much, but it will do in a pinch."

"It's better than a dusty dwelling that barely provides shelter."

Theodosia smiled at him. "And we can eat."

On cue, his stomach growled.

Theodosia did chuckle then. "It must already be midnight, I suppose." She fell back onto the bed. "I've missed a bed."

Silence.

She lifted her head to look at Saville. "What's wrong?" A silent Saville was never a good thing.

He stared at her. "You are a woman, and I am a man."

"You only realized this now?" She grinned. "I suppose late is better than never."

"Don't be smart. If word ever gets out that we shared a room, you will be ruined and I—well, I will be dead."

"Word will never get out, and besides, what are you so worried about, Gertrude? Tonight you are a woman, too."

He held her gaze for a moment before looking away without another word.

She laid her head back down, and teased, "Don't you *feel* like a woman yet?"

⇛⇚

FIELD FELT LIKE a damn fool. Feel like a woman? Little Field had something to say about that. The only thing he *felt* was that the world was mocking him, and this woman, lying on the bed all innocently, was provoking him. And delighting in her provocation!

"That Mrs. Latch let me pass for her entertainment, I'm sure of it."

"So what if she did?" Lady Theodosia murmured. "Older people do so love to be amused by the younger ones."

"I don't even know what to say to that. I made a damn fool of myself."

"You're not a fool. You're quite smart. Or you wouldn't be in this room with a hot meal on its way."

That reminded him. "Of course they would have only gin. An all women inn serving gin. How remarkable. Are you telling me they'd drink gin but not brandy? I would die for a glass of French Cognac."

"Just be grateful you are here. Mrs. Latch still has to give her guests the appearance of only allowing women to enter. Any spirits at all are a bonus."

"I still believe she did it solely for her entertainment. And it makes me uneasy."

"That you offer entertainment or that you are the only man in the inn?"

"Both. *Especially* the last."

"Why?" Amusement dripped from her tone. "Afraid you will be overcome by a gaggle of women?"

"I just escaped the clutches of a madwoman in London. A madwoman belonging to a secret club run by *only* women. Women who also run a criminal group with a wide network. For all we know, Mrs. Latch could be an associate of that damn club. Forgive me if I am a bit on edge."

"Ah yes, the club your sister wanted to join. The same one we need the betting book for."

Christ, the betting book.

Field had almost forgotten about the damn thing.

"Right." He drew the chair from the desk and plopped down, shifting uncomfortably as his thighs rubbed together beneath the dress. Not a comfortable feeling. He tugged at the strings of the bonnet, yanking the thing from his head and flinging it onto the desk.

"Our meal hasn't been brought up yet," Theodosia said. "What if the serving girl sees you like this?"

"You think she hasn't been informed that there is a man in the room dressed as a woman?" Field snorted. "She probably can't wait to come and catch a glimpse of the spectacle."

Theodosia lifted her legs into the air in a thoroughly unladylike fashion and tugged at her trousers. "If you are a spectacle, then so am I. And if you must know, I reminded Mrs. Latch of her daughter, which was why she made an exception for us. There are more things in Heaven—"

"Please don't quote Shakespeare right now," Field already felt as though he was in a tragic comedy.

She laughed, and his gaze fell on those long legs, tracking down to her mischievous face. The corners of her lips were lifted, and her features were relaxed into soft lines. A strangely beautiful sight.

Field paused.

Where had that thought sprung from? Then again, Lady Theodosia was pretty. And this *was* one of the rare times she was not shooting steel shards at him from her eyes. A novel experience every time it occurred, to be frank.

The room suddenly turned warm, and Field scooted the chair over to the window, reaching out to lift it a crack. Fresh air was required in such situations.

Cool, crisp night air blew across his face. Just what he needed. Boisterous laughter echoed over to their humble room from the inn across the street that had turned them away, the establishment that allowed both men and women.

"I'm surprised the men didn't retaliate by declaring that an all-male inn."

"Why would they?" She arched a brow at Field. "Don't men have certain needs that require the presence of women?"

"Oh," Field said. She forever startled him with her mouth. However, this was his chance to tease her back, so he settled back lazily and drawled, "And what needs are those?"

"Do you want me to say it out loud? Can you handle that?"

He probably couldn't. "How are you so much more knowledgeable than the average lady? It's not appropriate to speak of such things."

"*This* is where you draw the line? Now you sound just like Seth."

Her brother?

Ah. Of course.

He recalled that his sister had also picked up some things from him and his friends. In all likelihood it was rather naïve to think all ladies were guileless little flowers with no knowledge of the world.

"The line has to be drawn somewhere. Seems like a good place to start." He glanced at her trousers. "Where can I get a set of those?"

"Turkish trousers?" She smiled knowingly. "Why would you want a set when you bluster about them all the time?"

He cleared his throat. "They look more comfortable than this damn dress."

"They are. But don't worry, you can shed yourself of the discomfort when we leave in the morning."

"Let's swap for the night?"

She laughed. "Never!"

A knock sounded.

"Ah, the food is here," Theodosia said and sat up. "You may stay seated as a proper lady would. I'll collect it."

Field sent her a brooding look before snatching up the bonnet and pulling it over his head, averting his gaze.

Those trousers . . .

He wanted them off her. And *not* because of any nefarious reasons! It was just that they were forever on the surface of his mind—the shape of her legs beneath the thin material. Who would think that such strange trousers could still accentuate the lines of her legs in such an alluring way?

Two bowls of food were set on the desk as well as a small loaf of bread, a bottle of gin, two clean glasses, and two pints of ale. Field ignored the look of the girl and only turned to his bowl when the door shut behind her.

Lady Theodosia settled on the bed with hers. "Stew. I love stew."

"Me too," he murmured, inhaling the rich aroma. He had never been as glad to receive a dish filled with the sumptuous fare as he was now.

He broke a piece of bread and dipped it into the stew before taking a bite.

She did the same and let out a moan of satisfaction. "A rather simple dish, but there is something about its simplicity that is unquestionably delicious. My mother would have the cook make me stew as a child when I refused to eat anything else."

"You were a picky eater as a child?" Field asked.

She nodded. "I hated vegetables and preferred meat and potatoes, much to my mother's distress. She thought for sure I would bloat out as I grew older."

"Why distress? Meat and potatoes are the stuff true meals are made of."

"They also made my skin break out in pimples."

Field paused with his spoon midway to his mouth, his eyes finding her smooth, pale cheeks. "I can't imagine you ever having had a pimple."

"Oh, I was quite ugly as a child."

He could believe that even less.

"What about you?" she asked, her eyes sparking. "Did you have any pimples growing up?"

Did he? Field couldn't remember. "All children get pimples at some point in their lives. But I do recall my mother would always have stew brought up to my room whenever I fell sick." *Fell sick* meaning whenever his father raised a fist to him. Those moments were the only sweet memories he had associated with those events.

"Not chicken broth?"

"Can't stand the stuff."

"It's not for you to stand. It's to help you get better."

"Beef stew helped just the same." Chicken broth did nothing to help heal wounds.

"Your mother was quite indulgent with you."

Field's lips quirked. "She was. Now, her indulgence is directed at the Scot she married."

"You sound quite sour. Do you not approve of your stepfather?"

"As long as he treats my mother as a gentleman ought, I don't have a problem with him." He also didn't blame his mother for escaping to Scotland after his father passed. Selena, however, may have felt that loss a bit differently than he did. But she never said a word of grievance to him. On the surface, she accepted her mother's absence without shedding a single tear, though she had clung to him in those earlier years much more than now. He rather missed those days.

"As a gentleman ought?" Some dryness returned to Theodosia's tone. "I'm curious. What defines the term gentleman? Birth? Title?"

He couldn't argue against the implied criticism in her question. Being titled gentleman meant nothing if you didn't live up to the title. Even he at times didn't feel like a gentleman. He'd certainly done ungentlemanly things in the past. He was doing something shockingly ungentlemanly right now.

"As long as he treats her as an *honorable* man ought, then," he corrected.

"Well, I daresay it's a touch better than *gentleman*."

Field took another bite of bread, nodding absentmindedly. Quite right. He carried the title of gentleman, but he hadn't always acted from a place of honor. Like his father. But that man hadn't even tried to be a good person.

Let's not think about that.

He'd rather focus on the meal soothing his belly. They finished their food in silence, the sounds floating from across the street their only companion. Until Theodosia's head suddenly whipped to the window.

"What is it?" Field pushed his empty bowl to the side.

"Nancy."

Field sat up straight, his gaze following hers. "Your traitorous maid? *That* Nancy?"

"My maid no longer." She handed him her bowl and scrambled across the bed to the window. "But that is her laughter."

Field placed her bowl in his and bent over to lower his head next to hers as they both peered rather boldly through the window down onto the streets. They should probably be a bit more inconspicuous, but before he could urge Theodosia to lower a bit more, she exclaimed, "That's her!"

She pointed toward a woman who had stepped from the door to join a man smoking a cheroot outside, their silhouettes darker in the light spilling from with windows. Nancy laughed up at the man, her face, even from this distance, he could tell brimmed with delight.

Sure enough.

"It seems you were betrayed for love."

"Oh, hush. That's one of the highwaymen, is it not?"

Field nodded slowly. "He was the man to the Black Knight's right, if I'm not mistaken." Field recognized the shock of red hair.

"Well, I suppose we are fortunate that the inn didn't have any rooms left for us or who knows what might have happened! My carriage must be here somewhere. As must your horse," she murmured. "We are fortunate indeed."

Fortunate?

The very word offended him.

Field glanced down at the dress he still wore.

No, not fortunate at all.

Chapter Eight

THEODOSIA WANTED TO break out into a little dance of glee. They had found the highwaymen! And they'd found those two traitorous servants. Not that the last mattered much, but they could now swap horses and retrieve the book. After which they could alert the authorities of their whereabouts and put this adventure behind them.

"I wonder what they did with the carriage."

"It is probably around the back."

Theodosia scrambled to her feet. "Let's go have a look."

An arm stopped her. "You want to go now?"

"Is there a better time?"

"Yes, when they are sleeping," Saville said. "We need rest as well."

"Do you think I can sleep knowing those men are across the street from us? They could leave at any moment!"

"They seem to be drinking. Let them drink until they drop. It will strengthen our upper hand. We also have the perfect vantage point to keep an eye on the riffraff."

Theodosia leveled a narrowed-eyed look at Saville, wanting to push the matter, but couldn't muster up the daggers. Saville dressed up in all purple . . . in a *dress* . . . who could get angry at such a sight? The bonnet had once again been discarded, and the hard, grim lines governing his face fell in direct contrast, or rather could she claim perfect harmony, with the deep purple.

A comical sight, to be sure.

To think such a hotheaded man had once been indulged by his mother. He must not have been this surly as a child. Saville as a boy . . . Theodosia could scarcely picture it.

"Very well," she acquiesced. "We will wait. But one of us must keep post at the window." Only then would she relax.

He nodded and lowered back into his seat. "I'll keep watch. You rest."

"Don't you want to rest as well? You were exhausted earlier."

"I've been refreshed by the stew."

Liar. "Well, so have I."

He arched a brow but said nothing. And just like that, with her on the bed and him in the chair, they waited. She didn't want to take the chance that both of them would succumb to sleep and miss a golden opportunity, perhaps the only one, to retrieve the book. At least they were warm, and their bellies were full.

Half an hour passed.

Two.

Three.

Theodosia sighed.

Waiting was *so* hard!

"That's your seventeenth sigh."

Theodosia lifted her head to Saville. "Are you keeping track for a reason?"

"It's hard not to when you are being so obvious about it."

"If I'm obvious, it's because I'm impatient."

"Patience has never been a virtue of yours, has it?"

Theodosia averted her gaze. "Another thing we have in common, it seems."

"Me? Impatient? I'm not the one heaving sighs every few minutes."

"That's because you are only ever patient with matters you know will annoy me."

"That's hardly fair."

"The place has been silent for the past fifteen minutes," she countered. "Why are we still here if not to draw out my annoyance?"

"Just because it's silent doesn't mean they are sleeping." He rose to his feet. "However, we might as well get on with it. We will retrieve my horse and the book, then return to rest."

"Return? As in come back here? If we steal back your horse, we can't return. We must leave this town. The first thing they will do is search all the stables in town to make certain we are not hiding in plain sight, no?"

He dragged a hand over his face. "Damn it, I hadn't thought about that."

"Rest can wait, we shall get sleep in the next town. Let us first take back what was stolen from us."

"Fine." He grabbed the bottle of gin.

"What are you doing with that?" she asked.

"What else? Once this is over, I'm going to drink it."

"No need to be so snide."

"Says the mistress of mocking comments."

Well . . . "Let's put our taunts aside for one night, then. And if all goes well, we shall part ways at the next town."

"Then let us hope all goes well."

Theodosia followed Saville down the flight of stairs. Her lips quirked at his slow, awkward steps. If only she could capture this moment in her mind perfectly for future amusement!

When they reached the door, she handed him the bonnet he had left behind. "Why must I wear this thing again? It's pitch-black outside."

"Just in case anyone runs into us on the street. It's dark, so they won't make out your features if you wear this."

He snatched the bonnet from her fingers and wiggled it in her face. "I still don't believe this helps anything." Even so, he still put it on.

Theodosia bit down on her lips.

What a big grouch.

She would have to find a way to properly thank Mrs. Latch and her women-only inn. She would never have had the chance to experience this side of Saville if not for her. It was even amusing to how he went from grumpy to serious as they stepped into the night.

Quickly and quietly, they retrieved their horse, bundled up Saville's clothes to save time, and padded over to the back of the other establishment where carriages of the guests were kept.

Theodosia's eyes lit up as she found hers almost instantly. The crest on the door had been ripped off, but she would recognize it anywhere. She pointed at her carriage. "There."

"Thank Christ. That was easier than I thought."

"Almost too easy." She glanced at him. "Are you going to swap the horses?"

"We'll swap them once we retrieve the book from the carriage."

"You go swap them and I'll retrieve the book," she lowered her voice to a whisper. "If we split up we can save time."

"No. I am not separating from you."

"It's only a few yards. It will take me mere moments to get the book."

"Nevertheless, separating is a bad idea."

She pushed at his back. "You have the harder task of getting the horses swapped, especially if there are stable hands. Also, you also need to swap clothing if you wish to sit astride on your horse." And she would like to return his disguise to Mrs. Latch before they left.

He paused, sighed, then gave a reluctant nod. "Wait for me by the carriage and don't do anything foolish. If someone comes, hide inside."

"Yes, yes, I shall be careful." Theodosia nudged him on his way and padded over to the carriage, feeling the burn of his gaze on her back linger for a moment before it disappeared, along with him, in the direction of the barn.

In the darkness, with the only sounds of crickets and frogs,

Theodosia felt the loss of Saville's presence. She didn't care for the dark, yet she wasn't afraid of it either. She just preferred to either have her vision entirely unobstructed or to have someone at her side. She blinked a few times. Had she grown *that* fond of the earl that she didn't mind if he was the one with her?

"Focus, Theo," she whispered. She could think about such things later. Excitement of the moment aside, exhaustion tugged a bit at her eyelids. With her belly full of food, they were getting heavier and heavier, but she had no choice but to persevere. And for that, she required all of her wits.

She glanced left and right before she opened the door to the carriage as silently as possible and stepped inside.

Robbing the robbers! How grand!

Her heart pounded as she fumbled for the hidden latch, grasped it, and opened the secret compartment. She reached inside, her fingers brushed over firm leather. "There you are, you cursed thing."

She pulled the book from its concealed space, almost dropping it when a nasty cough echoed nearby on her right. Lord, it sounded like the cougher was almost right behind her!

She froze.

Another cough.

Not so close, then. *This* was why she hated the dark. All other senses were heightened, but she missed clear vision. Her fingers reached into the compartment again—a bit farther this time—to pull out a pistol she had brought along.

She grinned.

She hadn't told Saville about the pistol. Would he be surprised? Shocked? Scolding? She never knew with that man. Her hand felt into the compartment one more time, her eyes lighting up as pulled out a satchel with a spare set of Turkish trousers and a shirt. She would admit her brothers had the best tricks. She resolved never to have a carriage of her own that didn't sport a secret compartment or two.

The unsteady thud of steps suddenly joined the cough. Theodosia didn't think twice, she clutched the door and silently pulled it shut, ducking to the floor and huddling there, ears strained, pistol ready to aim.

The footsteps passed the carriage.

She let out a sigh of relief before her eyes widened. Wait, what direction were they heading?

Saville.

Even if the man was heading in the direction of the stables, the earl would be fine, wouldn't he? He had always been vigilant about his surroundings. And he could handle a drunkard.

I should wait.

She should do as she'd been told. Her fingers tightened around the pistol. But Saville didn't have a weapon to protect himself with.

That tongue of his is not a weapon?

Can his tongue protect him from a pistol? If the mystery man with the cough was one of the highwaymen, he could be armed.

Theodosia bit down on her lip. Hadn't he been shot by his sister in a duel recently? He hadn't once shown any reaction of pain since he'd turned up so unexpectedly, so she'd completely forgotten about it. Had the wound even fully healed yet? Drat it. She shouldn't be worrying about that hellion. Yet . . .

What would Saville do if he were in her shoes? Would he wait?

You aren't him.

And he'd asked her to wait.

She waited.

For all of about three seconds more.

No. No. No! So what if she weren't him?

That rapscallion would never wait. And neither would she.

FIELD HAD FELT conflicted many times in his life. More so in the past few weeks than in all of the rest of his years combined. And more so *tonight* than in all those years and past weeks combined. He shouldn't have left Theodosia all alone. Shouldn't have let himself be persuaded. It went against every instinct in his body.

He left the farmer's mare at the entrance, his gaze tracking across all the stalls for Dream as he passed them in long, urgent strides. He found him in the last stall.

Thank Christ.

Dream shook his and snorted at him, as though venting his grievances for having been stolen away from his master. Field entered the stall, tossing his clothing to the side and placing the gin at his feet, before stepping up to soothe his horse by brushing his hands along his neck in long, gentle strokes.

"I'm here, boy. I'm here. Let's get you saddled up."

Poking his head out of the stall to confirm that the way still remained clear, he grabbed hold of his nearby saddle and placed it on Dream's back.

"That's a good boy," the reassured in low whispers. "Let's get this done before anything else. We're going to leave here nice and quiet."

He led Dream out of the stall by the reins, his mind returning to Lady Theodosia, who should be listless with impatience by now. He couldn't help but smile at the thought. Had he ever met a more impatient lady than her?

"Who goes there?" a man called out, and then coughed.

Field cursed.

It seemed they might have to make a dash for it. He snapped up the reins and lifted his leg to mount Dream, only to be hindered by a skirt.

Confound it! He'd forgotten to change back into his clothes. His gaze flicked between the man and the stall. This was not a good position for him to be in.

"Who the bloody 'ell are you?" the newcomer demanded.

"None of your damn business," Field growled, his mind racing on how to settle this with the least amount of disturbance.

"Heh? A man dressed as a woman?" The man's gaze caught

on Dream. He frowned. "That's the boss's horse, you, you, *you* thief!" A finger wagged at Field before the man rushed over and flung his fist.

Field dodged the fist and kicked out, but was once more brought up short by the restrictions of a dress.

"Devil take it!" He nearly lost his footing.

"Aye, thief, I'll send you to hell, you unnatural he-she-devil!"

"What the hell did you just call me?" Field growled.

"He-she-devil!" The man pounced on Field, and they both tumbled to the ground.

A strong scent of alcohol swept up his nostrils. He would be grateful for the advantage of tussling with a drunk man, if the stench hadn't knocked the remainder of the breath from his lungs. And if he hadn't still been wearing this cursed dress.

"How dare you try steal from us?" The man scrambled to his knees and punched him in his injured arm, and Field grunted. The wound, shallow though it was, still hurt when it was aggravated. And he'd been deuced careful not to do so up to now. So much for that.

"Weren't you a thief first?" Field snapped as he gripped the man's hair and yanked. Hard.

A slew of curses sprung from the drunkard's mouth to a degree that even hurt *his* ears. "You devil! How dare you? Do you know who I am?"

"I don't give a damn who you are, you rotten blackguard." Field punched him in the jaw, the death grip on the man's hair not loosening. "Do you bloody know who *I* am?"

"You are a demon!" The man tried to crawl away, but Field jerked him back by his hair, drawing about another foul curse from the drunkard, who turned and seized his dress by the bosom and yanked. A stocking fell out. "A demon sent from hell!"

"Yes, I'm a demon, and as I go back from whence I came, I shall take you with me!"

"I'll never go!" The man tried to worm his way out of his hold again. "Not so long as I live!"

"Hah!" Field growled. "As if I'm giving you any choice!"

A glint flashed in the corner of his eye, and Saville rolled away just as pain slashed across his leg. *Not good.* Before he could throttle the blackguard further, another figure moved into sight, hitting the man over the head of some sort of object he couldn't make out.

The knife dropped to the ground as the man staggered to his feet, clutching his head. "What the hell was that?"

"Me," a sweet, familiar voice said. "And I am not happy that you hurt my partner."

Field blinked at Theodosia blankly from his spot on the ground. Had she just called him her partner? Did he hear that right? He watched in a daze as she strode up to the drunkard and delivered a swift knee strike to his crotch.

Field flinched in sympathy as the man dropped to the ground with a cry of pain, his hands moving from his head to clutch his groin. Field had half a mind to cover his own. She must have learned that from one of her brothers. He was rather glad, and somewhat surprised, that his own family jewels had not borne the brunt of this woman's wrath before now.

He dragged in a deep breath. "Christ, woman, I told you to stay put."

The bandit writhing on the ground glared at them with bloodshot eyes. "You will regret this!"

"I'm sure I won't," Theodosia said. She turned to Field. "Having fun?" Her eyes fell on his leg, where blood soaked the spot there the knife had sliced—a spot Field had avoiding looking at so far. She gasped and rushed to him, hunkering down to look closer at the wound. "Is it deep? Does it hurt?"

"I'm fine."

"Don't lie to me."

"Who says I'm lying?"

"The look of pain on your face says you're lying, unless your face has a reason to lie?"

Field instantly schooled his features. She ignored him and

bunched up the skirts above the wound. He shut his eyes. "See, it's not that bad."

"How can you say that when your eyes are closed?"

"I don't want to faint."

"*Faint?*" A hitch of breath. "Please do not tell me you faint at the sight of blood. No wonder your face is as pale as a sheet of paper!"

"Not a little blood no," he admitted. "But it's always hard to tell what is a lot and what is not until I see it." And he couldn't, under any circumstances, faint.

"Drat it! Very well, stay still and keep your eyes closed while I manage this."

Field opened his eyes but averted them to the man on ground, keeping watch on him.

"I'll use this stocking that fell from your bosom to wrap the wound."

Words no man ever wanted to hear.

"What about the blood on the skirt?" she asked as she quickly folded the stocking around his wound with deft but gentle fingers.

"I don't know." Perhaps if he could convince his mind that it was paint.

"Well, I'm not strong enough to tear the material, so you'll have to try not to look at it."

For the sake of getting away from this godforsaken town? "That I can manage. Don't worry, I won't faint and delay our escape."

"Delay? We shall be caught, not delayed, so don't you dare swoon now. I don't have smelling salts."

"Just wrap the bloody wound." Swoon his arse.

"Yes, yes, luckily it's just a nick, but the bleeding still needs to stop, and we need to clean the wound."

Field nodded. "Are you done? We should leave before his companions notice he hasn't returned."

"I'm done." She covered his legs with the skirt again. "Remember not to look. I won't be able to drag you out of here if you do."

"Warning noted." Field allowed her to help him to his feet. Dizziness rushed through his head, and the stew in his belly clamored to be released.

Settle down, body.

It was just the scent of iron, nothing more. He could handle the smell.

"How can such a big man as you be felled by the sight of blood? What a terrible Achilles heel to be in possession of." She cocked her head. "Did you faint when your sister shot you?"

He sent her a gloomy look.

"So you did. Never mind, I won't let you faint today."

"Well, I'm reassured," Field said a bit dryly. He couldn't help the fact that the sight of blood made him squeamish. It had ever since the day he stopped taking beatings and turned his fists back on his father. The mess he'd made that day . . . his belly still churned at the memory. He pushed the unwelcome recollection back into the box where it usually resided.

"Should we still rip the dress? I can guide your hands while you keep your eyes closed."

"No need. It's mostly blood on flesh that I can't stand." But he still avoided looking down. He'd rather not test if this still held true here. "My clothes and the gin are still in the stable."

She nodded and retrieved the items. "Luckily I found an old satchel in the compartment, too." She stuffed his clothing in gin in the bag. "We should pour some on your wound."

"Later. You have the book?"

She patted the satchel. "Yes."

"Then let's go." He glanced at the man, who at some point had lost consciousness still clutching his nether regions. Blood trickled from his temple. With what had Theodosia wacked the scoundrel with?

"I can't believe the scuffle didn't wake the stable hands."

Field shrugged. "If there are any, they probably wouldn't dare intervene." He motioned for her to come closer.

Her bows furrowed. "What about your wound?"

"It can withstand this much." He lifted her onto the horse first, ignored the sting of pain, before he followed. *Tried* to follow. But his leg hit the confines of the skirt. Again.

Field cursed, bent down while looking at anything but the bloody side of the dress, and ripped a slit into the fabric.

"I suppose I shall have to compensate the owner of those poor clothes with coin."

Field grunted and mounted the horse.

"And don't forget to thank me for my help."

Field stared at the back of her head. He could just imagine her pleased as punch expression. "Even though I had the situation under control, thank you."

A snort. "You were rolling around in the dirt, pulling his hair. Is that how all men fight?"

"It's a dirty trick, but one that's effective."

"Really? Is that not a girl's trick? Did you pick it from you sister?"

"So what if I did?"

A chuckle followed his question.

His scalp prickled as memories drew up to the surface of his mind. Selena had pulled his hair once when they were still children. It had hurt like the devil, and there had been no way for him to retaliate. He would never hit a girl. But she had also gotten into tiffs with other girls in those days who did fight back, and it always seemed to work with them.

He shook his head.

Well, the trick worked with men, too, it seemed. He nudged Dream forward. He wanted to get out of this damn town. At least he had his horse back. And the book. They could now safely conclude their journey together.

It was what he wanted.

Is it?

Field had no time to dwell on those two little words, as they'd only taken a few steps forward before another man stepped into their path, blocking their exit from the barn.

"That's my horse you're riding off on."

Theodosia leveled a pistol at him. "No, it's not."

Heavenly Christ.

Where had she found that? Was this what she'd hit that ruffian with? No wonder the man become insensible shortly after she'd also kneed him in the groin!

Field's first instinct was to snatch the pistol away from her, but he didn't dare. One wrong move meant she could accidentally pull the trigger. That wouldn't just alert the others, it would awaken the whole bloody town. She might also kill the man, and he didn't want anyone's death on her hands.

The man casually lifted both arms in the air.

He appeared sober, but he'd disregarded his jacket, which meant he might have been comfortable and confident enough to disregard his own weapon, too.

Field prayed to the skies this was the case.

"My man still alive, princess?"

Field scowled as the man defiled his ears with that endearment. "For now," he growled in her stead.

"Might wake up with a bit of a headache," Theodosia added.

"And a bit of something else," Field said. "Best stand aside, Black Knight."

The man smiled and, with his hands still in the air, stepped aside. "You made a mistake here today."

"We'll never see each other again after today," Field countered, spurring Dream into a dead run.

He prayed to God his word would hold true.

Chapter Nine

The next day

THEODOSIA BLINKED OPEN her eyes. Her gaze flicked over the room, her mind hazy for a minute before recollection returned of the previous night's events.

Book. Wound. Fleeing once again.

Saville had driven Dream nearly to death as they waded across the country roads, changing directions and roads so many times in hopes the highwaymen wouldn't pick up their trail.

They finally came across a farm and met a startled-looking Mr. and Mrs. Bell and sought shelter on their farm. She could only imagine what they must have thought at the sight of two strangers knocking on their door in the early hours of the morning. They'd spotted the house in the pale light just beginning to give shape to the landscape around them, and they'd been so tired—and her backside had hurt from riding for hours, first on the highwayman's horse and then on Dream—that Theodosia had decided to take the chance and ask if the older couple would take them in—maybe even for a few nights—as they were cousins on the run from a group of highwaymen.

The couple readily agreed.

Her legs had given out at that point, so it was then one rider standing before their door with her gathered up in his arms.

How embarrassing!

Worse than hanging onto his back?

She couldn't rightly tell.

But they were helped, that was all that mattered. And this spacious room they were offered had two narrow beds. They could comfortably sleep here, and they did.

She turned her head.

Saville was still sleeping soundly. If she recalled correctly, he lay in the same position he had first fallen into on the bed. Her lips quirked. He still wore the purple dress.

Her eyes drifted to his legs where the skirts had hitched up, displaying two legs layered with soft, sandy hair. Theodosia blinked.

How revealing!

She lifted her gaze back to his face. All scowls and frowns were smoothed out to highlight his handsome features. He should scowl less. He'd be almost irresistible if he did. He would certainly have more ladies flocking around him.

She slowly sat up and looked to the window. Bright light. How much time had passed? It should be more than a few hours, yet the heaviness in her head made it feel like she'd only slept a few minutes.

"You awake?" Saville asked.

She turned toward the raspy sound. His eyes were still closed. "Yes. It should be around noon if I had to make a guess."

"And we aren't surrounded by brigands?"

She smiled. "I don't believe we are."

"Then I'll sleep a bit longer."

You do that, Earl.

She rose softly, quickly darting a look beneath the bed to reassure herself that the satchel with the betting book was still stuffed beneath, before padding over to the door.

"Where are you going?" his gruff voice came.

"To let our hosts know we are still alive, and to ask if they've heard any whispers about our pursuers." She paused. "Mrs. Bell said she would set out some clothes for us. I'll ask if we can draw bath."

Theodosia slipped from the room, and after one parting glance at Saville, who still hadn't moved an inch, she shut the door quietly. Her heart wrenched in her chest. He looked tired. And he must be in some pain, too.

Not even one sarcastic remark had left his lips.

Even though the knife had only left a shallow scratch, the way he had driven the horse could not have been comfortable for any of his injuries.

The man was generally a pain in the arse with his demands and his rejoinders, but she could not stand a Saville that said nothing. One that didn't even have a breath to retort. That pained *her*. She would ask Mrs. Bell if it would be a bother if she used her kitchen to make a beef stew. She would repay their kindness tenfold later.

Mrs. Bell smiled when Theodosia ventured into the kitchen. "Ah, dearie, did you have a good rest?"

Theodosia nodded. The woman's welcoming smile was a fresh sight for her poor, heavy eyes. "Would it be possible for me to make a pot of beef stew for Field?" Theodosia switched to his name rather than title, which sounded almost foreign on her lips. They had merely told the couple they were cousins and hadn't been clear about their true identities. Mr. and Mrs. Bell hadn't asked either. A relief, really. They could both use a pause from all the demands their names and position made of them these days.

"Oh, have no worries, my dear. I could whip up some stew in my sleep, and you still look like as though you might collapse at any moment."

Theodosia gave a sheepish smile. "We've had quite the adventure. But it shan't feel right if I do not at least help with something."

"Then you can help me cut the carrots."

"Of course." Theodosia moved to the cutting board and picked up a nearby knife while Mrs. Bell rummaged for the carrots.

"Speaking of little adventures," Mrs. Bell said. "Do you wish for us to send for your family?"

Lord no. "That won't be necessary. Our families are a bit . . . It's best if they don't know—we wouldn't want them to excite themselves unnecessarily. Field and I just need a moment of rest and wait for the dust to settle on these brigands after us. Speaking of which, have there been any whispers about highwaymen?" Theodosia asked as she accepted the vegetables.

Mrs. Bell shook her head. "None that we've heard, dearie."

"I see." Could no news be accepted as good news?

"That's a good thing, dear. It's good that you found us. Those ruffians won't come looking for you here."

Theodosia nodded as she cut the carrots into chunky slices. It hadn't been that long since she'd left London, yet it felt like ages ago. She sent word to her aunt she would be coming to visit in Brighton a day before she left. By now, her aunt would be worried that she hadn't arrived yet and perhaps even sent word back to her mother. If not today, then tomorrow. After which time her mother would set the hounds loose on her.

A bunch of browbeating brothers breathing down her neck.

Yes, it's best to stay here for a while.

Her brothers wouldn't find her here, either, and she didn't want to get caught. It would be even worse getting caught together with Saville given the rumors that were circulating.

Those rumors. . .

She'd almost forgotten about them. She supposed they would die down with time. Just like these carrots would disappear into a delicious stew and then their bellies.

"Theodosia in the kitchen," a gruff voice said from the door. "Now this is a sight I never thought I'd witness."

She glanced over her shoulder to find Saville leaning against the doorframe, watching her. A sight she might have found handsome even, had he not still been wearing a purple dress.

"You really need to change your clothes."

Mrs. Bell snickered. "I've never seen Mr. Bell so startled before in my life as when he first caught sight of you. I shall cherish that memory forever, I'm sure."

"Why are you up?" Theodosia asked. "Didn't you want to sleep some more?"

"Couldn't."

Mrs. Bell chuckled. "I put clothes out for you. You can give me yours to wash. Let's not give Mr. Bell another fright."

"Thank you, Mrs. Bell," Theodosia said. "I still have a set of clean clothes with me And clothes for him, as well, though they aren't clean."

Mrs. Bell waved a slight hand. "We can wash everything that needs washing, dearie."

"Well, I for one, can understand his sentiment, which is why I haven't glanced into a mirror yet."

His gaze shifted back to Theodosia before he dragged both hands through his hair. When he dropped them to his side, his ruffled tendrils were sticking up in all directions.

Theodosia laughed. "You look a bit wild. A damsel in wild distress."

He frowned, and it wasn't his normal scowl. It was perhaps a little bit *less*, the furrow not as deep as before.

"Oh, yes," Mrs. Bell said suddenly. "Your horse—Dream, was it? He has been fed and rubbed down. A perfectly happy beast. And a nice name, too. Very apt. He looks fierce, like you, but he has a calm temperament like you, as well."

Calm?

At this, Theodosia did laugh. Were they talking about the same man? How had Saville managed to gull the Bells?

"It must be the dress," Theodosia said. Barring the rip and the patch of blood. "Softens the features. Purple really is your color, it seems. If you find you are becoming attached to dresses, you must have more commissioned for you once you get back to London. I can recommend a wonderful modiste."

"Excuse me? Could you repeat that?"

Theodosia shook her head, instead remarking, "Dream is an interesting name for a horse, wouldn't you say?"

"What sort of name do you think I'd give a horse?"

"Demon? *Savage*? Devil?"

His lips quirked, then a shrug. "I when I was a boy I dreamed of a black horse often. Then I found one that looked exactly like the horse in those dreams, so I called him Dream."

Theodosia blinked. Of all the reasons she might have guessed, that was not one she'd ever have thought of. Even the note of sentimentality that clung to his answer was unexpected. Unexpectedly lovely, too.

"Are you shocked?" he asked.

"Extremely."

Mrs. Bell laughed. "I am happy to see your spirits have not been crushed after what you two dears went through. It would be terrible if circumstances were ever to dim that affection."

Theodosia nearly choked. Affection? Was Mrs. Bell secretly foxed? She cast a suspicious look at Saville. Mrs. Bell didn't even seem to find it strange that he still wore the dress. In fact, both Mr. and Mrs. Bell had accepted their attire, her with her Turkish trousers and he in woman's clothing, with hardly a second glance.

"Just what did you do to get into Mrs. Bell's good graces?"

"Oh, no dear. When you knocked on our door asking for help, I could simply tell with one look you are most precious to your cousin. It's rare for cousins to care this deeply for each other—just ask me and mine. You should always cherish your relationship."

By Jove, just what sort of familial feeling did Mrs. Bell think she could glimpse between them? Theodosia would rather not ask for more details. "Well . . . we," she looked at Saville and gave an awkward laugh, "aren't *that* close."

"You can't fool me, my dear," Mrs. Bell said over her shoulder. "Just look at you wanting to make beef stew to give your family strength. So lovely."

What lovely? The man was hurt. That was all.

She met Saville's unrelenting stare.

"You asked Mrs. Bell to make me beef stew to give me strength?" he asked.

Theodosia snorted. "How else are we to get your weak body back in the saddle?"

He returned her snort, but it was almost teasing. "My weak body? I recall carrying you all the way to the doorstep when we arrived, and you are heavier than three sacks of potatoes."

Theodosia cast him a dry look. *Three* sacks? *I shall get you back for that one, Field Savage.* "You must cherish potatoes a great deal if you know their weight." She turned to Mrs. Bell. "Forget the beef, we can just make a plain potato stew."

"I take that back," he said instantly. "One sack."

She laughed. "You think that's better?"

He suddenly bent over to clutch his leg. "I think my leg is throbbing."

Rogue. All that was throbbing was his palate!

"Ah, you youngsters of today." The older woman tsked, then said dreamily. "If all family could be this way, it would be nice, don't you agree?"

Theodosia's appalled gaze met Saville's equally appalled eyes.

Theodosia was convinced. Mrs. Bell *was* secretly foxed. She had a stash of wine, or gin, or whatever in the kitchen somewhere and added it to her tea.

"That's right," Saville, the beast drawled with a smile Theodosia had never seen on his face. "We do love boldly, do we not?"

She wanted to throttle the man.

Hellion.

SAVILLE CHUCKLED AS the minx stared at him as though she wanted to chop him to bits instead of the carrots.

That was better.

Familiar.

All this talk of affection gave him chills. Staying in such close proximity with her was dangerous. It was those eyes—it was nonsense that he'd ever said they were the devil's own, but they did pierce straight through his soul. Every single time. Very dangerous. And after she'd helped with the ruffian in stables . . . no one had ever helped him fight a battle before. No one had ever come to his rescue.

But she had.

Without any hesitation.

Field couldn't deny it was a sensation a man could become addicted to. Dangerous indeed.

The hot stares were much better than playful banter, though they did fall a bit short from her usual glares. But having shared in a battle together, it seemed they had become comrades of sorts. Even Field felt the usual annoyance born from their bickering hardly surfacing. His own seemed to have changed tone as well. It all made him rather . . . uneasy.

Uneasiness aside, how could his heart not palpitate at Mrs. Bell assessment?

It didn't matter that the context was familial. It called to a deep, almost forgotten part of him.

"Would it still be affection if I pretend he is a carrot and slice him up for the stew?" Theodosia asked with a raised brow.

Field mirrored her look. "Would that be all of me or just *parts* of me?"

She pointed the knife at him in mock threat. "Care to find out?"

Mrs. Bell laughed. "You are done with the carrots, dear. Why don't the two of you go wash up? There's water in a basin with cloth in the next room. Unfortunately, we haven't boiled any hot water yet, so that will have to do for now. There are also fresh sets clothes are on the table."

Theodosia set the knife down on the table. "Thank you, Mrs. Bell."

Field nodded. "Much obliged. And I'm happy to help where I

can."

"Me as well." Theodosia looked over to him, her gaze dropping to where he got hurt. "You might have trouble removing the dress. Shall I help?"

A chill skittered down his spine. Theodosia helping him undress? There were several things wrong with that image, not the least of which being that he found it oddly fascinating. "No need, no need. You wash up first, I shall wait."

"No, go ahead." She smiled. "I'm sure you want nothing more than to get out of that dress."

Field didn't argue, and with a nod at the women, he turned on his heel. Exhaustion still tugged at him, but the moment she had left the room to find Mrs. Bell, he couldn't sleep. A restlessness had settled into his chest, prompting him to rise as well.

Now, she was quite right—he wanted to get out of this deuced dress. If he could simply rip it from his body, he would.

Footsteps sounded behind him.

He cut a fleeting glance over his shoulder. "Why are you following me?"

"Can't I?"

"I'm going to change clothes and wash." Field collected the items of clothing from the small drawing room.

"I know." She snatched up the washbasin and cloth. "You might need my help."

Field didn't bother to argue any more and returned to their chamber. "So rude." She placed the washbasin on the table and plopped down onto the bed, eyeing him with interest. But it was that smile that made the hairs on the back of his neck prickle.

"What are you doing?" Field asked suspiciously.

"Acting the rogue."

"Rogue?" Had the Heavens fallen?

Her teeth flashed. "You seem to be the one in a dress, and I seem to be the one in trousers, so I thought I'd see how the title of rogue fits on me."

Field didn't want to entertain this conversation. All instinct told him he would lose. "Speaking of trousers, just how long *are* you going to wear those?"

Her brow furrowed slightly. "I don't take your meaning."

"Let me put it this way, then: How are you going to act the rogue?"

"I see." Instead of answering, she leaped from the bed and sauntered over to him. "I suppose, given the circumstance, and to spare water, I should wash up now as well. Do you mind if I join you?"

Field stilled. "Theodosia."

"Oh my, my name sounds positively evil on your lips. Shall I play the devil? Apparently I already have the eyes."

"Do not play with fire if you do not wish to be burned."

"What's so fiery about this?" Her smile turned playful. "Are you perhaps hot? You might cool down if you remove that dress."

"Are you not afraid that I might act the rogue right back?" Field crossed his arms over his chest. "I may even lose control."

"Perhaps *I* am in the mood to lose control as well."

Field arched a brow, assessing her, the trousers she wore. "I suppose it takes a brave *man* to admit that he's in the mood to lose control over a pretty *woman*."

She chuckled. "A man, you say . . ."

He shrugged. "If the trousers fit."

"Shall I rip open your bodice, then?" she murmured with a twitch of her lips.

"Just how much time did you spend with those brothers of yours?" Saints, he was just a man, after all. One with a rather visual imagination. And God help him, what she was saying brought an onslaught of provoking imagery to his weak, male mind.

"Enough," she said simply.

Field thought back to his sister and Warrick. "Brothers seem to be the true corruption of ladies."

"It's rather naïve to assume we ladies grow up all innocent and that our mothers have to explain how the world works."

"For some ladies that still holds true."

"Ladies without brothers, you mean."

"Ladies who—" Field decided to clamp his mouth shut before he stepped into a minefield of glares and tart comments.

"*Who?*" she urged.

He averted his gaze. "Never mind."

A small chuckle. "It's a wise man who is quick with learning new skills."

"Dodging tricky conversations is a skill?" His gaze locked onto hers again. "I suppose in our case, it is. Now, if you are done with acting the rogue and loitering about . . ."

"Actually, I followed you to check on your wound."

His wound? He'd almost forgotten about it.

"We haven't cleaned it yet. We should do so before it becomes infected," she continued.

"I'm about to wash up. I'll clean it."

"You forget, I grew up with six brothers. If there are three things I know about men, it's that they detest doctors, play the infant when they're sick, and don't care a whit about scrapes and scratches. Lie down on the bed."

"Why should I lie down?" That sounded more dangerous than an infected wound. "Why can't I just sit?"

"Because then you'll be glowering at me from on top. I prefer to you glower from the bottom."

Bloody hell. "If you even know what the picture that provokes, you'd not say stuff like that."

She pressed him down on the bed when he stubbornly remained upright. "Behave."

Field lay down grudgingly, not sure whether he should be impressed or concerned that such a statement didn't even give her pause. "I can't believe you just said that to me."

"Believe it." She hiked up his skirts.

Field scowled. "You are doing this on purpose, aren't you?"

"What exactly am I doing on purpose?"

"There!" He lifted his head to scowl at her. "I detect suspicious humor in your voice."

She scoffed. "Quite sensitive, aren't we? I won't do anything roguish to you, so settle down."

Field bit down on his jaw as she removed the stocking she'd wrapped around his leg. Easier ordered than done. Because she was touching him again.

So damn gently.

Gooseflesh broke out of his skin as she removed the cloth, and Field shut his eyes, savoring the sensation way too much. When last had someone taken care of him so tenderly?

When he was a boy?

Before his father passed? After that, since there were no beatings, there was no more care. Then his mother remarried, and left Selena in London with him. No more care. Just sibling bickering.

He sighed.

"Does it hurt?" She dipped a cloth in the water and washed the wound. "Luckily it was not deep enough that you require stitches."

"No. It doesn't hurt."

Just . . . don't stop.

Never stop.

Chapter Ten

THEODOSIA SHUT HER eyes and enjoyed the flavor of gin rolling over her tongue. And by flavor, she meant the burning sensation that nearly robbed her of all her breath!

So strong.

The Bells had already gone to bed, and she sat at the kitchen table, the tension in her shoulders draining with each sip of gin. After she'd played a bit of a rogue in the bedroom, she'd escaped and let him wash up. Then returned to wash up a bit herself. Then escaped again. But that was beside the point.

Why had she done that? Act the rogue?

More importantly, why had she liked it?

Cleaning his wound had almost felt like a sort of seduction. Which sounded truly ridiculous, but her body had turned hot all over.

She took another sip. Saville was probably not going to be happy that she'd nicked the bottle from the room.

Again, what did she care anyway? The more she could annoy him and pay him back for all the annoyance he'd caused her, the better. Right?

Ah, Saville, Saville, Saville.

Over the course of the season, she'd learned he loved to quarrel with his sister. He loved to act the hero. His favorite waistcoat was purple—one she'd taken delight in snipping up with Selena before her trip. He also was also rather dramatic at times. Stubborn. Once he set his mind to something, he might compromise, but he wouldn't change paths. He had a gruff exterior and a foul mouth, but beneath all the bluster, a tender heart. Sensitive to anything that touched it. Just the merest brush might raise his hackles. Or should she say quills? He did remind her of a hedgehog at times.

Her gaze tracked around the small room.

So peaceful. And quiet. Perhaps she should marry a farmer. Such a simple life would not be all that bad.

Footsteps approached, and her lips quirked when Field entered the kitchen. He still looked rather wild, with nothing on but a pair of ancient brown trousers and a shirt with sleeves rolled up to his elbows. His gaze darted left and right before falling on the bottle. He scowled. "You cannot drink that."

"Why not?"

"Ladies don't drink gin."

"Ladies don't sleep in the same rooms as men, but I did that, too."

"Can I never win an argument with you?"

"You can try," she eyed him askance, "if you wish to waste your breath."

"Well, that I don't wish to do tonight."

She let out a small belch.

He arched a brow. "Are you all right? How much did you have? Should I rub your back? It always helped Selena in the past."

Theodosia blinked at him. If he were Lord Chance, he'd probably have vanished like a puff of smoke at the very idea of a woman belching. Saville was truly different from all the rest. Was that good or bad? Most likely a bit of both.

"I'm fine, but thank you for your concern," she told him. He lifted the bottle to inspect. "I didn't have that much."

"But you did have enough."

She semi-rose to snatch the bottle from him. "Are you one of my brothers?"

"If I were, I'd have taken you over my knee by now."

"Does that work with your sister?"

"No," he said.

"I didn't think so. So why do you believe it would work with me?"

"You are right, why would it ever work on you? Minx."

"Hellion." She pushed out a chair with her foot. "Are you going to join me?"

He retrieved a glass before lowering himself onto the stool, his big body looking out of place at the small table. He poured himself a glass, tossed it back and poured another. "There is something I am curious about."

"Do tell."

"Do I still make your skin crawl?" he suddenly asked her, sitting back, crossing one leg over the other.

Theodosia drew back. Make her skin crawl? She seemed to recall she had said something to that effect. Was the man a grudge-bearing hound, destined to sniff out all of her rudest comments over the season? Perhaps she'd underestimated his prickliness. He never seemed to forget even the smallest of insults she'd hurled at him.

Did he still make her skin crawl? She couldn't say yes, for that was no longer the case. She also didn't want to say no, for she didn't want to admit to something she couldn't quite understand herself. She settled for, "A little bit."

"In a good way or bad way?"

"Not a good way. Not entirely bad either. I suppose somewhere in between."

He nodded. "What a compliment coming from you."

Hah! She knew there was a reason she didn't want to outright say no. "It's not a compliment."

"I'll take it as one."

"Please don't," Theodosia said dryly.

His chin raised a notch. "You can't stop me."

Theodosia tossed back her gin as he had done earlier, thumping the empty glass down onto the table. She poured another.

"When you wake up tomorrow feeling like shite, don't say I didn't warn you."

"Do you always speak that way in front of ladies? Or is it just me?"

He flashed her a grin. "Am I in front of a lady?"

"Hah! That barb has little sting coming from you." With *that* smile.

"Probably because it's received with acceptance."

"Do not make me laugh. Let's just drink tonight. That way I can forget all about robberies, sour apples, and knife-wielding bandits."

"It wasn't all that bad," he muttered. "There was also a pistol-wielding princess."

"You could even say that after being sliced up by a brigand?"

"I wasn't sliced up, for Christ's sakes. It's a mere scratch." He shot her a look before drinking another swallow of gin.

"What's wrong?" Theodosia asked, eyes narrowing on him.

"What do you mean what's wrong?" He raised a brow.

"Your lip just twitched.'"

"Why does that mean anything is wrong?"

"It never twitches. It curls."

He tossed another sip back into his throat, a motion so smooth Theodosia thought she should try it, too.

"Is there a bloody difference?" he asked.

"Yes."

He actually huffed out a laugh. "Fine. Nothing is wrong, but I was just thinking about your impressive moves back in the barn. Bringing down that man in one fell swoop. Your brothers taught you well."

"They've always been worried about me. Some men have tried to take advantage of me in the past." She eyed him. "And don't say I give them reason to worry. I've not always rebelled against my family."

But she *had* always felt trapped by her station. Which might seem ridiculous to most since there were so many others who would give anything to trade places with her.

"Now what's wrong with you? Why are you scowling?" Saville asked.

Theodosia sighed. "When you're in my presence I always scowl."

"While I do believe that's true, this scowl is different."

Theodosia met his gaze. Oh? "Different how?"

"As though you have just thought about something deeply unpleasant."

Unpleasant? "I suppose I do have something I find unpleasant at times."

"Care to share?"

"Care not to judge me if I do?" she countered, and couldn't help but bite back a smile when a smidgeon of thunder flashed across his face.

"I won't."

"Very well, I feel confined by my role as a lady."

"That's all?"

That's *everything*. "What do you mean that's all? Aren't you shocked?"

He shrugged. "We all feel shackled by our roles at one point or another. It's up to us to place the right meaning on those shackles."

"I . . . have not words."

"Why not? Are you rendered speechless by my wondrous reasoning?"

"I shall reserve the right to decide whether it's wondrous or disastrous." She took another sip of gin and said, "So even the Earl of Saville feels trapped by his station."

"I am just a man."

And she just a woman. A curious one to boot. "May I ask why you felt trapped?"

He opened his mouth before closing it again.

"You don't have to tell me."

He shook his head. "It's not that I don't want to tell you, it's just that when it comes to this topic, words oftentimes fail me. Let us just say that my father was rather . . . temperamental."

"I hate to point this out, but you are temperamental, too."

"He was much worse than me. So much so, that I've often wondered what it would be like if I had been born to a simple family. Less entitled. Perhaps not even titled at all." He glanced around the kitchen. "Perhaps a place like this."

She shook her head. "You would have hated it."

"How so?"

"No gossip here," Theodosia said simply.

He sent her a flat look. "I am not a bloody gossip."

"If you say so."

"What about you?" he countered. "Why should a lady with all the privileges in the world feel trapped?"

"Six overbearing brothers are not enough of a reason?" Theodosia thought a bit. "It's the damnedest thing. I love my family, but I want to push back against all that is expected of me. Yet at the same time, I don't want to disappoint them."

"Selena could learn something from you."

"She and I aren't all that different," Theodosia remarked. "Ultimately, I still rebelled against my family by dispensing copies of the betting book. In a way, I'm still rebelling. Just like her."

"I can't argue about that."

She cocked her head to the side. "Tell me something, Saville. Are you disappointed in her?"

"In Selena?" He shook his head. "I could never be."

"Even with all her shenanigans with Warrick?"

He pulled a face. "I'm mad as hell at *him*. But also not disappointed. I suppose if I'm disappointed in anyone, then it's in myself."

"Because you behaved like a lunatic?"

"Now it's your turn not to make *me* laugh." He snorted, then considered. "No, it's because I couldn't protect her as a brother should. Because she is disappointed in *me*. A godawful feeling, that."

"Yes well, she did feel betrayed, but that turned into anger, not disappointment. I daresay she knows you did your best."

His grin returned. "You are complimenting me?"

"No," Theodosia denied. "What's there to compliment?" Expect for a *smiling* Saville. He's more handsome than a sleeping Saville. But she would chomp down on her tongue before she admitted that to him.

"I'm pretty certain you are complimenting me."

"Really? Since your best was subpar at most, how can it be a compliment? At most it can be considered as a concession."

"That is still a compliment."

She laughed, deciding not to argue with the man. For some reason, tonight, Saville looked, or rather appeared even more *something* than usual. "You are hopeless." She paused to consider. "At any rate, it seems that we must add another thing to the list of all we have common. We both have felt, at one point in time, trapped in our lives."

"But you still do," he remarked.

"A bit."

He poured them each another cup of gin. "Well, let's drink. This stuff has been known to free a trapped person right up."

"Really?" She stared at her gin. "I don't if that is how it works."

"True, tomorrow we will feel wretched, but tonight we shall both feel free. What do you say?"

"Let's be free." Theodosia clinked glassed with him, ready to unburden herself of any traps and shackles. "And let us not forget to forget."

GIN HAD NEVER tasted so sweet. Or perhaps an exchange with a woman had never tasted so sweet. Field had always been of the opinion that he couldn't hold a deep conversation with a woman. They either informed him of what was to be or not to be, or they bickered with him—especially in the case of a sister, as personalities clashed. And that was that.

But a conversation?

Speaking about *things*?

This was a rather pleasant revelation.

And something shifted inside of him.

She'd said she wanted to forget about robberies, apples, and knife-wielding bandits. Let us not forget to forget? An appealing yet almost hopeless idea. He didn't want to forget anything about these past few days, because every moment had her in it.

But there were other things he wanted to forget.

He wanted to forget his father's wrathful fists. He'd like to forget the back of the carriage as his mother set off to start her new life without her children. He'd even like to forget the sight of his sister pointing a pistol at him.

He'd done his best to protect his mother and his sister from his father's temper. He had usually succeeded where Selena was concerned, but he couldn't always protect his mother. That had never sat well with Field.

He never wanted to become like his father, yet the more he lost his temper at the smallest of things, the more he couldn't help feeling that he was doing exactly that—becoming like the man he despised.

Liberation came in many forms and memories were one. Yes, there were many things he'd like to forget. That was exactly why he couldn't forget them. They kept the conviction be different—to try—alive inside of him. And, all the things he'd rather forget notwithstanding, there were many, many more things he wanted to remember.

Field took a swig of his gin. A good drink was another form of liberation—short lived but rather more appealing. Forget to forget . . . "It's certainly possible not to forget to forget but still ultimately remember."

She laughed. "Which shall then give us a sense of freedom. At least for a while."

"A sense is all we need."

"I suppose," she murmured. "After all, breaking free from this trap is like breaking free from life, and that is not something we can do."

Right. The aim was to *feel* free rather than to be free, since, as she said, one could not break free from life. Only in death. "Quite an astute observation, if I may say so myself."

"You shall be free in another way soon, too."

Field cocked his head, swirling his drink. "And what way is that?"

"Selena. When she weds Warrick, you shall be free of your sister. You must be quite excited about that."

His drink stopped swirling.

Ah, yes. Selena would set up her own home with Warrick once they'd spoken their vows. Those two had been flaunting *their* affection so boldly since they got engaged that he hadn't even considered that once they actually tied the knot, they wouldn't be in residence anymore.

"Field? Are you all right? You look a bit pale."

Field cleared his throat, tossing back the contents of his glass. "I'm fine."

"Are you sure?" Her brows furrowed. "Is it something I said? Is it about Selena? Do you not want to be free of her?"

"I . . ." What did he want to say? No, he didn't, damn it. With freedom from her came a different sort of confinement altogether. One he hadn't even considered. "If she leaves . . ."

"You will be alone?"

"Christ, I need another drink." He poured himself another. "Does that make me pitiful?" He certainly felt pitiful.

"No, of course not."

"But?"

"There's no but."

"I know there's a but," Field growled. "You don't have to lie to spare my feelings. Tell me."

"There's truly no but. However, you do make it sound as though Warrick is dragging her off to another continent. She will still be in Mayfair."

True. He caught the sudden glint in her gaze. "What's with that look?"

The corners of her lips lifted. "Nothing." A soft chuckle followed soon after. "I just didn't know the mighty Earl of Saville also felt the lesser human emotions."

"I'm not mighty." He sounded like a complete fool. "Forget I said anything."

"I can't forget." Her grin inched upward a notch. "It's etched in my mind now, whether I want it to be or not."

"Unetch it."

She laughed. "Is such a thing even possible? Besides, this does give you a more manly aspect."

"That doesn't make a whit of sense."

"Sense is for the senseful. I feel quite senseless at the moment."

Field cast a skeptical glance at her glass. "You've *drunk* yourself senseless, is what you have done."

"Senseless means freedom, and we decided on freedom."

"In that you are right." He lifted his glass again to clink hers. "To drink as a form of liberation. At least for one night." Though he couldn't promise to forget. He would cherish this moment in this ordinary little kitchen, probably forever.

"At least for one night," she repeated. "To freedom from emotional constraints." She peered at him from beneath her lashes. "Or is that too boring? Should we add freedom from physical constraints?"

"I don't even know what that would entail." Not unless it involved a bed. Christ, what he was thinking now would never even cross her mind. His gaze dropped to her lips. Not that he wanted to imagine what brewed in that beautiful head of hers.

Well, he could—

"What are you looking at?"

His head snapped back up to meet her gaze. Mischievous. The minx was provoking him again. Damn it. What was he thinking? She knew very well what she was talking about. "I'm not looking at anything."

"Are you sure? It looked like you were staring at my lips."

"Even if I were, do you not think it's inappropriate to point out?"

She wiggled her glass at him. "Is it not inappropriate where you were looking?" She smirked. "Do you perhaps want to kiss me?"

"Don't be ridiculous. That would be disastrous."

"I wager many a man has grasped for the chance to kiss me," she said. "Why, do you know how many men my mother has roped in to meet with me on blind matchups?"

"Blind what?"

"Blind matchups."

"What the hell are those?" His brows scrunched together. "Why haven't I heard of this?"

"Ah, that is simple. Because you've not been selected by my mother." She suddenly laughed. "I suppose this means my mother doesn't approve of you as a suitor."

"I've never called on you, either," Field pointed out. "More likely because no one would think I could be paid off to go on one of these matchups with you."

A mock gasp. "Are you accusing my mother of *bribing* the gentleman of the *ton* to meet up with me?"

"How else do you explain their enthusiasm for the chance of being flayed by your not-so-subtle insults? You are a blunt instrument, I tell you."

She leaned in closer, elbows resting on the table. "You know, I wouldn't put it past Margaret King to bribe the weaker of your sex into putting up with me for fifteen minutes."

Field ignored the taunt and asked, "That's how long they

last?"

"The longest one held out was fifteen, the shortest was two."

"Two?" Unbelievable. "How did he manage to excuse himself that quickly?"

"He leaped up and fled the drawing room claiming his belly was acting up."

Dear Christ. "Whatever did you say to the poor chap?"

"Nothing. I just stared."

Field chuckled. Ah yes, a stare that could quell many a man. "Your mother must hope that you will find a gentleman who can stand his ground."

"Not if she's bribed them," Theodosia said. Then shook her head. "Which, of course, she would never do. However, I know she wants me to find a gentleman I do actually like and can see myself marrying."

Admirable. "You've never found such a man?"

"Such a man has never found *me*."

Ah. "Then do you want that man to find you?"

"Well, I cannot be much bothered to search, so he'll have to. I suppose, in this way, I'm rebelling against my family, too. This might also be my mother's way of rebelling right back against me."

"Smart woman."

"So everyone claims," Theodosia said. "But everyone forgets,"—Her smile slid into her eyes. A magnificent spark—"I am my mother's daughter." That grin was dangerous. "So how about it, Saville?"

He leaned back into his seat, his ankle brushing the leg of the table. "How about what, exactly?"

"A kiss."

"What about a kiss?" Field asked slowly, almost unwilling to believe what he was hearing. What she was suggesting.

"Since you've been staring at my lips, why not kiss me? I'm rather curious what a kiss from the likes of you would feel like." She puckered her lips.

"The likes of me? You sure know how to set the mood."

"A mood should be set for a kiss? Do you men not steal kisses left and right without setting any mood?"

"You're foxed." She *must* be foxed.

"No, I'm not," she argued, shifting in her chair. "Give us a kiss."

"And just who is *us*?"

"Me and I?"

He shook his head. "You're not in your right mind." He absolutely could not kiss this woman. Could he?

"If I'm not in my right mind, then neither are you."

"I'm not going to argue with you there." Because he wanted to smack his lips right onto hers.

She lifted up a finger. "*One*. Just one kiss. Only one. I want to see if your kiss is as sour as your temper."

Provoking minx. Very well, if she wanted a kiss so badly, who was he to refuse? He leaned over the table and pecked her on the lips before lowing back to his seat, its creak filling the kitchen along with her slightly startled look.

She blinked at him. "Is that all?"

"Yes, that's all. There will be no more kisses." Or there would be much more than kissing.

"But I couldn't tell if it was sweet or sour."

"It was neither."

"Well, it was something. If I had to put a name to it, I'd have to say it was rather bitter."

Christ. He took another sip.

She cocked her head to the side, smiling. "What harm can a little kiss do? There is no one else here. It's the perfect setting. Pots and pans don't kiss and tell."

A little kiss? Field didn't think so. No little kiss with Theodosia King would ever be little, no matter the setting. "No."

"Are you sure that is your final answer?"

"Absolutely sure." He nodded for emphasis. "In case it hasn't sunk into your *little* brain, there will be no further kissing, at no time and in no place."

"So doing it again now would be foolhardy, you are saying?"

What did this woman *not* get?

"More than foolhardy." Dangerous. So damn dangerous. "Not. Happening."

"I disagree," she said happily. Her voice sounded all kinds of sweet that it sent shudders down his spine.

And then she leaned over, grasped him by the lapels, and kissed him again.

And Field was lost.

So damn lost.

Chapter Eleven

THEODOSIA'S MIND TURNED hazy as her lips pressed against Saville's. Her mind could scarcely keep up with her actions. That she was actually kissing the Earl of Saville. A man she never thought she would ever kiss in her whole life.

But it felt wonderful.

Clearly her mother had brought all the wrong sorts of men to each and every blind matchup she'd arranged. Or perhaps if her mama had arranged them in a more intimate setting such as this, rather than a drawing room where the space loomed larger than the presence of the people within, it all might have been more enjoyable.

"How did this kiss taste to you?" she asked, her face still very close to his.

"Not bitter." His gaze swept over her as he pulled away.

Oh? "I taste like gin."

"It tasted like the sweetest cake on the dessert table." His eyes were hot like two fire pokers. "Did it satisfy your curiosity?"

"It did." But not nearly enough. She wanted to satisfy her curiosity more. She wanted to satisfy it *fully*.

As her first kiss, Theodosia had no other kisses to compare his kiss with, true, but she just knew in her heart, in this moment, no other man would be able to compare. No other man had tempted her to be *free* before. How many would be likely to do so in the future?

What on earth is wrong with me?

His mocking smile captured her, each look cast her way charmed her, and his touches—a mere lift onto a horse, riding caged in his arms, carrying her to the Bells' doorstep—had excited her even though she had refused to dwell on them at the time. Could not this be just the effects of the drink?

Must be.

Can't be.

She hadn't been tipsy all those other times she felt awareness flood her body. No, she'd been all too sober then.

However, another effect came into play as her mind bounced back between all the *must be* parts and *can't be* portions—she didn't care about the why of them, why they might or mightn't matter, what lay beneath them, or what even lay behind them.

Tonight was all about embracing freedom.

She pushed her chair away and stepped around the table, up to him. "Tell me, how many ladies have you kissed in your life?"

The gin he'd just sipped sputtered from his mouth, and he brushed off his legs. "That's not a question you ask a man."

She put a hand on his shoulder when he moved to rise, keeping him in his chair. "Because there are too many? What about this—if you share your number I shall share mine."

"What the devil?" He crossed his arms. "Just how many men have you kissed?"

Her lips lifted along with her brows. "You tell me yours and I'll tell you mine."

He cursed. "Would you believe me if I said five?"

"Do you believe yourself when you say five?"

"Damn it, it's not like I keep count of how many women I've kissed."

"Then there are more than five. Did you just pull that number from your arse?"

"Where the hell did you learn such a saying?"

She held up six fingers. "Brothers."

"Of course," he said sourly.

She leaned closer. "Just own up to the fact that you're a rogue who has kissed many women."

"Fine, this is me owning it. Now out with it. What's your number?"

Theodosia sent him a toothy grin. "A lady never reveals her cards."

"Didn't we have a deal?"

"I can hardly recall such a deal. Did we shake on it? Sign an agreement? And did you give me a true number?"

"Vexing minx."

"Shall I tell you a secret, then?" she asked conspiratorially.

He shot her a moody glance. "If you mean to appease me with some ridiculous nonsense, don't."

She rested against the table, staring at him. "I've even been thinking about marrying below my station. It's mostly a passing thought, but after meeting Mr. and Mrs. Bell, I might give it more consideration."

His mouth opened, then closed. "You want to do *what*? Why the devil do you want to marry below your station? Your brothers will never allow it."

She waved a hand over the kitchen, passing over his outburst. "Say, a farmer. I'd be a farmer's wife."

"Are you being serious?" he grumbled. "Or is this the gin taking the lead in the conversation?"

"I'm always serious when it comes to my life. I know what I want." For the most part.

"And you want to marry a farmer."

"I want to be valued." She leaned back to grip the table with both hands. "To the men of the *ton* . . . I am an object to be used. I am simply there to make an advantageous marriage. produce an heir, be obedient. I'd rather take charge of my own life."

"You don't need to marry beneath your station to become valued," he pointed out. He suddenly arched a brow. "Do you think you will be valued more as a farmer's wife than a gentleman's wife? Does a man not remain a man?"

"I want to argue with you," Theodosia said slowly, rather amused at her own answer. "But my tongue won't form the words. You've rendered me speechless."

"I never knew I was *that* powerful."

"You're not." But he was powerful enough. Enough that she found it rather refreshing to turn scathing retorts into teasing remarks.

He scoffed, but a smile formed immediately after. "Do you ever lose your sass?"

She crossed her arms. "Would I even be the woman you love to hate if I did?"

He barked out laughter, and Theodosia blinked at the rare sound. If his smile had been blinding, this outright laughter was almost hypnotic. His face softened when the corner of his eyes crinkled in amusement. She never knew he could have such an expression.

"I was wrong," she murmured. Why was her heart suddenly beating so fast? Lord, any moment it would burst from her chest.

"About?"

"My curiosity has not begun to be satisfied." Theodosia made a bold decision. "I want another kiss."

Dark eyes blazed into hers. "I am curious, too."

"About?"

"How it would feel if Lady Theodosia kissed me after so boldly declaring her desire."

Theodosia leaned closer to Saville, pulled by a force she couldn't explain. Blame the drink, the tipsy dizziness that claimed her body—Lord, blame the stars—but she could not help herself. She placed her lips softly on his.

Lightly but boldly, she traced her tongue over his lower lip. Suddenly unsure, she started to pull back, only for him to seize control with both hands on her cheeks, sweeping her into a ravaging kiss. His lips were warm, much softer than she expected. His tongue glided along the seam of her lips, demanding entry.

She gave it, and he didn't disappoint. The kiss turned into an unrestrained devouring, and all her senses faded until there was nothing left but *him*.

He pulled away just as quickly as he had taken charge, eyes burning into hers once again. "Theodosia," he breathed. "Christ. What are we doing?"

"Living in the moment."

"That's dangerous. I'm just a man."

She nodded, her face still clasped between his palms. "I know. You've said as much. But let me ask you this, is this more dangerous than being chased by highwaymen?"

"Can you even bloody compare the two?"

Theodosia laughed "Come now, I haven't felt this free in a while. Don't spoil the mood."

"Then don't regret this." The lowered timbre of his voice sent a new wave of shivers down her spine.

I won't.

Proverbial chains had never felt this good snapping. His lips found hers and this time he didn't pull back. The man might have poison on his tongue at times, but his lips were magic.

He rose, pressing himself even closer into her body, as close as he could manage. Theodosia wrapped her arms around his neck, embracing his warmth. He lifted her up into his arms, and she wrapped her legs around him as he set her on the kitchen table.

Was she really doing this?

Yes, I am doing this.

"A life as a farmer's wife would never suit you," he breathed against her mouth.

"Why not?"

"You are much too vibrant to be bound to the country. You're far too brilliant to be tucked away in a solitary, pastoral life."

He claimed her lips again, his tongue dancing and teasing hers. It was as though their mouths had fused together and could hardly be parted. She held onto him for dear life, finding comfort in the solid surface of the table beneath her while the blood pumping through her veins took on an unsteady rhythm.

When he pulled away again, Theodosia took a moment to slow her breathing before she asked, "Is kissing always this wild?"

"No," he said. "Only with you." His gaze drifted over her face. "We are both foxed. I think."

"You think?" A bubble of laughter spilled forth. "I think we might be, too. Does that matter?"

"It means we are both primed to do something we might regret later."

"What is life without a little regret? Lord knows, we have enough regrets already, what will one or two more matter?"

"Damn it, you are not helping." His eyes narrowed. "And that's a problem."

"Well, it sounds like a problem for tomorrow." She tightened her legs around his waist. This was madness, utter madness, but for once in her life, gin or not, Theodosia didn't want to hold back. She wanted to take what she wanted. "For the most vexing man in England, your kisses are sure good."

His lips were on hers again. Demanding. Searching. Claiming. He molded their bodies together once more, and Theodosia felt his arousal press into her.

Theodosia jolted.

A glass crashed to the ground.

Their eyes met. Without a word, he picked her up and carried her all the way to their room while trailing kissing down her cheek, her jaw, the arch of her neck.

"That is not my mouth," Theodosia breathed.

"Your mouth isn't the only place I can kiss."

Her breath caught. And the moment they entered the chamber, their lips met once more. This time, she didn't know who kissed who first. Maybe she kissed him first, maybe his lips claimed hers first. But they were greedily devouring each other now like they each were each other's last meal.

A rush of excitement washed over her.

She tightened her arms around his neck as he pressed her against the door. The kiss went on until they both ran out of air. Her feet suddenly touched the floor, and the cage of his arms lifted away from her, as though giving her one last out.

Theodosia didn't want it.

She wanted another taste. The wanted all the tastes.

"You're not escaping," he said in a low, raspy voice.

"I'm not escaping," she agreed.

"What are we doing here, Theodosia?"

She ducked away from the door and sauntered to the center of the room and turned to him. "Having fun? Being free? Daring to take what we want even if it's only for this moment."

She sat down on the bed, smiling at him. He started to stride over but she stopped him with a lift of her hand and gestured to the chair.

"Sit."

He stared at her for a whole ten seconds before he slowly lowered himself onto the chair.

"Now, where were we?" Theodosia had no clue what she was doing, but she allowed instinct and her mood to lead her. It was as though they had entered a world of their own, and she decided she wanted to make a few of the rules here. Could she make the man before her lose himself? The idea was wildly alluring.

She undid the buttons of her shirt one by one.

"What are you doing?" A low growl.

"Teasing you." The shirt dropped to the floor, leaving her only in her corset and Turkish trousers. "Is it not working?" She laughed when his eyes clouded over. "Are you not in the mood to tease?"

His gaze held hers, as though a battle had ensued as they challenged each other with this one look. A challenge he lost when he shut his eyes and cursed. "Damn it, of course it's working."

She laughed.

This tiny bit of power. It felt marvelous.

She lifted her chin and slowly dragged her fingertips over the arch of her neck, the swell of her breasts, and stopped below the material of the corset.

The veins in his forearms bulged, and Theodosia came alive beneath the restraint in his gaze.

This is so bold, Theo.

And perhaps he was right. Perhaps they would regret abandoning all the rules tomorrow. But she didn't want to live her life on what ifs and what nots.

Regret? She'd regret it if she stopped now.

She reached behind her back, expertly yanking on a ribbon, loosening her stays, observing the bob of his Adam's apple as she pulled the corset away from her body and dropped it to the ground, exposing her breasts to his view.

So, so bold!

A deep, gruff curse.

She cupped her breasts in her hands. "Do you like what you see?"

"God yes."

Belatedly, Theodosia wondered where all the embarrassment that ought to be there had fled to, but then, she supposed this was the magic of gin—the *freedom* it promised. Even if this freedom lasted only this night.

Theodosia arched a playful brow. Except for the bulging veins in his forearms and now his temple, the man hadn't moved an inch.

Given the man's usual character, his restraint in the face of her teasing was quite impressive. Too impressive. She wanted to test that. She wanted him to feel what she was feeling in this very moment. Alive. Amorous. Almost roguish. Ready to seize this rare moment of freedom they'd decided together to claim.

One last garment to go.

Theodosia traced a finger over the hem of her trousers, noting with satisfaction as his lips parted.

Yes.

She lifted off the bed slightly to shimmy out of the trousers in what she hoped was an alluring manner, but given her slight unsteadiness, she thought she might be a bit off the mark. No matter. The end goal was to fully grasp the moment.

And it worked.

Theodosia's lips twitched as crossed her legs and leaned back on her arms, watching him.

What now, Field Savage?

FIELD SWALLOWED.

The minx half sat, half lay on the bed without a stitch of clothing, without so much a lick of shame. Staring at him. Tempting him. *Taunting* him.

It takes two to play this sort of game, sweetheart.

Saville didn't bother with sensibilities; he gripped his shirt and yanked it over his head. Her eyes widened before narrowing to slits, but no daggers appeared in their depths. Instead, he found, for the first time since they met, a new look in her eyes.

Field wanted to grab hold of that look and never let go. No . . . that didn't sound right. He never wanted to *forget* that look.

Much sweeter than all her other dagger-like looks. How many other looks did she possess? Were they as . . . *beautiful?*

Had she always been *this* alluring? Was she even real, or was this a dream? He didn't know which would be more disturbing. Theodosia the temptress or Theodosia nothing but a dream. He was afraid the sight of her would disappear. He blinked a few times. It didn't.

Her grin widened.

Field almost swayed at that smile. He gripped hold of the chair to steady himself. She smirked. "One yank of your shirt and you're stumbling."

"I didn't stumble." *I was struck by a revelation.*

He knew it, because he could feel the knowledge battling through his veins, trying to burrow into the very core of him. But he couldn't describe it, couldn't put a name to it, this fire raging in his blood.

But he knew he wanted this woman.

He had wanted her for whatever mad reason since the moment they were stuck close together on that horse. No. Even before that. In truth, he couldn't really say when it had started; he just knew it had at some point.

His eyes had formed the habit of forever hunting for her. If she were not in his sight, he would set out to chase her down. And the moment he'd started this chase, he couldn't stop it.

Just like he couldn't stop himself from removing his boots and tossing them to the side. His trousers went next, male satisfaction rushing to one particular section of his body as her cheeks flushed bright red.

He flung his trousers with his foot toward the minx as he took his member in his hand. She swatted them away, her eyes turning to saucers as she watched him.

This time Field smirked.

She didn't disappoint. In fact, she exceeded any and all his expectations when the startlement in her eyes softened to intrigue.

"I must admit, this is a sight not even six brothers prepared me for."

Field sneered. "I would bloody hope not. And don't mention those heathens at a time like this."

She laughed.

"So what do you want to do now that we are both naked?" Field asked.

She cocked her head. "You mentioned something about kissing."

Field dragged his gaze over her pale body. Christ almighty. He wanted to taste every inch of her. He squeezed his cock, not sure how long he'd be able to hold back. "Yes," he said, his voice coming out hoarse. "I can kiss the entire length of your body."

"The entire length? Is that a promise?"

Christ. "Yes."

She chuckled. "Only if I can kiss your body first."

Field's jaw went slack. Kiss him first? Could he survive that? No, no, he couldn't. Could he? Her lips on him, trailing kissing everywhere? No, that would be the purest of tortures.

She patted the bed. "Come lie down, if you dare."

Field could no more resist the challenge that sparked in her gaze than he could the temptation she presented. He strode over, lowering onto the bed as she instructed, not letting his gaze slide away from hers even for a second.

This is madness. Madness you'd better not regret in the morning.

But even though that brief thought flashed through his mind, Field didn't stop. Regret? What regret? He could never regret this moment, this night. Regret was so far out of reach that even the word sounded strange to him now.

She placed her hands on his shoulders and leaned over to lay small kisses over his chest.

"Hard. Muscled," she noted.

Yes, very hard.

"Also warm."

So damn hot.

She kissed him all over his body. The muscles of his chest, his belly, shoulders, and even the cords of his neck while her fingers left trails of gooseflesh along his upper leg. Her attention moved downward to his torso, and her mouth veered very, very close to his manhood. Field's entire body stiffened.

He would never be able to handle that. Not tonight.

Field couldn't take it anymore. In one smooth motion, he flipped her over. "My turn."

"What? But I wasn't done."

"Christ, woman, any more of that and another kind of liberation will happen and I want to taste you fully before it does."

"You're that desperate?" she teased.

Field couldn't deny it. "That bloody desperate, yes." His lips went straight for her breasts, those pale globes with their rosy tips he'd been itching to claim since she'd removed her corset.

So good.

His hand inched to her center and all the beauty to be discovered there. By no means could he claim to be inexperienced, but at this moment, as he searched for the spot and pushed one finger in, he was startled to find his whole body was trembling.

She gasped, arching into him, her arms circling around his back.

"Field."

"I'll say this only once more, Theodosia. There is no going back after this."

"If I didn't know that, I would never have teased you." She wiggled the lower half of her body. "Put it in me already."

"Christ, your tongue knows just how to set the mood. Where did you learn to speak such words? No, wait, don't answer that. I don't want to know."

He inserted another finger.

"That is not enough," she breathed.

Was there another woman on earth capable of driving a man crazier than this one? It was as though he had stepped into an otherworldly realm.

"We need to prepare you. I'm bigger than two fingers."

"You don't say," she teased, grinning up at him, a sparkle of mischief laced with desire in her eyes.

"Why does it feel as though you are questioning my manhood right now?

"Is your manhood compromised of two fingers? Then yes, I'll question this manhood."

Field nipped at her neck with his teeth. "I can't believe we are discussing such things. The size of my manhood is not in question."

She laughed. "Because size *matters*, isn't that right? Do you know, when my brothers were boys they once jumped into a lake naked—"

"Stow that tongue, woman! Do not dare compare me to your brothers!" His eyes burned with fire when they locked with hers. "They have no place here tonight."

"How right you are. Besides, I quite like the size of your manhood."

Field nearly choked on air. So, his cock was impressive to her. Good.

"*Field*." Lord, the way she said his name made him even more hard, if that were at all possible. "I am prepared. Don't keep me waiting."

"Damn minx."

"Always."

He gripped her chin and dragged his mouth over hers "I can't wait anymore either."

"Then don't."

Field allowed instinct to take over his mind and body, and he unleashed all his desire into that moment with her. His tongue swept into her mouth the same time he entered her, and everything he knew about himself turned inside out. He hadn't known just how much he wanted her until that night, until that moment. Until he saw a side of her he never believed he'd be permitted to glimpse.

God, it feels good.

"Theodosia, are you all right? Is this good?"

"Yes," she murmured, then added provokingly, "Is this it? Or is there more?"

Teasing wench. There was so much more, even the entire night would not be nearly enough to explore everything he wanted.

"Give me more, Field."

All his restraint snapped, and along with it everything that made him a gentleman. *Don't fool yourself, Field. Your control withered to nothing a long time ago.*

Her moan escaped onto his lips.

He claimed it, just like he claimed her body with every thrust. Sparks of pleasure trickled over his skin as her nails dragged over his back.

This woman.

Theodosia King.

She always gave as good as she got. In life. In battle. Even in bed.

"Field," she cried, and his name on her lips sent him over the edge of a cliff he could never climb back up from. His thrusts deepened, pounding as he swept his tongue between her lips.

That cry belongs to me, too.

She belonged to him.

Chapter Twelve

THEODOSIA EYES SLOWLY flitted open. A splitting ache stabbed at her temples. *Where am I? Who am I? What year is this?* And why was there a heavy object pinning her down? She blinked a few times until her vision cleared. Hunger stabbed at her belly, but more than that, a touch of nausea claimed space alongside hunger.

And thirst.

So thirsty.

Water. She needed water. An entire gallon, if possible.

A large chest came into view, a carpet of soft sandy hair coating the surface, tickling her cheek when she moved.

What on earth?

She wasn't being pinned down. She was the one doing the pinning! No, not pinning. Laying? Wait . . .

Was she *on* Saville?

She inwardly took stock of her body.

I'm lying on Saville. I'm certain neither of us is wearing any clothes. My body has a mild ache. He is so warm.

Wait, the last had nothing to do with her. She shut her eyes as the memory of the previous night suddenly rushed back, and she stilled.

She and Saville . . .

She and him . . .

They . . .

Theodosia rubbed her eyelids. Perhaps if she went to sleep and woke up again, the man beneath her would disappear. The memories would disappear. The sensation between her thighs would disappear. And this wretched beat of her heart would settle.

Memories, some hazy, some startlingly vivid, burst into her consciousness, causing that already wretched beat to quicken until it all but exploded into a frantic pound.

Oh, God, what have I done?

But there was no denying the pictures flashing through her mind. The claim of freedom. The writhing of naked bodies. Field. The look of his flushed face while he captured and imprisoned all her senses.

She assessed her current position.

She shouldn't go back to sleep like this. She should slip into her own bed.

Is that even possible?

There was no way to inch out of his embrace. His arms shackled her, trapped her in this awkward position. She would wake him, and that would hinder her plan of escape. And she wanted desperately to escape and gather her wits.

Her eyes couldn't help but open once more, tracking his jawline until they settled on his lips.

Her cheeks heated.

What those lips hadn't done to her body.

Oh, Lord.

How could this happen . . .

How could this happen . . .

How could this happen . . .

Calm yourself, Theodosia. You are a levelheaded woman. What happened, happened. It cannot be undone. And first things first. Remove yourself from his body. Then remove yourself from the bed. Rest a bit more. Then remove yourself from the chamber. Eat. Then remove yourself to Brighton, as planned.

The book.

To perdition with that book. Saville could take the thing and do with it as he pleased.

Field.

A memory of her moaning his name made an unwelcome intrusion into her mind. How could she have uttered his name in such a tone? Ah, how mortifying. Was that what gin did to a woman? She was never touching the stuff again.

He'd told her she'd feel wretched.

He'd also told her she might regret things in the morning. Did she? Though the memories were quite embarrassing, she could not claim she regretted clinging to a sense of freedom last night. It had been ridiculously liberating.

Her gaze lifted a scant few inches and met two dark eyes looking back at her.

Theodosia stilled. Everything except for the pounding of her heart that slammed against her chest and right into his.

He merely stared at her, as though his brain were still turning the events of last night over in his mind. Theodosia understood, which was why she gave him a few seconds to loosen his arms around her, but the man had turned into a statue. A hard one. With smooth, softer edges.

What to do? What to say?

"Your arms . . ." She found her voice before he did.

No comprehension filled his usually sharp gaze.

"Field?" Had the man finally lost his senses? "We are naked."

Still just a stare.

"Your *thing* is pressing against me."

That earned some response. "That's normal," his gruff voice finally spilled out.

"How is that normal?"

"It's an early morning thing."

Theodosia didn't care to know any more. So men had early morning things. Not strange *at all*. "Just . . . make it go away."

He went back to staring.

She arched a brow. "Can you not make it go away?"

"Why are you on top of me?"

Was he still drunk? "Why do you think I'm on top of you?" She squirmed. "You are holding me in place."

He blinked, then slowly retracted his arms, as if their placement confused him even more.

Definitely still foxed.

But then again, she must be, too. Why else was she still lying atop him even after he removed his arms?

Move, she ordered body. Theodosia simply rolled onto the mattress, and then wished she hadn't. The pain in her temples jerked across the plains of her mind. They lay next to each other as another stretch of silence spanned between them.

"I feel like shite," he said.

You don't say.

Her gaze darted to the scattered clothing on the floor. The gin bottle was nowhere to be seen. It must still be in the kitchen.

Thank heaven. She didn't want to even catch a glimpse of that bottle.

Mrs. Bell!

Mrs. Bell probably wouldn't think much about the bottle, and perhaps even the glass she now recalled shattering on the kitchen floor, but the house wasn't all that large. What if the couple had heard them? If the ruckus they'd heard was anything like the cries and grunts that screamed from all corners of her mind . . .

It would be mortifying!

Theodosia threw a hand over her eyes and groaned. Could she just disappear already?

The silence between them filled the space with an indescribable tension. Theodosia thought she might suffocate from it. Should she casually sit up and dress? Should she wait for him to casually sit up and dress? Or should she wait for him to say something other than this *thing* is normal and he felt like shite?

How awkward!

Come to think about it, it was rather surprising he hadn't

already demanded they marry out of some sense of duty. Her brows gathered in thought. The Earl of Saville she knew would have demanded it by now, wouldn't he? He had such a righteous sense of duty he wouldn't be able to help himself.

Yet he appeared rendered senseless.

Did that mean he didn't want to marry her even out of duty? Did the man loathe her so much that he would not even consider the possibility? No, that couldn't be right. Could he loathe her and still do what they had done last night with that much passion? It hadn't felt like loathing. Could *she* loathe *him* and still do that?

Or did he simply regret it that much?

Stop.

She had wanted last night. She'd wanted to experience the freedom of doing what she pleased and for once not caring about the consequences. If there was blame to be assigned, she was just as much at fault for last night as he was. If fact, he might even believe she had used him, if the embarrassing, contorted scenes of her memory were to be believed.

Then she should strike first before he could do or say something they both might regret further and turn the moment from awkward to unbearable. Because there really was only one outcome for last night, one course of action to take—pretend it never happened. That was for the best. They'd shared an intimate moment of freedom. They both enjoyed it. And that was that.

Now it was time to pretend that moment possessed no consequences at all, and for that to work they had to view it with a sense of indifference. Overlook its weight. Handle it causally.

Could she do it?

There is no other way.

Theodosia inhaled a deep breath.

Last night . . . "Last night never happened."

FIELD DRAGGED BOTH hands over his face. He felt like *shite*. His body, his head, and this damn organ beating in his chest. That felt the worst. His heart hadn't stopped racing from the moment he opened his eyes as memories raced and stumbled against the inside of his skull. No matter how mysterious and otherworldly last night had seemed, today it was cold, hard reality that awaited him.

Gin. Bed. Theodosia's matching haggard look.

What the bloody hell did I do?

Field wasn't that much of a martyr to claim full responsibility for last night. Neither of them should have had so much to drink after all they'd been through—the excitement, the lack of sleep. But he was older by nine years. He should have been able to handle his damn drink better. Should have been stronger. What man at nine-and-twenty would allow themselves to be seduced in such a—

He stopped.

That would be every man, no matter the age.

Ah, Christ.

He'd entered uncharted territory. But he could no more step back than he could step forward. He'd lain with an innocent. He knew what he *should* do. Duty had been ingrained into his bones since the moment of birth. He ought to offer for her hand. But this was Theodosia King. The chit might find him attractive, but she didn't like him as a man.

Which left him at a loss for words.

"Field, are you listening to me?"

He turned to her. "Did you say something?"

"I said we should pretend last night never happened."

Pretend it never happened? Was that even bloody possible? He could no more forget their bodies intertwining than he could forget every single thing that made him a man.

"*Field?*"

"Last night never happened," he repeated dumbly.

"Yes, it's our little secret. It stays between us."

Little secret? *Little?* Christ, it was bigger than the Queen's

House! "What the devil do you take me for?"

"A man who would demand the heavens to kneel out of a sense of responsibility."

"You have the wrong man," Field muttered, albeit a bit begrudgingly. He was exactly that sort of man. But not with her. With her, he couldn't demand anything.

Bile rose in his throat. *Not now.* "I think I'm going to cast up my accounts."

She arched a brow. "Is the memory of us sleeping together so wretched?"

"Did I say that?" Would he ever say such a thing? Damn woman.

"You didn't *not* say it."

"Are you bloody listening to yourself right now? A night with you could never be wretched. It's the drink."

"Oh." Her gaze roamed over his face. "So, are we in agreement?"

"To pretend our night together never happened? Do you think I can do such a thing?"

She narrowed her eyes. "Why not? Do you not see this is for the benefit of us both?"

"Why *not?*" Field matched her look. "For one, I cannot purge my mind at will." Dear God, he clutched his chest as bile burned up his throat once more. His body did want to purge something.

No. More. Time.

Field leaped from the bed and darted straight to the chamber pot in the corner of the room. Everything in his belly emptied into the pot as he heaved, which wasn't much since he hadn't eaten last night. Only gin left his body. Vile stuff. There was a reason he never drank it. He forgot his body didn't accommodate it well. Damn poison.

His throat burned as he emptied his stomach. He should have eaten. Perhaps then he wouldn't have lost complete hold of his senses. But no, he knew that wouldn't have been the case.

He'd lost himself gladly, hopelessly.

He groaned as he sat back on his arse, reaching for a towel to wipe his mouth.

A glass of water appeared before him. "Here," a concerned voice came. "Wash your mouth."

Field sighed.

He took a large swallow, rinsed his mouth and spit into the chamber pot. "I'll take this out."

"You should put on some clothes first."

Field cursed. Ah, hell. Not a stitch of clothing covered his body.

A pair of breeches hit his face. She tossed him his shirt as well. The corner of his gaze caught her clutching the bedlinen to her body. A body he had explored thoroughly last night. Memories rushed back with that one glimpse. No, he'd never be able to forget.

Field dragged a hand through his hair.

"Aren't you going to dress?" she asked him when he made no move to clothe himself.

"My body needs a moment to settle." He cast a glance at her and tossed her words back to her. "Aren't *you* going to . . ." He trailed off as a section of the linen slid down and exposed one of her breasts.

The daze Field had been feeling since he'd woken suddenly cleared up. Memories were one thing but . . . reality was quite another, and that reality sank into him like a ton of bricks plunging to the bottom of an ocean.

He had sucked on that breast.

They had slept together.

She followed his gaze and gasped, hitching the linen up again. "What are you doing? Stop staring at me like that!"

"I am a man. Can I help it?"

"Is that your response to everything? So what if you are a man? Does that give you leave to gawk at me?"

"Minx, you're the one half exposed. Any man would gawk at a beautiful woman."

"You're naked and fully exposed!"

"Any woman is allowed to stare at an Adonis-looking man."

A pillow hit his face, and he laughed. "Turn around and let me get dressed. Christ's sake."

She whirled, giving him her back.

"I cannot believe you called me beautiful," she muttered. "Has all the gin not left your body?"

"It has nothing to do with gin or anything else." Field tugged on his trousers. "Just the truth."

"You have never thought me beautiful."

He arched a brow, his hands pausing in fastening his pants. "What the devil gave you that idea? I slept with you, didn't I?"

Wrong thing to say. Wrong. Thing.

Her tone whipped at him, lashing into his nerves. "So you slept with me because I'm beautiful? How shallow, Field Savage!"

He flinched. "I didn't mean it like that."

"Such a shallow man," she repeated.

"Such compliments so early in the morning."

"I can supply you with more, if you want," she said sweetly, too sweetly, causing a shiver to trickle down his spine. "And like I said, we shall pretend that last night never happened."

Field peeked at her. "But it did."

"But we shall pretend that it didn't."

He dragged a hand through this hair. How could he accept such a thing? Every single cell in his body bellowed to take responsibility for his actions. He knew his duty. He should marry her, protect her, stay with her forever.

Yet she wanted to pretend last night hadn't happened. She wanted him to compromise this principle and, by extension, her own self. Could he do that? Did he have a choice? No matter how last night had come about, he had ruined an innocent lady. Her life might take the worst sort of turn if this ever came to light.

I can't deal with this right now.

He wouldn't put it past the minx to end him in his sleep if he did anything she didn't want. An image of her six brothers came to mind. Christ. Why did it suddenly feel as though *his* life hung in the balance?

He thought of his own recent behavior regarding Selena and Warrick. He knew his friend had believed himself to be cursed, but Field was the true curse. Whenever he attempted to do the right thing, he made it worse. Why, whenever he wanted to protect someone, did he hurt them, or himself, even more?

And this was going to hurt.

He could feel it in his gut.

His temples were already throbbing.

Could the heavens give him a damn break for once? Was that too much to ask?

"Excuse me?"

Field stilled. Had he just muttered that out loud? By the look on her face, he had. A sigh blew through his lips.

"Did you forget that you're the one who said we should be free for at least just one night?" Theodosia pointed out.

Free.

He had said that, but he hadn't imagined innocence would be lost when he did. Last night hadn't freed either of them. It trapped them within a secret. But now was not the time to argue. She wanted to forget, so while the sentiment was still too fresh, he wouldn't press.

Patience is your friend, old chap.

"Fine," Field said with the same amount of difficulty it had taken to win the war against France. "Let's pretend last night didn't happen." *For now.* "We shouldn't ruin our lives over it." He really shouldn't have said the last, but he couldn't help the surly words from breaking free.

She studied him. "Are you sure, as in *sure*, sure? You will forget that you and I," she motioned to the bed, "ever happened?"

Not in this life.

He gave a curt nod.

"I need to hear the words, Earl."

Earl.

So much distance in that one small word. He wanted to smash his fist into the wall. Damn it. She wanted to pretend last night had never happened? Well, he could pretend.

No, you can't.

He could pretend all damn day long that he never touched her.

Impossible.

Never dragged his lips all over her body.

That will never happen.

Never entered her or brought them both to unimaginable heights.

Never.

Christ, he couldn't. Not even if his life depended on it.

Chapter Thirteen

REGRET.

A bittersweet emotion. Theodosia had never tasted it to the magnitude that she did now. And at this moment it was rather more bitter than sweetness as she recalled how she had acted that morning with Field Savage, the Earl of Saville. They should have had more of a discussion. They were both adults, weren't they? Yet, while they *said* things, they hadn't truly discussed anything. Now everything felt awkward. Awkwardly so.

Her gaze tracked over the farmlands. No bitterness dwelled within these fields. There was only sweet in the natural world's untroubled affairs. She'd hoped a walk would give her some clarity, and it did to some degree, but also brought other things to light.

She had always been stubborn to the bone. She never cowered under a man's gaze. She would not be pushed into an unwanted corner. And today, she hadn't asked Saville what he wanted, only thought about how pretending nothing happened would benefit them—but mostly her.

Was pretending really the right answer?

Or was it just another form of cowering?

But what else am I to do?

Now that she had calmed down a bit, more of that night

flickered through her mind. Quite frankly, she couldn't decide what shocked her more about her own behavior—the conversation they'd had before they kissed, the fact that she'd asked him to kiss, everything that happened after that, or demanding that they pretend it never happened.

Could she truly forget?

She'd insisted he pretend that nothing had happened. But she had quickly come to understand something. Just because one pretended something hadn't happened, didn't mean one forgot it. In fact, since the moment she'd decided to pretend last night had never happened between them, she had been unable to push the memories out of the forefront of her mind. They refused leave her be.

They danced across her inner vision as if to taunt her.

You can't pretend.

You can't pretend.

And perhaps she didn't want to pretend either. But what else do?

She glanced back at the small farmhouse.

You are much too vibrant to be bound to the country.

She threw her head back and shot a prayer up into the sky. A prayer not just to pretend better but to forget. To escape this man. To settle down for a peaceful remainder of the season. It didn't seem at all possible anymore.

She blinked. White puffs of clouds littered the sky. One in particular slowly shaped into a . . . heart?

Urg!

For heaven's sake!

Even the sky mocked her this day.

Damn that man.

Bless him, too. Because Field, *Saville*, had been keeping his distance from her. She supposed he had his own thoughts to sort through, as well, since she'd asked him to pretend. Her request must have stuck in his craw like a branch with sharp edges. The man was nothing if not driven by a desire to protect, however flawed his attempts to do so might be. He would want nothing more than to *protect* her from ruin, even though he—well, *she* was the cause of that ruin.

Why am I so conflicted?

Everything that had happened last night had been her choice. She had been the one to initiate the kiss. She had seduced him. Yet now she demanded they both forget it ever happened.

I'm never drinking again. Full stop.

Theodosia didn't regret their night together in the sense that she wished they had never spent a night with their bodies entwined. Other than in her management the situation this morning, her biggest sense of regret, she had come to realize on her stroll, was in the sense that now, no matter what, she could never forget how it felt. How *he* felt. His body against hers. His kisses. His touches.

Saville.

Her nemesis! Or previous nemesis. Or her perhaps-still nemesis? She now knew him on a whole other level. And she didn't hate it. What was she supposed to do with this *not*-hate?

Like him?

God, no.

Enjoy his company?

That was even *more* unfathomable.

But what else was she supposed to feel? She knew now she wouldn't be able to pretend nothing had happened. Had he come to a similar conclusion, or was he finding it easier to forget? How had things become so unimaginably complicated?

You know very well, Theo.

She kicked a pebble in her path and peeked at the house once more. Yes, it all began with her request. Should she return and have a true conversation with the man? She hadn't ventured all that far, mostly just up and down the lane leading up to the main house. They could be discussing all this in a matter of moments . . .

This is not like you, Theodosia.

She did not enjoy this skulking, *lurking*, outside the house while he skulked and lurked inside.

She patted her cheeks. The entire world seemed so far from their reality that Brighton, the book, the highwaymen, even her brothers all felt like a distant dream.

"You all right, lass?" Mr. Bell asked.

Theodosia turned to the elusive husband of Mrs. Bell. She loved how he called her lass even though the man didn't possess an ounce of Scottish blood. But apparently, he had grown up in the Scottish Lowlands, and picked up some Scottish habits there, too.

"Ah, yes, all is well," Theodosia said, a bit embarrassed. She hadn't seen much of Mr. Bell and assumed he was quite busy, but the man reminded her a bit of her father. Calm, and solid with a kind smile.

"I'm enjoying the midday sun."

"Be careful not to enjoy it too much, lass. The sun's rays are sharpest this time of day."

Theodosia smiled and nodded. Sharp though they may be, they didn't sting as much as the not-so-subtle looks Field had been shooting her before she'd decided to escape outside. The bright sun seemed like the lesser evil.

"I expect you've been in the fields this morning, sir. Will your crops be abundant this year?"

The man wiped sweat from his brow. "Just came from the potato fields, lass. They are doing well."

Potatoes . . .

Another reminder of Saville.

"Well, that is good, Mr. Bell."

His smile softened his features. "Also had a chat with our neighbors over yonder," he said with a vague *over yonder* gesture. "There have been whispers of robberies but nothing near here."

Her eyes widened. "Oh? Well, I suppose that is good news."

Mrs. Bell came around the corner of the house with a basket. "There you are, Mr. Bell. Ah, dearie, you are here as well. I've set lunch in the kitchen for you. You didn't even have a bowl of the stew last evening."

"Oh, yes, I'm afraid we got a bit . . . distracted, Mrs. Bell. My apologies if we left a mess in the kitchen."

"Oh, it's no bother, dearie. Youngsters must have some fun as well. But do eat something. Mr. Bell and I will take our lunch outside." She glanced up at the sky. "It's a marvelous day, don't you think, Mr. Bell?"

The old man's gaze lit up as it fell on his wife. Theodosia's heart pinched. What a sweet sight.

"Oh, and do tell that fierce fellow the news about those whispers," Mr. Bell said.

"I shall, and thank you." She gave a nod and smiled at the couple. "Is Field inside?"

What an absurd question, Theodosia.

Of course he was inside. What she really wondered was whether she would run into him in the kitchen. She hadn't eaten yet today, having been too busy with her thoughts to even think about food. And they'd risen quite late. But now that lunch was mentioned, the hunger from earlier returned tenfold. And she'd much rather eat alone while she sorted her thoughts.

Mrs. Bell nodded. "I told him about lunch, as well. He looks a bit pale. Distracted, too. Make sure he eats something, will you?"

"Of course." Theodosia nodded.

Right. Well. It seemed they would have to face each other again sooner or later. She'd hoped to have her wits collected by then. But a smidgeon of worry brewed. Was he in a state to face *her*? Did he still feel sick?

She waved as the couple walked off, arm in arm onto a path that led to big tree in the distance. Would she have that one day? Lunch with her husband in a field beneath a tree? How envious she suddenly felt.

Now, on to her own partner.

Of sorts.

Behind her, in that little farmhouse, was a big man with an

even bigger presence. Time to face him and the reassurance he hadn't given her. But a more maddening question arose with that. What reassurance did she want?

Infuriating creature. She. Him. Them both!

There was no doubt in her mind that Field Savage would not let this matter go. The man hardly ever agreed with anything she said, though to be fair, they had been agreeing more lately. It still came as a surprise, however, when they did agree on something. Plus, her request went against his protective nature—she was sure of it.

Something was brewing in the air. Something that would crackle, hiss, and explode the moment she walked through the door of that house and came face to face with him. He'd given her time, but probably just to calm her nerves, as some men were wont to do. That was what her brothers did, at any rate.

Am I ready for this?

She would stay outside the entire day if she could, but the decision wasn't up to her. Her belly held all the power at the moment, and hunger won.

Theodosia straightened her shoulders.

You can do this.

She just hoped that Field's hunger would keep his mouth stuffed with food long enough that she could eat and stall for more time.

LIBERATION.

There was nothing that liberated a man as much as alcohol. There was also nothing that brought more trouble for a man, either. In hindsight, he should have remembered that. The list of heiresses that had been butchered at their hands served forever as a prime example. Though not as prime an example as the momentous miscalculation he had made after this particular bout of freedom had been dispensed by a bottle of gin.

He had gravely miscalculated how much he had wanted Lady Theodosia King.

He had never stood a chance.

The calm he had regained throughout the morning was rapidly draining away as he stared through the window, watching Theodosia converse with the Bells. Field still hadn't come close to coming to terms with the depth of the shite he had gotten himself into now and how to deal with it. Forget about pursuing her to Brighton, the highwaymen, the town, and everything in between—the simple fact was that they had been traveling together alone.

Had slept in the same room. Alone.

Had got foxed. Alone.

At what point had he thought all that was a good idea? He hadn't. Because he hadn't given any of it *any* thought. He had been so doggedly pursuing his own goals that he hadn't stopped to look at anything else.

Field scowled at his reflection in the window. "I can't believe I did the very thing I dueled my best friend over."

Very well, he hadn't actually dueled with Warrick. His sister had commandeered Warrick's place. But the reason he had issued the duel in the first place was because his friend had kissed his sister.

Kissed.

A mere kiss! Perhaps two.

And now he had done so much worse. He'd turned into a ravenous beast, some creature that acted as though it had been starved for all its existence and then lost control at the prospect of tasting a delicious morsel to alleviate the tormenting hunger. Much like the devil Theodosia and Selena had turned his portrait into, no?

By all accounts, six holes, one for each King brother, should riddle his body over what he'd done.

But she wanted him to pretend it had never happened?

I can't do it.

Won't do it.

Had she even thought about her future? What if she married? Wait, could a woman even pretend to be chaste on her wedding night? Was that possible? Did it matter? Did it not? Was she not *worried*? Or did she not plan to marry? Wait, why was *he* so worried about her wedding? Her wedding night?

Slow down, Field.

Field dragged a hand through his hair.

He racked his brain over and over about what the hell she wanted but couldn't come up with an answer. The woman was too damn elusive. Perhaps the better question to ask was what *he* wanted. Perhaps he was hopeless in every last respect. No, *helpless*. He didn't know what the hell to do.

Warrick would laugh his arse off.

Field's brows crinkled.

Perhaps he wouldn't laugh. More likely he'd merely lift a dark, infuriating brow with eyes full of judgment and would never let a day go by without reminding him of it.

His eyes narrowed on her through the window.

Was this how she pretended nothing happened? By *avoiding* him?

A snort.

Just how long are you going to keep it up, you little minx?

His back straightened as she glanced back at the house before beginning to make her way to the door. Mrs. Bell had informed him moments ago that they would lunch on the stew she prepared yesterday, and they could help themselves in the kitchen. She should have informed Theodosia by now as well.

His eyes moved in the direction of the kitchen, and his feet soon followed suit.

She should be famished.

He lowered himself into a kitchen chair, tapping the table with a finger. He didn't have to wait long before she appeared in the doorway, jolting to a halt when her gaze landed on him. His body did a little jolt of its own.

"Mrs. Bell set out the stew you requested." Christ. What was that? Stating the glaringly obvious?

She gave a brief nod and entered, taking a seat opposite him. As if they were commonplace acquaintances and not lovers in . . . in . . .

He froze.

Lovers?

Field almost groaned.

She gave a small cough. "A marvelous day, is it not?"

A marvelous day? Field cast her a worried glance. *Who are you and what did you do to Theodosia?* "It would have been a touch better if we had the papers to read up on some gossip to chew on alongside our food."

Lord, who the hell was he?

Field reached for the bread. It was about the only thing he could stomach at the moment.

Her throat cleared. "You miss the gossip columns that much?"

He shrugged, buttering his slice. "I like to keep updated on what trouble stirs from certain heiresses."

She paused before giving a thoughtful nod while spreading butter over her own. "I'm also curious to know if anything has been said about my brothers lately."

A chill shot down Field's spine.

By now word would surely have reached her family that she hadn't arrived in Brighton. He couldn't be sure about her family dynamics, but he was certain he didn't want to be caught by Kingsley while traveling alone with his sister.

He valued his life. Or, more to the point, he wanted to continue living.

But that was a worry for another time.

"Oh yes, Mr. Bell mentioned that he has heard rumors about robberies, but apparently not in this area."

"I see," Field said thoughtfully, taking a bite of food. It seemed the threat of the Black Knight might have passed.

However, the look in that man's eyes before they blew past him in their escape . . . It was hard to believe he would just give up.

"It should be safe to leave soon, shouldn't it?"

He nodded, swallowing. "We should get a good rest tonight. Our heads will be clearer tomorrow." He just didn't know how he would pass a night with her in the same bedchamber with him.

She cleared her throat again. "Would you care for a cup of tea? It's still hot."

Field's brows furrowed. The awkwardness between them seemed to have settled in a most disconcerting way. He hated this. He preferred the biting comments over this, to be honest, so he said with just a hint of devilry, "I shall love a cup of tea, so long as it's not poisoned?"

Her gaze flew to his. She blinked. "What's with the smile?"

He pointed at his cheek. "This smile? It's my best one."

An odd look crossed her features. "It's really not." She poured them both tea, but he detected a hint of a smile emerging. "Drink the poison. It will help settle your stomach."

He accepted the cup. "Thank you."

"Field Savage, you are being rather too nice to me. It's un-nerving."

"What about you?" he prodded. "To be blunt, this awkward-ness is even more unsettling to me. This whole morning has been." He'd almost marched down that damn lane and dragged her back to the house because the tension in their distance had been more unbearable than any tension that could run between them together.

"Well, I do agree." She took a sip of tea. "About my request this morning . . ."

"The one to pretend our night together never happened?"

Her eyes darted to his before she averted her gaze again. "Yes, we should—"

"Wait," Field interrupted. He wasn't ready. He wasn't ready to hear whatever she brought up on the matter. God help him, he might just demand everything she didn't want to hear. Perhaps more. He shot to his feet, swallowing the tea in one go, but losing all other appetite. "I need to leave."

Her head snapped back. "You are what? When? Why?"

"Not to worry, I'm just going to ride out and see if I can confirm what Mr. Bell has heard. We'll talk later." His gaze dropped to where a smidgeon of butter glistened on her lips. He wanted to capture spot with his tongue.

Field inwardly groaned.

What the devil is wrong with me?

An adult man didn't act like this. Grown men had discipline, strength, sound-mindedness. Could he ever again claim such qualities for himself after forcing his body into a dress and wearing a bonnet? After being called "bonnet man?"

Ah hell, why did he have to remember *that* of all things?

"I wish to go with you." She suddenly interrupted his thoughts.

Field started, then shook his head. "No."

"No?" His answer seemed to have caught her off guard. "Why ever not?"

"It's too dangerous."

"Honestly? We stole a horse back from highwaymen. How can ferreting out word of them be more dangerous?"

"The danger doesn't lie with highwaymen." It lies with me. You.

"Then what is the problem?" she asked.

A sudden, delightful thought occurred to him. "Theodosia King, are you worried over me?" He smiled rather suggestively. He couldn't help it.

"Do not be absurd," she muttered. "Why would I worry about a big, surly hellion?"

"Perhaps you don't hate me as much as you thought."

"Don't get your hopes up, Saville."

He chuckled. Just who was the surly one here? "Get some rest. It's better to just have one fatigued frame setting out than two."

It would give him some time to cool down, too. He had thought when she was keeping her distance that more space was simply more unbearable, and while true, even being in the same room with her to eat a bit of lunch was also wreaking havoc on his emotional equilibrium. But he could admit that he didn't want to widen the gap between them. He just needed to gather his wits, decide how to handle what happened between them.

Only then would he be able to calmly talk.

Because he couldn't pretend what happened never happened.

He didn't want to.

"I still think I should accompany you," she said.

Field arched a brow. "Very well, if you keep on insisting, who I am I to deny you?" He shrugged. "But what if your brothers are scouring the countryside and we run into them?"

Her face flushed. "You go, then, but don't come crying to me if you get hurt."

"You say that now, but . . ."

Field chuckled at her frosty stare. This was the stare he'd grown fond of. Teasing Theodosia King might become the greatest pastime of his life.

Perhaps it already had.

Yes, a ride in the countryside would be just what he needed to get his head in order. And the sooner the better. Before he they really were found by the Kings and he lost much more than his future.

✦ ✦ ✦

Chapter Fourteen

T HEODOSIA HAD LONG considered food to be a cure-all for all
foul moods, and now, a hangover. What it did not cure,
however, was the urge to hit a certain earl, or the desire to kiss
him. A desire, Theodosia told herself, that was surely born of an
even deeper urge to shake him senseless.

Where was the blasted man, anyway? It had been three hours
since he'd left to hunt down information on their pursuers. Three
hours she'd been left to her own devices. Left obsessing whether
she should have insisted harder to join him.

She peered into the empty stall in Mr. Bell's barn where
Dream had been merrily nibbling his hay before Saville had
saddled him and ridden away.

She'd much rather have plodded along on one of the other
horses than wonder whether Saville was all right.

Worry if he was all right.

They had to leave soon unless the news he brought back
wasn't favorable, which she couldn't imagine it would be. Also,
unless her mother had achieved a miracle, her brothers—at least
Seth—must be on the move in search of her by now.

Oh, Lord, what if Field, *Saville*, did run into her brothers?
They wouldn't suspect they were traveling together, would they?

Theodosia sighed.

If she were to be caught here alone with him . . . Even if her brothers looked past that difficult-to-justify fact, Theodosia was a terrible liar and her brothers knew all her tells. Even now, just thinking of her body entwining with Saville's, her face flushed with heat.

Yes, she was fighting a losing battle.

She'd done fine before lunch, or she thought she had, but the moment he'd dashed off atop Dream, the edges of her nerves had begun to fray.

Urgh! *I hate waiting!*

She should use this time in more productive ways, shouldn't she? Such as resting, not wearing the floor of the barn thin with her restlessness. Lord, the only thing more unbearable than traveling with a handsome enemy was being *aware* of him on a level that defied any level of attraction she had experienced before.

Perhaps this space between them was good, after all.

Or perhaps not. She hated to admit that earlier—when he was still at least on the property—she had felt rather calmer.

Theodosia paused.

She would never admit this to anyone—absolutely anyone— but the man did have a way of making his presence thoroughly felt once his incessant, aggravating looks and playful smirks were absent.

"What am I even thinking? Surely I don't feel nostalgic for his vexing mouth." She shook her head. "Impossible."

She tapped her foot, her gaze darting to the empty stall again. That vexing mouth had turned rather sweet of late.

"Lady Theodosia?" A voice pierced through her woolgathering. "Is that you?"

Theodosia started and whirled around to find George Clifton, the Earl of Sandgrove striding over to her.

"Sandgrove?" She peered around the yard. She hadn't even heard his carriage approach. "Where did you come from? More the point, what are you doing here?"

"Mr. and Mrs. Bell are distant relatives of mine. This is my land. I visit them ever so often to enquire about their health."

Theodosia's mind raced. Of all the rotten luck. "Well, this is certainly a surprise."

"I'll say." He beamed at her. "What about you? How are you here?"

"I . . ." Lord, how to explain. Of all the places she and Saville could have landed, it was suddenly looking like this might turn out to be one of the worst.

Lord Sandgrove was their longtime neighbor in Brighton. They were friends, *of sorts*. Good acquaintances. Did she tell the truth? Weave a clever lie? Would he leave before Field returned? She didn't want to spin a tale only to be caught in its web later, with no way to extract herself.

"I was set upon highwaymen," Theodosia admitted, deciding to stay as close to the truth as possible. For the most part, her life wasn't any of his business, and she did not owe Sandgrove any explanation. But it would be very awkward to say nothing, especially as this was his land, and whatever she did tell him, she'd have to be comfortable with reaching her brothers. "Mr. and Mrs. Bell took me in."

The blood drained from his face. "Highwaymen? Wait, don't tell me . . ." His eyes widened. "No, it cannot be."

Theo went on alert. "What? Have you heard anything about the highwaymen?" Had something happened to Field?

"Well, yes, I have. I've just come from the magistrate of this area. He is a friend, you see, and he mentioned that a famous highwayman that goes by the moniker Black Knight is searching these parts for a woman dressed as a man and a man dressed as a woman." He suddenly laughed. "How preposterous is that?"

"Yes, how preposterous." She gripped the skirts of the plain frock she'd borrowed from Mrs. Bell while her trousers were drying after being washed. It was fortunate that she wasn't wearing them now. "How did the magistrate come to learn that this Black Knight is looking for such an odd pair?"

"Oh, he is quite clever. One of his men has recently infiltrated the band. They are just waiting for an opportunity to apprehend the brigands."

"You don't say," she murmured. "Is that all you've heard?"

"Only that they robbed the Black Knight and injured one of his men. The band is now scouring the countryside for their thieves."

Field . . .

Would he be safe?

Sandgrove strode over to her and took her hand in his. "Are you all right? You weren't harmed?"

"No," Theodosia said, a pinch of guilt forming in her breast at his concerned gaze. She'd never known the man to be anything but nice, so misleading him, even with partial truths, felt like tricking her youngest brother to do her bidding. "Rest assured, the only thing harmed was my dignity." At his frown, she clarified, "My maid and driver betrayed me to them, but they left me unharmed. Also . . ." She paused.

How to tell him about Field?

Sandgrove looked past her and stilled, the sound of trotting hooves reaching her ears at the same time his mouth gaped like a fish before he spluttered, *"Saville?* What the devil are you doing here?"

She looked over.

And her breath caught.

His hair had become windswept, and at some point in time he had rolled the sleeves of his shirt up to his elbows. Since he wore no jacket, it only magnified this untamed appearance of his.

"Could ask the same of you, Sandgrove." Saville's gaze dropped where the earl was still clasping her hand.

Theodosia snatched back her hand as though she'd touched a hot iron, and then cursed herself for acting as though being caught in an illicit affair. "I see no introduction is necessary." Thank the Almighty Lord he was also dressed more appropriately today. Field in a bonnet would be telltale indeed.

"Indeed," Sandgrove said, returning his attention to Theodosia. "But I'm rather confused by his presence, Lady Theodosia."

Saville's lips lifted in a sneer. "Likewise."

Lord, save me.

She inhaled a deep, fortifying breath. She smiled at Sandgrove. "The earl encountered me on the road. He helped me when I had no one else."

Sandgrove glanced between the two. "Helped you?" came his skeptical probe. "Then how did you end up here? Why not send you back to her family? He didn't hurt you, did he?"

Theodosia frowned at Sandgrove's choice of words.

Saville's careless shrug belied the hard edge that entered his gaze. "I was robbed by the highwaymen, too."

"I see." Sandgrove gave them an uncertain look. "I suppose there was nothing else to do but seek shelter at that point."

Theodosia couldn't take the tension rising between the men anymore, so she said to Sandgrove. "We also encountered a suspicious group of people on our way and offended them, as well. That is another reason we sought shelter here."

Sandgrove once more reached for her hand. "What a travesty! You must be quite exhausted from shock!"

"Theodosia is exhausted, all right," Field said, dismounting from his horse and sauntering over. She caught his look at their hands again. "But not from shock."

"Saville," Theodosia bit out, shooting a warning look his way while she extracted her hand from the tight grip of Sandgrove once more.

"My apologies, I must have misspoken," the rogue said innocently. "My recollection is a bit jumbled."

She snorted, trying hard not to notice how Sandgrove's gaze flicked between the two of them. "I'd say they more than jumbled," she muttered.

He suddenly grinned at her, and Theodosia's pulse leaped at the glint that spread to his gaze. He reminded her of a cat that found a mouse to pounce on. "Well, I am trying very hard to pretend about—"

"Oh!" Theodosia exclaimed, cutting the scoundrel off. Was he set on causing her heart to stop? "I think I heard Mrs. Bell!"

Not wanting to cause suspicion by lingering, and wanting to get away from Sandgrove's questioning *and* the burning wickedness of Saville's gaze, she turned and made for the kitchen. She made it as far as the door of the house before a hand gripped her arm.

"Why are you running away?" Saville asked in sweet voice. "You and Sandgrove seem quite close, holding hands and all, yet you leave him in the dust?"

She scowled his way. "Are you jealous?"

"Perhaps I am."

Oh, what those words did to her pulse. It made her want to giggle with delight and laugh at the absurdity of it all at the same time. Field Savage. Jealous. Her heart could skip at that thought all day. But because of *Sandgrove*? Because he took her hand? Honestly! "He and I are not close at all!" She poked a finger at him. "And just what were you thinking saying those things?"

A sheepish look crossed his face.

A throat cleared.

Theodosia glanced at Sandgrove, who had followed them. All good nature had left his face. "There seems to be something I'm missing."

Before she could answer, Saville interjected, "Well as you've only just arrived, wouldn't it be normal to be missing nearly everything?"

Sandgrove looked at Theodosia, raising a brow.

Oh, dear lord. Why Sandgrove of all men? She might as well have run into her brothers!

Saville's large body moved, obstructing her view. "She doesn't need to explain herself to you, Sandgrove." He glanced back at her. "You don't have to explain yourself to him."

"She will still have to explain all this to her brothers."

Theodosia could practically see Saville's feathers ruffling and shooting in all directions.

"Are you threatening us?" Saville demanded.

"Us?" Sandgrove's tone turned mocking. "Aren't you just Lady Theodosia's savior?"

Theodosia frowned, stepping out from behind Saville. This was the first time she'd ever heard such a tone from Sandgrove. "Yes, he is my savior. And I daresay our predicament is no real concern of yours."

"How can you say that? When I heard you'd suddenly retired from London—and deduced why—I knew I must call on you in Brighton when you arrived. Thank God I had the foresight to call on your family this morning—you can't imagine their worry. And I resolved to search for news of what might have become of you as I made my rounds today. Who knows what might have happened if I hadn't."

Theodosia stared at the man, not quite sure what to say. What might have happened if he hadn't come here today looking for signs of her? Hah! She might have gotten away with everything. Now, no matter what, her brothers would learn of this, and that she had Saville at her side the whole time.

"What do you think would have happened if you hadn't arrived, Sandgrove?" Saville asked before she could find the words to respond.

"Do you even need to ask?" Sandgrove retorted. "You will be the ruin of her."

Saville snorted in answer.

Well . . .

"Lady Theodosia." Sandgrove turned his gaze to her. "I understand this man saved you, but you don't have to put up with him anymore."

"*This man* takes offense at being called *this man*." Saville crossed his arms over his chest. "Especially coming from a pup with dismal taste in clothes." His gaze dropped to Sandgrove's waistcoat. "Who is your tailor? I shall have to avoid him at all costs."

"Timothy Britton." Sandgrove straightened his shoulders.

"And I'll let you know, he is a tailor with exceptional skill."

"You can say that with a straight face with stitching like that?" Saville arched a mocking brow. "I've heard of that infant Timothy Britton. He is the cheapest in the industry."

Sandgrove puffed up like a pufferfish. "Hogwash!"

What on earth were they going on about?

"Anyone who has done their research on tailors knows this, which is why he is popular with the impoverished."

Sandgrove bristled. "You are a menace on society, Saville. Have you not caused enough trouble? And now you cling to Lady Theodosia."

"Sandgrove," Theodosia admonished.

Saville shrugged. "I'm not offended, Theodosia. If the earl is referring to my involvement in the list, he is not incorrect. The clinging part is true, too."

Her gaze swung to his, and he winked, causing her butterflies to erupt in her belly. Why on earth would he admit to something like that?

"So the rumors are true," Sandgrove said flatly.

"There are so many, you shall have to be more specific, Sandgrove."

"Lady Theodosia," Sandgrove spoke. "I beg to have a moment of your time alone."

Must I? She'd rather just listen to him and Saville bicker. She'd thought before that she didn't want to weave a web she couldn't untangle herself from, well, here it was. The web. And she had no idea how to untangle herself!

Saville shook his head. "That's not happening.'"

"I beg your pardon," Sandgrove said in a huff. "I need to have a word with Lady Theodosia about the blackguards who are best to be avoided at all costs."

Saville snorted. "We were just discussing that very topic before you interrupted us with a nose that—"

"Field!" Theodosia hissed.

Saville shot her a quick glance, but his lips quirked upward.

Oh, Lord.

She shouldn't have outright called him by his name, and one glance at Sandgrove's wide eyes confirmed it. Theodosia pinched the bridge of her nose.

"Well, Sandgrove, if you will excuse us, Theodosia and I have matters to discuss."

The earl's face hardened. "You have such an overbearing demeanor for a man of your ilk. No wonder your father beat you."

Theo's eyes widened. *"Sandgrove."* How could he say such a thing?

Saville's face went blank. "What the hell did you say to me?"

"Ah, Sandgrove, dear," a soft voice entered the fray. "You're here, too?"

Thank goodness.

Saved by Mrs. Bell.

⇛⇚

FIELD SUBJECTED SANDGROVE to his most menacing glare, but he swallowed his fury and held back the urge to punch the man in his face. Memories flashed, and he tried his damnedest to push them back down. He didn't want to falter now. Not with Theodosia next to him. Not with this halfwit's eyes on them. What conclusions would she draw from what Sandgrove had said?

Christ.

He still hadn't processed what happened between him and Theodosia last night, and now he had to deal with this fool? A dolt who was now purposely goading him?

Did he *know* Field?

Despite the emotions raging inside him, Field managed a smile for Mrs. Bell.

"I didn't know you were acquainted with our Sandgrove, here," Mrs. Bell said. "How marvelous."

Field inclined his head. "Marvelous indeed."

"Yes," Theodosia murmured politely. "We are well acquainted."

Sandgrove said nothing.

"Oh, yes," Mrs. Bell said. "I forgot to tell you that your clothing has been washed. I placed everything in your room. Unfortunately, the dress is ruined beyond repair. There is no helping it."

"Thank you, Mrs. Bell," Theodosia said. "We are in your debt."

Field also nodded his thanks. *You are in my debt, boy.* Damn it. He viciously pushed that distasteful thought back into the far reaches of his mind.

The woman laughed. "Oh, it's nothing. You are both most welcome."

"*Their* room?" Sandgrove questioned.

"Quite right," Mrs. Bell said. "No harm, no harm. Family is family."

"Aren't there three bedchambers in the house?" Sandgrove demanded. "What's wrong with the third?"

"It's being used as a storage room, so we placed that bed in the second chamber as well. Why? Is anything amiss?" Mrs. Bell asked.

Theodosia glanced at Field.

He smiled at her before directing to Mrs. Bell, "Nothing is amiss. We have been most grateful you had a room for us." He ignored Sandgrove's narrowed look. But a tiny part of him couldn't help but feel a tiny bit of satisfaction, the vision of Sandgrove holding Theodosia's hand still burning in his mind. Theodosia may have forgotten about his hands, but Sandgrove would not have forgotten about hers. The man deserved to feel rather less sure of himself when it came to Theodosia. Quite a lot less.

What rotten luck was this anyway? He'd only left for a few hours and returned to find a sight that quite literally hurt his eyes.

Quite frankly, it reminded him of her wish to pretend nothing happened. How it might *look* if they didn't pretend. He could play along for a while, but given his well-known explosion after he'd discovered that his sister and his best friend had kissed, he couldn't get past how he seemed to be turning into the world's worst sort of hypocrite.

Warrick would be shaking of laughter right about now. However, he now had firsthand experience of what his friend must have felt like after his sister had rejected him.

What had Warrick done?

Ah, yes. He had acquiesced to Selena's wishes to the point that it had almost killed Field. Should he do the same with Theodosia? The alternative was even more frightening. Damn it, one night. One night and his world had turned upside down.

Sandgrove straightened his shoulders, and announced, "I'll be staying tonight, as well."

Field's eyes narrowed on the man. And now this clod entered the fray.

"That won't do, dear," Mrs. Bell said. "There is no room."

Hear that, Sandgrove?

"I fear it is already growing too late for me to return home. so *we*, Saville and I, can sleep in the room you are using for storage. Allow the lady some space."

Late? What utter nonsense. Field refrained from rolling his eyes in front of Mrs. Bell. "And what shall we sleep on? The floor?" Next to Sandgrove? Not happening. Ever.

"I'm sure we can make a plan," Sandgrove pressed.

"Sadly, I have this affliction where I cannot share a chamber with anyone I do not know as well as I know my own family." And certainly, if he was going to go to hell at the hands of her brothers, which seemed all the more likely with Sandgrove's arrival, he was not spending what might be his last night with the man whose grubby hands had pawed Theodosia.

Sandgrove turned to stone. "Or we could all retire to the nearest inn."

We all? No, thank you. How to get rid of this damn nuance?

"That won't be necessary," Theodosia stepped in to say. "We've already settled in here, and Mrs. Bell has kindly insisted that we stay here as long as is necessary."

"Yes," Mrs. Bell agreed. "Though it will certainly be more comfortable for you if you wish to go find lodgings for the night, my dear."

"And leave Lady Theodosia with London's biggest villain?"

"That's a bit harsh, Sandgrove," Mrs. Bell admonished. "They are family."

Sandgrove's jaw clenched, but his only response was to shoot daggers at him.

"Thank you," Field said, ignoring that look. His gaze touched Theodosia, and he lowered his voice to a whisper. "Did you hear that? I'm the biggest villain in London."

A soft brow arched. "You only realize that now?"

"Minx."

"Hellion," she shot back.

Field shrugged, the tightness in his chest unclamping a bit. "Or a hero, depending on your frame of mind."

Mrs. Bell chuckled. "See, Sandgrove, dear? They are most beloved of each other."

Hear that, Sandgrove?

"Enough," Sandgrove said with a touch of annoyance. "I will stay here, Mrs. Bell, whether I sleep on the floor or the roof."

The older woman sighed. "Very well, dear. As you wish."

The blackguard smirked at Field.

Field turned to Theodosia. "A moment please," he sent a provoking look back at Sandgrove, "in private."

Theodosia nodded. And this time, Sandgrove didn't protest. He also hadn't outed them to Mrs. Bell, but that didn't mean much to Field. Instinct told him the earl had other intentions.

The moment they were out of earshot, she complained, "That Sandgrove. How annoying."

Field's sentiments exactly. He stilled. Then again, how novel to witness an earl other than himself being on the sharp edge of her ire for a change. "Right. I don't get a good feeling from him, either."

Her gaze lifted to lock with his. "What feeling do you get from him?"

"A true weed that's sprouted up."

She laughed. "Really?"

Field lifted his shoulders dramatically. "What can I say? He is an unpleasant sight." Sandgrove definitely rubbed him wrong. "How do you know each other?"

"He has a neighboring estate in Brighton."

It was even worse than he thought. "He is going to send word to your brothers, isn't he?"

"Most likely."

As he suspected. He might as well give up slipping through the fingers of her brothers. Sandgrove would run straight to Kingsley the moment he turned his back.

Theodosia clutched his sleeve and pulled him into their chamber. The moment the door shut, she cast him an uncertain look. "What Sandgrove said . . ."

The tightness in his chest returned. Damn it. "Don't give it any thought."

"It was unforgivably rude to say such a thing."

Field bit down on his jaw and averted his gaze. "But it's true, and even worse than you might imagine," he admitted, almost instantly regretting it. Why the devil did he say that? While it wasn't exactly a secret that the late earl had loved to use his fists on his son, he'd never spoken about it to anyone. Not even Warrick.

"I'm sorry."

He shot her a hard look. "I don't need your pity."

She shook her head. "It's not pity. No child should go through that. Parents should protect their children."

He searched her gaze. Her eyes had softened, but no it was true—no pity was reflected in them. Some of the tightness in his chest eased again. "Yes, well, it's all in the past now. I don't like to talk about it." He paused. "You're the first person with whom I've ever touched on the subject."

Her eyes widened. "Me? The first? What about—"

"I don't talk about the past with anyone, Theodosia," Field interrupted. He needed her to understand that this was not a topic he discussed lightly—he didn't discuss it ever. Not even when he was a boy and his mother nursed him back to health did he utter a word about what he had gone through, even though the bruises on his body were evidence enough. God only knew why he'd opened his mouth to speak the truth of Sandgrove's biting comment into existence now. "Not even Selena."

"She doesn't know?" Theodosia asked softly.

Field shook his head. "She deserved a childhood free of pain and worry."

"What about now?"

"Now it's still not her burden to bear." He would protect her from the truth no matter what. "Our father has been dead for a long time, and my mother is happily married in Scotland. Selena is on her way to being happily married. There is no need to tip a boat in still waters."

"Very well, I understand." Her voice lowered to a whisper. "Thank you for telling me."

Field eyed her askance, unsure what to make of that soft tone. "I didn't tell you anything much."

"And yet it feels like you revealed it all."

Field honestly didn't know how to respond to that.

"We need to leave, don't we?" Theodosia continued after a pause.

Field nodded in relief, both for the topic change as well as what the topic changed to. "He will stick to you all the way to Brighton, or to Kingsley, whichever comes first."

"Then what do you propose? If we just leave, he will also send for my brothers the moment we disappear."

"Yes, how troublesome," Field half muttered, half grumbled,

thinking over their options. There weren't that many, though.

"Any grand plans?" Theodosia asked.

One. "We leave tonight." A smile suddenly tugged his lips. "And we *borrow* his carriage."

Her eyes widened. "What about Dream?"

"We can tether him to the carriage. That's not a problem.'"

She suddenly sighed. "My brothers . . . While I do not wish to be caught by them, it seems that we already have."

She wasn't wrong. If ever there was a time to give up on this adventure, this was it. They had the book, after all. They had completed their mission. But Field didn't want it to end. Not like this. Not before they figured out how to go forward without having to pretend last night had never happened. "What will they do if they find you?"

"Lord, I do not even wish to contemplate that."

"They won't let you out of their sight again, that is for certain. We got the book back." His mind raced. "Now all we need is to guarantee its safety before we face Kingsley's wrath. At least maybe—hopefully—it will make their wrath worth facing."

Theodosia strode over to her cot and pulled the satchel out from underneath. "This book . . ."

"Yes. That book," Field murmured. The object of much vexation. "Now that I think about it, it might not be the worst thing if your brothers are scouring the countryside for you while highwaymen are on the prowl."

She looked over to him. "You mean to use them?"

"Well, it wouldn't exactly be using them."

A sparkle returned to her eyes. "Nevertheless, I take your meaning. We might slip through the cracks." She nodded her agreement. "Where will we go?"

"Are you not on your way to Brighton?"

"That was the plan at first, but . . ."

But . . . a great deal had happened since. "Perhaps we should consider getting the book back to London," Field suggested.

She scrunched her brow in thought. "Louisa should take it for safekeeping. Lord knows it doesn't seem to want to stay in my hands, cursed thing."

"Mortimer should take the bloody book. Seems he should just take it since he is the one who needs it for evidence."

"Yes, but we don't know where the duke is, and I do know where Louisa is."

"Where is she?" Field asked, hoping to the gods it wasn't too far from where they were now.

"Ashford."

"Ashford? What is she doing there?"

"What am *I* doing here?" she countered.

"Fair point."

Field inhaled a deep breath, feeling as though the pit that had formed in his stomach earlier that day was finally easing. "Then we leave for Ashford."

Chapter Fifteen

The next morning

THEODOSIA GLANCED AT the once again brooding earl opposite to her. She supposed it couldn't really be called brooding, since he was resting with his eyes shut and looked more tired than anything else. But not one word had left his mouth since he'd bribed Sandgrove's driver and they had set off for Ashford in the early hours of the morning, leaving a note of thanks for Mr. and Mrs. Bell and the promise to repay them for all that they'd done for them. And that was rather unlike him.

Perhaps he was still out of sorts about his admission last night. Now that she thought about it, he hadn't talked all that much after declaring they would leave for Ashford.

It must be about his father, then.

Her heart melted all over again.

Lord, she never thought this man would have such a painful past. She would be lying if she claimed she didn't want to know everything that had happened to him as a child, but she would never ask him to crack open the painful parts of his soul lightly. Yesterday, he had merely admitted that his father had beat him, but that was more than enough to know that what happened to him as a child was painful to a degree that even admitting to it out loud caused pain.

But he had.

It must have been such a lonely burden to carry. And she would hold that admission dear and share the burden he carried as much as he allowed her to.

On another note—and welcoming the distraction of the thought—servants were too easily bribed.

And if her brothers by some stroke of luck still didn't know that she'd yet to reach Brighton, and that she'd been betrayed by their servants, they would soon enough. Sandgrove would certainly let them know as quickly as he was able—and a few other things besides—and remaining in his company wouldn't do them any favors. They had dawdled and been distracted for long enough—they had a quest, and he was not part of it.

She should have boxed Sandgrove's ears when she had the chance. The man left a sour taste in her mouth after his cruel comment, and just knowing he could tattle to her brothers set her teeth even more on edge. Honestly, what had gotten into the man? What had happened to the pleasant neighbor from the past? Anyhow, good riddance!

And now here she sat with a silent Saville.

It seemed almost miraculous that she had gone from trying to rid herself of Field Savage to voluntarily staying at his side. She never thought such a day would come.

Yet, Field was the least of her worries.

Well, not the least. Her body was so vividly aware of him that goose flesh had trailed over her skin the moment they'd entered the carriage together—alone once again—and continued to flare up again at virtually every movement the man made. Which made her *biggest* worry all the more alarming.

Her brothers.

What would they do once they discovered that she had been alone with Field for days *and* nights? They would be livid. And running off after Sandgrove found them, stealing his carriage . . . Her brothers would never understand.

They would pressure her to marry.

They would pressure Field.

They might do more than that to him.

Now, given what she knew about his past . . . Urgh, she didn't want to think about that! Fortunately, neither of them was the sort to be browbeaten into situations. But neither did she want to fight with her brothers. It seemed unlikely to be helped, however. Consequences had to be faced.

She studied the man across from her. He didn't want her pity, so she wouldn't give it. in any event, pity was the last thing on her mind when she looked at him. In fact, seeing him, understanding him, a bit better now, she found him more . . . endearing.

Her gaze dropped to his lips and flicked across his jaw before lowering slowly to his ungloved hands. Beneath his clothes was a body too magnificent to be described by words. A body that had loved hers to extraordinary heights.

She suddenly recalled his pale look when he'd been nicked with a knife. It seemed rather impossible that such a big, blusterous man could ever faint from the sight of blood. But then, she'd never truly taken the time to try to understand him before. She'd always just found him annoying.

But there was much more to him, a much deeper depth, than she'd first believed. In a way, he reminded her again of Seth— stubborn, overbearing, and so damn *male* that it made her want to grit her teeth most of the time, but beneath all that lay a soft, sweet center.

But enough of this silence!

She narrowed her eyes on him, and nudged his foot with hers. "Why aren't you saying anything? Did Sandgrove anger you to the point that you've lost your tongue?"

One eye shot open. "No."

She arched a brow. "Then what?"

He rubbed his temples, his eyes closed again. "I don't have anything to say, so I'm not saying anything."

Theodosia blinked at him. "That is a first. If it's about Sandgrove and our disc—"

"That fool has nothing to do with it. Nor what we discussed. I'm merely tired, 'tis all."

That could be true. But she sensed something different beneath this exhaustion of his. If not Sandgrove or his admission, then . . . She regarded him a moment before asking, "Is this because of what happened between us? Me asking that you pretend that the matter never happened?"

His lips quirked. "The matter?"

Theodosia grimaced. Well. "What else would you have me say?" That they had made love? The mere word kissed her body with chills.

Hot eyes locked with hers. "*The matter* is our engagement in pre-marital affairs."

Pre-marital affairs? Lord, and here she was worried about the *love* in "made love." How foolish of her. How *inexperienced* of her.

Oh, yes. That's right.

This man must have much more experience than she did, and yet he seemed the one most plagued by what had happened between them. Not that she wasn't plagued at all. There were just too many things to be plagued about. However, one thing she could not deny; she regretted the entire pretending conversation, but it was already out in the air and she couldn't take it back now.

Theodosia parted her lips to respond but shut them when he added, "Let us get one thing straight, however. I never agreed to pretend it never happened."

"I know you didn't, Field." She inhaled deeply before admitting clearly. "I don't regret it, you know."

"Lying little minx."

"I don't!" She couldn't help a smile from forming at the obvious suspicion on his face. "God's truth. I don't regret our pre-marital affair."

"Then why make such a request in the first place?"

"I don't know. I panicked. I was in shock. I was embarrassed at my boldness in the name of freedom. I was most certainly feeling the aftereffects of the gin. It just seemed . . . the best thing to say at the time." For both of them.

"Then how do you feel about it now?"

She met his gaze. "Like I cannot discuss it yet." She wasn't ready for *that* discussion. She hadn't even sorted through all her thoughts yet.

"Why not?"

Because then I fear I'd want to do it all over again. This time sober. This time with all my faculties intact. Where would they go from there?

She gave him a long look. "Let me ask you this, Field. What happens if we *don't* pretend that night didn't happen?"

"I can't just forget out it."

"Meaning you want to do something about it, correct? Like what? There are only three options here, don't you agree? Move on and remain friends, continue the pre-marital affair with unimaginable consequences, or marry and continue an after-marital affair with little to no consequence." Theodosia blinked to herself. Had she just said *after*-marital affair?

Field arched a brow, yet it appeared lined with a smidgeon of amusement. "Well, I can't say the after-marital affair sounds all that bad."

Her eyes widened. "*Us?* Married? The two most hot-tempered people in England? What would our life look like?"

That brow remained high. "What, indeed?"

"Do not give me that tone. We claimed a moment of freedom. You, more than anyone, should know once you claim a moment, any moment, you must live with it."

"But are you allowing any of us to live with it if you wish for us to pretend it never happened?"

"Then pretend or don't pretend, but we still have to live with it separately."

He studied her. "So the choice is my own, but whatever choice I make, it has nothing to do with you. Is that what you are saying?"

Theodosia nodded slowly, her heart pounded in her chest. Do *not* look away. She had to be clear. She already knew how difficult that would be to pretend or to try to forget, because she couldn't free herself from that night either. It had almost completely taken over all of the space in her brain.

But her and Saville?

What future could they truly have? She didn't like him. Or hadn't at least. And he didn't like her. So they had discovered that they were somewhat attracted to each other. That wasn't affection. That was an inflamed sort of madness that would die out until nothing but their incompatibility remained.

She didn't want that.

Perhaps one day they could be friends. Friends who had once known each other intimately. Friends who were bonded over a shared secret. Didn't those sometimes become the closest of friends?

One glance at his face and she scratched that notion. Even if they had started to form a sort of bond, albeit a reluctant one before, it had been crushed by one bottle of gin. Field wasn't the sort of man to be friends with a lady whose innocence he'd taken and who had rejected the possibility of an after-marital affair. It would probably drive him mad, and he would look like he looked now. Rather exhausted by it all.

The aftertaste truly was bitter.

"He might be fool, but Sandgrove seems to be your ideal match, does he not?"

His remark snapped her right out of her reflections. She caught the slight tilt of his lips, as though he was trying to lighten the mood somewhat. Well, he should have chosen a better topic! "Why on earth would you say that?"

"He is a farmer."

"He is *not* a farmer."

"He owns farms."

"He has tenants who farm his land. Don't you own farmland,

as well? Does that make you a farmer?"

He pursed his lips, and some of the tension seemed to leave his face, though Theodosia could never be entirely sure. For all that he felt free in expressing his emotions, his face could be remarkably difficult to read.

"I suppose you are right," he said after a moment. "I'm a farmer, too."

Her heart caught in her throat. "I . . ." She inhaled deeply and smiled. "I cannot imagine you as a farmer." The memory of him atop Dream, sleeves folded back, hair windswept, flashed across her mind. "It's the most ridiculous thing I've ever heard."

"And the country would never suit your vibrancy."

They stared at each other, and Theodosia was reminded of *that* night, when he had looked away, and she had won. She had thought herself powerful at the time. But that power had been short-lived. What did she even win? What was there to lose? This time . . .

She averted her gaze first.

FIELD COULDN'T EXACTLY describe the emotion that pressed against his chest at that very moment, only that it resembled a fiery hot whirlpool of fire and brimstone.

Hell. It felt like hell.

It also felt damn good. But in a way that would bring trouble more than it would bring peace—the threat of an obsession to keep this warmth from burning out. It would run out soon enough the moment they separated.

And they would separate.

She had made that clear.

Damn it. Even though he felt like shite, her *move on and remain friends, continue the pre-marital affair with unimaginable consequences, or marry and continue an after-marital affair* almost made him laugh.

Probably because it was true—those were the options forward. And he might have teased her about each one if had he not, in the little sleep he'd managed to get before setting out, had a nightmare about the late earl. One he hadn't had in years, though it was always the same. He could never recall every detail of the dream in perfect clarity, but what remained clear long after he'd awoken was the sound of fists hitting flesh, bones cracking, and cries of mercy.

Damn Sandgrove.

His underhanded comment was responsible for this.

He peeked at Theodosia, who was staring out of the window in thought. She hadn't given him any pity. Not yesterday. Not today. Christ, that made him want her even more. Even though he was in the mood to brood, one look at her and all the nightmares faded until nothing remained but her voice.

So damn beautiful.

She was not afraid to march into danger for what she believed in. She was impatient as hell, yes, and also had a viperous tongue, but she was trustworthy and dependable. Kind, loyal, and a touch mischievous with those she deemed her friends. She was a partner who would kick foes in the crotch and ride on the back of a horse for hours without complaint.

Perfectly flawed.

And flawlessly perfect.

He certainly didn't want to continue on to be friends. In time, they would revert right back to what they were before. He wanted more—he knew that now. He just didn't know what to do about any of it.

So for now, he'd wait.

He would bide his time until they had delivered the book into Lady Louisa's hands, sent word to the duke, and he'd escorted her to Brighton. That ought to be, if he were a lucky man, enough time to persuade her that a conversation about their mutual options *was* the best option—better than pretending or not pretending. By then they'd have no mission between them then and could talk about how to manage the future with clear minds.

Good plan.

If only patience were one of his virtues.

"Halt!"

Field stiffened, his gaze whipping to the window. "What the hell now?"

Theodosia straightened up. "Sandgrove couldn't have caught up to us, could he?"

"No," Field said. Then muttered, "I never trust a man with such rotten taste in waistcoats to behave sensibly, but I am certain that I left him with no means to be able to catch us."

"Lord, were you a peacock in your last life? Why are you so pompous and proud?"

Peacock? Well, he supposed it was better than being called a weed. He leaned over to peek through the window. "Damn it. I can't see who dares to stop us."

"The highwaymen?"

"I don't know."

She leaned over to peer out the window as well. "If not them, then who? Certainly not my brothers?"

God, he hoped not.

The carriage drew to a halt. "We're about to find out." Field didn't stall like the first time. He opened the door and stepped from the carriage, shaking his head when Theodosia would have followed.

"Wait!" she hissed softly, grabbing his arm while reaching into her satchel and pulling a pistol from it.

Field cursed. He'd forgotten about that damn pistol. He accepted the weapon from her hand and tucked it in the back of his trousers surreptitiously before turning fully and facing two men atop horses, staring down at him.

Not highwaymen, from what he could see.

Not gentlemen either.

They wore rough country attire and both sported beards that should have been shaved months ago. They very much reminded him of the people on the farm outside the abandoned village.

"Gentlemen," Field said imperiously by way of greeting. His tone made it clear: *Why the devil are you bothering me?*

"Sorry to trouble you, sir," the older of the two said. His hair was nearly completely grey. "But I must ask, is that your horse?"

"*Who* is asking?" Field countered.

"Watchmen, sir," the younger, brown-haired lad answered.

Watchmen? In the countryside? Didn't they patrol towns at night? These parts would have parish constables or landowners who kept an eye out for suspicious activities. Instinct warned him. No. Which meant they were more than likely the Black Knight's men or in league with them in some way.

"It's my horse," Field played along. "Is there a problem?"

"This horse fits the description of one that was reported stolen."

What in the everlasting hell was *this* strategy? "By whom?"

"We can't reveal that information, sir."

"Well, there are many horses that look like mine. I assure you, I am the owner. I have his papers."

The gray-haired man nodded. "Do you have the papers with you?"

"Who the hell carries such papers with them?" Field snapped. "Allow me to introduce myself. I am the Earl of Saville, and you can enquire after *my* horse from my man of affairs in London."

"I'm afraid we shall have to bring you and the horse into our offices while we confirm your identity."

They had offices? He snorted. "Are you even watchmen or are you just posing as watchmen?" he sneered. Both men reached for their belts, but Field was faster. His pistol clicked. "I wouldn't do that if I were you."

The men froze mid-action.

Field inhaled a deep breath. "Toss your weapons to the left, dismount to your right, or else I shall shoot now and ask questions later."

"You are outnumbered."

"Am I?" Field asked, glancing to the driver. "The way I see it, we are three against two."

The driver nodded, reaching beneath the seat and pulling out a shotgun. Thank God.

"And I've another in the carriage," Field said calmly. "Do you really wish to take the chance of starting a bloodbath in the middle of a country road in broad daylight?"

"You will be committing the gravest of crimes. We are watchmen."

"But you can't prove that you are, now can you? So I'd be a fool to take your word for it. I'm no fool. Remove your weapons slowly and drop them to the ground."

The men did as he asked, and two pistols hit the ground with a thud.

Theodosia stepped around the carriage and retrieved the men's pistols. Field stiffened, and she shot him a grin. "The more pistols the better."

"How the devil did you do that?" he muttered. "I didn't even hear a sound."

"I can be quite light-footed when the occasion calls for it."

"Good to know."

"Besides," she strode over to his side, "you're the one who said three against two. I'm part of that three."

Field had to admit, Theodosia was impressive on a normal day, but when she was determined, she practically glowed.

"How many more of you are out there?" she asked the two characters.

The men remained silent.

She looked at Field. "We should take their horses."

"Good idea." Field turned to the driver. "Do we have rope?"

He nodded.

Field grinned at the men. "Tie them to the back of the carriage and head to the nearest *real* constable you can find. Tell them we send them two possible highwaymen posing as watchmen."

"You will regret this!" the gray-haired man roared.

"I doubt that."

"Field, what if they *are* watchmen?" Theodosia murmured.

His scalp prickled at her use of his name. It wasn't the first time, but damn it, why did it sound sweeter? "Then I'll be proved wrong. In the meantime, it will keep them off our backs while we continue on horseback." He took one of the pistols from her. "Keep that one trained on them while I untie Dream and retrieve their horses."

"It would be my pleasure."

Field gave them a deadly stare. "I wouldn't act out if I were you. Not even a bit. The lady has a sharp aim." He moved to Dream. "And I have a fast hand."

He tucked two pistols into his waistband—one courtesy of Theodosia and one from these brigands—while he collected Dream and both of their horses. Fortunately, he was no longer in a dress, and Theodosia wore her trousers again.

They had come a long way and made a smart team on the road. All he had to do was make her see that they could be much more than that. And they could be that way forever.

Let's first make it to Ashford.

That damn Black Knight.

He was proving to be quite the thorn in his side. Was the damn highwayman going to follow them into hell if they decided to rush there with Dream in tow? The man had lost all his damn common sense.

Field half wished the man were standing before him now so he could watch Theodosia jerk a knee into his crotch. Wouldn't that be a glorious sight to witness?

Chapter Sixteen

THEY ARRIVED IN Ashford a few hours later, and Theodosia had never been so grateful in her entire life. While the journey had been faster on horseback, it had also been more nerve wracking being exposed in the open instead of in the protected cocoon of the carriage. No, that was not quite right. The cocoon might even be worse. In the carriage, her awareness of Field was so palpable it almost crackled. It was true that on horseback, Field made just as a fine figure, but at least when she was riding, she had her own horse to pay attention to and manage. A bit of a distraction.

Theodosia glanced at Field.

Such a handsome figure.

There would be no need for him to accompany her after this. She could visit with Louisa for a few days, send word to her family about her whereabouts, and then depart for Brighton when she'd had some time to rest and she was sure any zealous highwaymen had finally given up their search. She ought to be ecstatic, joyful, at the thought of finally being able to usher Field on his merry way back to London.

"This is it?" Field asked as he dismounted before Louisa's house.

"Yes."

"We're probably not going to be able to avoid scrutiny."

Saville's eyes swept over their surroundings. Several people were strolling here and there, going about their work.

"Scrutiny was guaranteed the moment we met Sandgrove." As for any others—well, there were already rumors she and Saville were engaged, and Theodosia was having trouble mustering up the strength to care just now.

Theodosia pulled the satchel containing the book and her freshly laundered extra trousers over her shoulder as she approached the door and knocked boldly. Then her gaze returned to her companion. They hadn't spoken much, since traveling horseback made that rather difficult, and his expression gave nothing away of his thoughts.

She should probably be grateful for that.

The door opened to reveal a lean young man. "May I help you?"

"I'm Lady Theodosia King, and this is the Earl of Saville. We are here to call on Lady Louisa. We are friends from London."

The butler dragged his gaze over them, but no emotion showed on his expertly trained face as he said, "Lady Louisa is not in residence at the moment."

At this time of day? "Oh, I must have my information wrong then. Is she not in Ashford?"

"I believe is attending a house party at the Viscountess of Moreville's manor. You may seek her out there."

That she couldn't do in her current state unless she wanted the entirety of England gossiping about her before the last note of the season struck, which might still very much be the case.

Instead, she asked, "Do you know how long Lady Louisa will be at the party?"

"I'm not sure, my lady, but my understanding is that Lady Moreville is hosting a three-day party that started yesterday. I believe Lady Louisa plans to return after the party concludes."

"Then, can we leave something for her?"

"Theodosia," Saville's low voice had a note of warning in it, and his eyes were questioning.

She leaned a fraction closer to him. "This is why we came to this town—to seek our friend out, is it not?"

"I thought you wanted to hand the *gift* over to our friend *personally*."

"I . . . did." She glanced at the butler. But unless they further extended their journey and ventured out to the Moreville estate where the vultures were roosting, she couldn't do so at this time.

The butler seemed to understand. "I shall personally make sure to hand your gift over to Lady Louisa."

Theodosia hesitated.

She hadn't expected Louisa not to be home, nor that she would have to leave the book, and possible evidence of a crime, with Louisa's butler. But the alternative was carrying it along while they had ruffians after them and risk losing the book again.

Or sending it back to London. Theodosia considered Saville. She could have him return it to London while she went on to Brighton. But she already knew he would be unlikely to agree to it unless he escorted her to Brighton first and then returned to London with the book.

No, she couldn't allow that—any of it. One way or another, it was time to part ways.

"I shall think about it a moment," she said to the butler before leading Saville back to the horses.

He frowned at her. "What's on your mind?"

Theodosia inhaled a deep breath. "Let's part ways here."

He visibly started. "I beg your pardon?"

"Let us part ways here, Field. That way, I shall go on to Brighton where I'm sure to meet my brothers, and you take the book to the London to the duke."

He stared at her, his eyes deep and probing. Theodosia wanted to look away, but she steeled herself and held his gaze.

"No." Short. Simple. To the point.

"What do you mean no? This is the best plan."

"What about the Black Knight?" Saville asked.

"He doesn't know what routes we'll choose, does he? And if

he's still searching for us, he'll be searching for two people together—he has no reason to think we'd separate. We should be well clear of him," Theodosia said. "I shall have Louisa's family send me back. I will be perfectly safe."

"I don't like this." His jaw clenched. "We still have matters to discuss."

Matters *she* would still rather avoid at present.

Maybe it was because this truly seemed like an endpoint of their odd journey, maybe it was the relief of finally being in a familiar space after so much danger and running, maybe she was just tired, but she suddenly grinned, finding it all—finally—a bit amusing.

"Why are you smiling?"

"Quite honestly, there were quite a few moments I thought we'd never make it to Ashford or to anywhere safe at all."

His lips quirked. "Me too."

"Thank you for all your help, Field."

The corner of his eyebrow twitched. "Things have been quite interesting in the countryside this year."

"I'd say."

"You trust me to take the book back to London?"

Theodosia nodded her head. "Yes. I'm not nearly as comfortable with the idea of leaving the book with a servant."

His lips pursed. "Is this really what you want?"

I don't know.

"Yes."

A throat suddenly cleared. "Theo?"

Theodosia started and whirled. She hadn't even heard the approach of the oncoming carriage or the disembarking of its inhabitant, so engrossed had she been in their parting.

"What are you doing here?" her friend asked.

"Louisa? Aren't you supposed to be at a party?"

"I was not feeling well and came back sooner." Her gaze drifted between Theodosia and Saville, and she briskly walked over. "Did something happen? Do you need my help?"

"I've come to deliver the *book* to you."

"The book?"

"Yes, you know, *the* book."

"*Oh.*" She cast a quick glance to Saville. "That book." In a whisper she asked, "What is he doing here? And why does he look so . . . *wild?*"

Theodosia glanced at Field. She hadn't noticed before, probably because she'd been in his company all this time, but he did look a bit untamed. A few days' golden stubble coated his jaw. His hair stuck in all directions, windswept from their travels. His shirt was partly untucked.

He caught her gaze and gave her a probing look before turning to Louisa. "I know all about the book. I escorted Theodosia here so she could hand it over to you."

"Why me?" Louisa asked uncertainly.

Theodosia shrugged. "You're the only heiress who hasn't taken a turn to experience the curse, and you also happened to be the closest."

"Curse?" More scepticism.

"The book is a curse." An everlasting nuisance.

"Very well then. Shall I have two rooms prepared for you?"

"No," Theodosia quickly said. "The earl is heading back to London."

A noticeable clench of his jaw. "Yes, I have business to see to."

"You can use my carriage if you want to," Louisa offered.

"No need."

Theodosia watched as Saville turned on his heel, stiffly strode back to Dream, and hoisted himself onto the horse's back. He gathered her horse's reins as well.

With one last look at her, he spurred the horse into a gallop.

And that was it.

She had never expected it to be *this* easy. How could he walk away with so much a hint of a fight? Not even a backward glance as he rode away?

Her fists clenched at her sides.

⟫⟫⟫⟪⟪⟪

FIELD CURSED AS he brought Dream to a halt no more than a hundred yards away from the bane of his thoroughly upended existence. Not far enough to be distant, but far enough to be out of sight.

He dragged a hand through his hair.

To say he'd been startled when she suggested they part ways would be a gross understatement. He could scarcely breathe. But if he left, what did that mean for them? Christ, nothing he ever did seemed right. All he wanted was to . . . was to . . .

Field cursed.

What he wanted he couldn't yet say. Couldn't yet dream of. Fine, he could dream. But without question, what he *didn't* want was to ride off into the sunset without Theodosia.

Damn it.

They'd had a mission. One they completed.

No.

Weren't there still brigands looking for them? This mission wouldn't be over until she was safely escorted to her family in Brighton. He couldn't just abandon it—abandon her—like that. No, by God, he couldn't just leave. It went against every instinct and principle he held dear. It was even more impossible than pretending the night they spent together had never happened.

Field turned the horses and raced back. She was still there— thank God she was still there—just about to enter the house.

"Theodosia!"

She turned, her astonished gaze on him. "Field?"

Once again, a long ripple of awareness shot down his spine at the use of his name. Did she even realize she'd started calling him Field? Just like he had started calling her by her name. They were so damn familiar with each other and yet so still far apart.

He dismounted in one smooth leap. "I need one moment of

your time."

She glanced back at Louisa and nodded. "You go; I'll speak to the earl and follow."

Lady Louisa shot a glance at him before entering the house.

"What is wrong?" Theodosia asked.

Field walked up to her.

How the hell do you expect me to leave like this? he wanted to roar, but all that came out was a trailing, "I . . ." He grabbed a fistful of hair and tugged. "This entire affair is wrong."

She blinked at him, seemingly searching for a response.

"Do you really just want me to leave like this?" His gaze searched hers. *Tell me you do not want this.*

"What is the alternative here, Field?" she asked him.

"The alternative is that we stay together until we reach Brighton."

Her mouth opened and closed, then she lifted her shoulders in a shrug. "Why?"

"Why?" *Steady.* "You might think little of the fact that there are dangerous men on the hunt for us, but I do not. I won't feel at ease until you are safely handed over to your people."

"Is that really what this is about?" She sounded suspicious. Sharp woman.

"What else?" Better not to answer that question if he could avoid it.

"I am perfectly safe with Louisa. I suspect you just don't want to leave without talking about what happened *that* night."

"No," Field said. "That's not what this is about. We . . . we still have . . ." He glanced at Lady Louisa's house. With her back, could he truly claim they still had a mission? "I just want to know . . ."

She looked away then back again. "What do you want to know?"

"What do you want, Theodosia King?"

She blinked. "I beg your pardon?"

"What do *you*, Theodosia King, *want*?"

"I . . ." She stared at him with wide eyes. "What do I want?"

Field nodded. "Forget about anything else. Pressure. Consequences. That damn book. Do you truly want a life in the country? To live in Brighton? London? Do you want to have a family? Start a women's club? Hunt highwaymen?" He inhaled deeply. "I'd love to hear what your life looks like to you."

And hope I'm that life. Hope I could be.

"I . . ."

"It's all right if you don't answer me now, even though I'm about as impatient as you are," he smiled, "and would love nothing more than to push."

"Well then what about what you want?"

I just want you.

"What I want . . ." he stepped closer and leaned into her, whispering, "is less important than what I know."

"And what do you know," she whispered back, tilting her head slightly toward him.

"Your touch haunts me. It's driving me bloody crazy."

She gasped, hurriedly retreating a step and glancing around, her cheeks flushing. "Don't say such things."

"Why not?" Field questioned, grinning. "I need you to know." *And I need to know if it's the same for you.* Any damn hint will do. "And so that you know, so that there is no doubt, even if your brothers christen me, I will never demand we marry."

That earned her a smile. "You demanded it of your sister," she pointed out.

He straightened, nodding. "I've learned my lesson." He wouldn't make the same mistake again. He had no idea what might happen next, but he hoped she was open to exploring.

"Well, your waistcoats will be glad to hear it."

Field stared at her beautiful face. *Do you want to marry her?* It didn't matter, because, at this current moment, *she* didn't want to marry *him.*

"Yes, well, my waistcoats will be safe once Selena moves house."

She looked away, then threw her head back and sighed. A long deep sigh that punched straight into his gut. "I do think about it, you know—you and me," she looked at him, "to the point where all I want to do is forget."

The blow struck his soul. "Is it really so"—he cleared his throat—"bad?"

"Yes," she answered without any hesitation. "Because you and I are two kegs of gunpowder, waiting and ready to explode. Do you wish to spend any more of your life waiting for a match to fall?"

"Then this is the end?" Field didn't want to accept that.

"This is where it must end."

He didn't want to . . . "What if I'm not a powder keg anymore? What if I don't want to be?"

"That would mean you'd have to change. I don't want you to change, Field—not just for this, not just to please someone else. You deserve to be accepted with all your strengths and all your faults, powder keg or not."

Field wanted to protest, but before he could, the word *waste* sprang to mind, and he swallowed back the fire that threatened to breathe through his lips even though he wanted nothing more than to rant and rave and stomp his feet.

Only a waste of a man threw fits over not getting what he wanted. He was no *waste*.

He had to think.

He had to give her space to think as well.

She was right—this was where he walked away. Like a calm, responsible adult. This was where their current journey ended.

"Very well. But I still mean what I said. When you are ready, I'd love to hear what you want, Theodosia."

Her brows drew together. "You . . ."

"Think about it." He inclined his head even though he wanted to pull her into his arms. "Safe travels on your journey to Brighton."

"Goodbye, Field."

He bowed, no doubt startling the hell out of her, before turning on his heel and heading back to where Dream and the other horse waited for him patiently.

If he stayed . . . if he stayed . . . he might do something *wasteful* that would come to bite him in the arse like all his other mistakes.

It was better to walk away now.

Even though he wanted to do nothing but stay.

Chapter Seventeen

"WHAT ON EARTH happened between you and the Earl of Saville?" Louisa said as she plopped down onto the sofa of the drawing overlooking the street.

Theodosia sighed, her heart still frantically beating in her chest. Honestly, what *had* just happened? Her mind still lingered on Field's question in a daze. Had she done the right thing sending him away? She was safe, the book was safe, and he had long ago received the answer he pursued her from London for—everything was settled. How many hours had passed since she'd seen his face—three? Yet his voice still echoed in her ears.

It felt as though a big, gaping hole settled in her heart where it ought to have been full of conviction and life and spirit.

She'd had lunch with Louisa and her little brother almost immediately after arriving, so they couldn't talk freely, but now the two of them were in the drawing room, and her friend's gaze probed her with unrestrained curiosity.

She plopped down next to Louisa, the strength draining from her body.

He wanted to know what she wanted. He'd said he was haunted by her touch. By Jove, hearing Field say such things, ask such things, was like being in a hurricane, ravaging her wits and almost destroying all good sense. That one little sentence, that one question, the memory of his gruff voice along with all the images of that night . . .

She cast a glance through the window.

Your touch haunts me, too.

Would he come back again?

Your words haunt me.

Would she send him away if he did?

Everything about you haunts me.

What on earth did he expect her to do?

What do you want, Field Savage?

"Louisa, let me ask you a question." Theodosia looked to her friend. "What would cause you to decide against marrying a particular man?"

Her friend shrugged. "I wouldn't marry a fortune hunter, a criminal, or a man with too much power."

"Goodness, you certainly know what you don't want," Theodosia muttered. "But men with too much power? How on earth do you determine that?"

"Kings, princes, and dukes."

"Are you saying men with lesser titles have lesser power?"

"Of course not—and I hope I would use good judgement in those cases—but men who are kings, princes, and dukes are powerful by way of their titles alone. A mere mortal such as myself can never compete with them."

"You want to compete with such power?"

"No, I don't want to. That is why I won't even entertain such men."

"I understand kings and prices, but a duke is the most sought after title in the *ton*. Would you not also have power as a duchess?"

"Perhaps, but I've seen too many people abuse their powers. I'd rather not have power at all if there is even the slightest possibility I might abuse it in the future."

Well, to each their own, Theodosia supposed. Yet this did not help her at all.

Louisa tilted her head thoughtfully. "What about you? You

must have a reason for asking me this. Are you perhaps thinking of a certain earl?"

"Lord, no." Yes . . . "We would never suit."

"Well, you are right on that score."

Theodosia's back shot straight. *Why not?* "Then you agree?"

Louisa shrugged. "The earl was one of the main men responsible for listing out our best and worst traits on the heiress list. He also hounded your every step thereafter. You've loathed him forever."

She did.

She had.

Though not so much anymore. To be honest, the book, the hounding—they didn't bother her much at all anymore. If they still did, even foxed, she would never have instigated a kiss that led to a night of fire. Images filled her head again, and she shut her eyes against them.

"So, are you going to tell me why it looks as though you both just stepped out of Napoleon's war?"

"Get comfortable. It's a long story." Theodosia proceeded to inform her friend of all that had transpired since she'd left for Brighton, except for some intimate bits. Though she did confess they'd kissed.

"You kissed Saville? *The* Saville? As in *you* kissed *him*? The man who was outside my house mere hours ago looking like an untamed warrior?"

Well, she wouldn't go *that* far. "Shocking, I know."

"Well, I suppose I can see it happening."

"You can?" Theodosia asked skeptically.

"You are both rather like twin tempests clashing with each other. Such a clash could either have disastrous results or perhaps be filled with explosive passion."

Explosive passion?

She thought back to the night they became intimately acquainted with each other. Nothing about that night had been disastrous. How they both had handled it after—now that might be another story.

"It seems to me I might have been wrong." Louisa smiled at her. "Perhaps you are more suitable for each other than I thought."

"I certainly have much to think about."

What do you want, Theodosia King?

"In the meantime," Louisa said, "you should get some rest."

Field's bow, the look on his face as he left her filled her mind. "No, I must . . ."

Louisa cocked her head. "You must?"

His back as he walked away. "I must . . ."

"Theo?"

Theodosia leaped to her feet. "I must borrow your carriage." She must find Field Savage this moment. Chase him down. She must . . . must . . . tell him! Lord, this was the most ridiculous thing ever. In truth, she didn't know what she wanted to tell him, but she *needed* to tell him . . . something. She'd know the *what* of it the moment her eyes fell on him.

She was sure.

"You wish to travel to Brighton so soon?" A knowing glint entered her eyes. "Or chase down a certain earl?"

Theodosia pulled Louisa up from the sofa. "Well, he has certainly chased me down more than enough times. I see no reason why I can't do the same."

"I don't think you'll have to chase far."

"Don't be so sure about that." The man must be annoyed with her. He was probably well on his way to London already, driven to speed by vexation.

And she didn't want to tarry. Her legs felt restless, as though a thousand red ants crawled over them.

She needed to move.

"My carriage is at your disposal."

"Thank you, Louisa." She tapped the satchel, which had not left her side since she'd arrived. "The book is here. Don't lose it."

"So I just keep it safe?"

Theodosia nodded. "Yes, just keep it safe until further notice."

"I can do that."

"Oh, and if the Duke of Mortimer appears on your doorstep for the book, you can hand it over."

"The Duke of Mortimer? Oh, yes. You said the book is important for a future investigation." She clutched the satchel to her chest and peered through a window that looked out onto the street. "Ah, splendid. The carriage is still . . . still . . ." A pause. "Ah, Theodosia?"

"What? Is something wrong?"

"I don't mean to alarm you," Louisa said slowly, poking at the window, "but aren't those your brothers?"

Theodosia whirled, ducking down out of instinct. She craned her neck to peek through the window.

Lord, oh, Lord.

They . . . How? Here?

"How did they even think to come to your house? I cannot let them find me here!" She couldn't get caught. Not now. Not at this moment. They would demand answers, answers she couldn't give until she had figured them out for herself.

And . . . was that *Sandgrove*? How was it possible that he could even be here? And with her brothers! He was still asleep when they left. Had he woken up and noticed they were gone? Oh, what did it matter, Theodosia? He was *here*! With Seth, Joshua, and Broden! By now Sandgrove would have told them she was with Saville, which would at least account for them beginning their search for her so quickly. But why come here? Unless they gathered that Saville would take her to her nearest friend. Or perhaps they found Sandgrove's carriage and driver.

That might be more plausible.

Needless to say, she was dead. Dead, gone, alive no more.

Her gaze flicked over the faces of her brothers. Yes. Definitely dead and gone.

"What should we do?" Louisa asked, her wide eyes flying to

her. "We need to leave this drawing room!" The words scarcely left her lips before Louisa was dragging her from the room by the arm.

"Louisa." She pulled her friend to a halt. "I need to leave here."

"Yes, of course." Louisa patted her shoulder. "We shall sneak out the back. Then I shall distract them for you while you make a dash for my carriage. What do you think?"

She thought it brilliant.

⫸⫷

SAVILLE TOSSED BACK a brandy and glared at nothing in particular in the tavern he'd come across. He hadn't been of a mind to do anything but stop, collect his thoughts, and have a drink to settle the nerves that wouldn't stop wrecking his chest. Four hours later, he hadn't come to any sort of epiphany. Should he bellow up to the heavens and demand his answers?

Why the hell did his chest feel so tight?

Why the hell did he feel like shite?

And why, just why the hell, couldn't he get that minx from his mind?

Was he in *love* with her?

Field gave the question some serious thought. He'd followed her about after the list had become public to atone for his sins. They had bickered throughout that ordeal, and she'd led him around by the nose more than once. And yet, there was something about her that he hadn't been able to break free from. And when the time had come to move on—the day she'd left London, his opportunity to release himself from the burden of the heavy weight of his mistakes—he'd given chase after her.

Christ in Heaven.

Why else would he think a woman flawlessly perfect and perfectly flawless if he didn't . . . if he didn't . . .

Love her.

He was in love with Theodosia King.

Field slammed his glass onto the table. *I'm in love with her.*

Smitten. Besotted. Bewitched. And not even damn slightly. Head over deuced heels.

He glared at his empty glass, then refilled it from the decanter on his table.

What a shambles.

How could he fall in love with the one woman who loathed him beyond reason? Oh, very well, she might not loathe him beyond reason anymore, but she certainly didn't accept him. If he had to hazard a guess, he would say she tolerated him more than anything else.

The only time she'd ever appeared taken with him was when she'd been foxed. But the next morning she'd been so alarmed by him that she wanted them to pretend nothing at all had happened. As though he had been a mistake.

Field sighed and took another swallow, then he lifted the glass to his eyes. This smooth golden liquid was much more appealing than the sharp, biting, translucent stuff.

What would Selena do if she were him?

Field shook his head. Hell must truly have descended upon him. How else could he ever have come a point where he missed his sister's insights? Plus, Theodosia was her friend, was she not? More than likely, Selena would just torture him for a while and only after that consider helping him.

The doors of the tavern opened and a group of burly men entered.

Everlasting hell.

Could an earl not catch some luck? He ducked his head to the side, averting his gaze.

How? Why?

A familiar feeling filled him. He hadn't seen them when he'd hidden beneath his own damn desk in his study, but he had *felt* their presence. And he recognized them instantly now. Kings.

"Let's get a drink before we decide our next step," one of

them said. Wait. Why did he find that voice so annoying?

Sandgrove.

Field whispered another curse.

Luckily he'd chosen the corner that most reflected his mood—the darkest.

He ruffled his hair, wishing he had a damn cap. Or hell, even a bonnet. But angling his face away would have to do. He could do nothing but stay. Leaving would mean he'd have to rise. And rising meant catching their attention.

My chances of death today just raised a notch. Or six. Or fifteen.

A shuffle of chairs. "Do you think Lady Louisa was lying?" Field recognized Kingsley's voice.

So they had been to Lady Louisa's? Had they found Theodosia there? No. They wouldn't be here if they had.

"Just how the devil did our sister get caught up with that lout?" a deep voice asked.

Lout? Were they speaking about him?

"An apt description, my lord," Sandgrove said. Field rolled his eyes. The man was a toad.

A grunt. "Call me Joshua. And being held up by highwaymen is one thing, but why didn't she come home? Why didn't that arse escort her home?"

Ah, well. Field had wondered the same thing. But there had been the betting book and his horse. Not to mention what he now understood to be his desire to stay by Theodosia's side longer.

"It is clear he's attached himself to your sister," Sandgrove said.

If I am attached, then what the hell are you? I, at least, don't cling. Or did he? He ground his teeth. He was *not* Sandgrove.

"Where do you think they've gone?" Kingsley asked.

Field furrowed his brows. So they believe he and Theodosia were still together.

"London? Brighton?" Another voice—low, constrained—suggested. Another King, but which one, Field could not be sure.

"I don't bloody know," Kingsley muttered.

"Or they might have found another farm or cottage to hide at?" Joshua suggested. "What exactly do we do about the lout? What if he's kidnapped her?"

Kidnap his arse! *You're the lout, you King blackguard.*

"I'll snap his neck," the low voice said. God help him, but Field believed this low-voiced King meant to do just that.

But it won't be that easy, pup.

"Don't worry, we'll deal with him," Kingsley said. "Together."

Then again, there's *that familiar sense of doom.*

"I saw you speaking with that messenger. Did he bring news of the highwaymen who robbed Theo?" Kingsley asked. "The servants responsible?"

Field's ears perked up.

"Yes, Biorn sent word that he and Caleb are working with a constable to find their whereabouts," Joshua said.

Biorn and Caleb—they must be the twins.

"Good," Kingsley said. "I want the maid and driver found and dealt with accordingly."

Good.

"Oh, don't worry, brother," Joshua said. "They shall have their comeuppance."

"What about the sketches?" Kingsley asked. "Can we trust them? Do you truly believe they're Theo and Saville?"

Sketches? What the devil was *this*?

"If they were drawn by the constable's man you've been in contact with," Sandgrove said, "then it's probably so. As I said, he's been traveling as one of the highwaymen himself and would have seen with his own eyes the pair that the band is chasing."

Three curses met Field's ears. He silently added another few in his head. They already knew a lot more about his adventures with Theodosia than he thought they ever would.

"We should be sure it's them. Sketches can be vague," the low timbre came again.

"A woman dressed as a man?" Joshua said. "Come now, Broden. If that doesn't sound like Theo, I don't know what does. But you may have a point about the lout dressed in women's clothes. I cannot envision it as Saville."

"I can," Kingsley's tart tone came.

Field pulled a face.

"Either way, it's still Theo. It must be," Joshua said. "Remember how she dressed up Caleb and Biorn when they were boys? She would put on their clothes and she forced them into hers. Poor twins."

Field raised his glass and took a long swallow.

Good for you, Theodosia.

But having been subjected to that particular nightmare, he had to admit he did have some sympathy for the pups.

"Let's not get off track," Kingsley said. "About the highwaymen—what did Biorn's note say?"

"Well, this Black Knight has his men scouring the countryside," Joshua answered. "The boys believe they followed them, or who they *believe* to be them, to Ashton."

Field frowned.

"Impressive," Sandgrove said. "How did they discover that?"

Good question.

A moment of silence. Then Joshua said, "I believe the note said that there's a farmer, his wife, and their boys looking for two people with similar description—different dress, though. Apparently, Caleb ran into the group."

Those people were still searching for them, too?

Kingsley cursed. "Are you certain? How the devil could you lose their letter?"

"He's an idiot," Low-voice said flatly.

Field snorted, then cursed. Quietly.

If the Black Knight was in the area, in Ashford, then Dream—Dream was a big, fat beacon. At the moment, he was tethered in the dedicated stable outside, out of obvious public sight. But that didn't mean those ruffians couldn't ferret him out.

Then there was Theodosia.

Was she still at Lady Louisa's? Had she hidden under a desk like he had? She would stay at her friend's house until she was ready to leave, that much he was certain of. Unless she believed arriving in Brighton before her brothers would give her the advantage of pretending nothing about their trip had happened.

The simplest course of action would be to hide rather than risk traveling to Brighton and getting caught by her brothers midway there. She would want to hang onto her freedom for as long as she was able. But there was always a *but* with Theodosia King. And she never took the simplest course of action.

And that meant . . .

She was probably on the road.

"Then do we travel to Brighton?" Broden asked.

A short pause. "No," Kingsley said. "We caught up to Theo quickly. Whatever her reason for coming to Ashford, I'm not sure she's had time to accomplish it yet. And you know how determined she can be."

"So what then?" Joshua asked. "We station ourselves on every street?"

"No," Brodan's low voice dropped another octave. "We turn over Ashford first."

"I agree," Sandgrove said, and Field could just imagine that fool eagerly nodding his head. Or something.

"Agreed," Kingsley announced. "We'll put a man on Lady Louisa's house. I'm still not convinced that she was telling the truth."

Field took a swallow and sent a peek to the door.

Once again, he was struck by the same inescapable urge to hunt Theodosia down. Only this time it wasn't to demand answers, or collect fake dues, or settle baseless rumors.

This time he didn't have any false excuse.

But he did have a proper reason: ensure her safety until the very end. At the very least until the matter of the highwaymen and that other posse was settled. He'd do what he needed to do and stay at her side whether it killed him or not.

A drunk man stumbled up from a table, causing his chair to tip over and ale to spill over the person at the table next to him. Field's eyes were drawn to the spectacle—as were everyone else's.

His chance.

Field slipped from tavern.

Chapter Eighteen

FIFTEEN MINUTES.

Fifteen minutes was how long the carriage rattled on before it slowed to a stop. A familiar feeling spread through Theodosia as a memory flitted through her head, one from another day on another country road where she had been stopped by the Earl of Saville at the beginning of her travels to Brighton.

Field? Had he found her even as she sought him?

Anticipation filled her at the prospect of him once again chasing her down. She'd decided to head to Brighton, hoping to all the hopes and betting on those hopes that he would leave Ashford and set himself that way, too. That they can meet on the road again. The man had been following her around for weeks. She refused to believe he would stop now and head back to London just because she had sent him away.

A knock came on the carriage door.

Theodosia pushed it open without thought.

"Well, hello, my lady." Theodosia's breath caught. "Seems my men were correct."

"Black Knight," she breathed.

His face split into a magnificent grin, one that belied the ruffian he was. "In the flesh."

Theodosia stilled. What a rotten turn of events. She patted

for her satchel where the pistols were located, only to come up short. Drat it. She'd left the entire bag with all its contents at Louisa's. She turned back to the man.

"You know, I never believed that man would leave your side. A pity. I was hoping I would find him here as well." The Black Knight stepped aside and extended his arm, inviting her step out.

"What are you going to do?" Theodosia asked, stepping from the carriage since she had no other choice.

"Well, that depends on you." His grin never wavered. "You and your companion are as slippery as eels, I must say. I have never had to work as hard at tracking someone down as I have with you two."

"Why find us at all?" Theodosia shot back. "You received more than enough blunt from us."

"I grew quite attached to the thoroughbred."

Theodosia stared and the man.

He shut the carriage door, patting the vehicle. "And this carriage will bring us a marvelous penny or two."

Lord. Exhaustion suddenly tugged at Theodosia. All she wanted to do was return to Mr. and Mrs. Bell, fall onto her narrow cot, and forget about highwaymen, horses, and betting books. To let her eyes close and be taken by a dream.

About *him*.

Field Savage.

Just where are you?

Of course, it was her own fault she even had to ask that question. She had let him walk away. She had *sent* him away. No matter how Theodosia looked at him, no matter how much she said it was for the best, she wished she hadn't done that.

"*Also.*"

Theodosia caught the bandit's gaze.

"Nobody steals from the Black Knight."

God, can I punch him in the nose?

Just one jab. One.

"Honestly," Theodosia muttered. "Is this the peak of arrogance? 'Nobody steals from the Black Knight,' says the Black Knight who must be permitted to steal from everybody. And just so we get the facts straight, *we* did not steal anything. We only retrieved what already belonged to us."

"And you cannot see how that is a problem for me?" he asked.

"I cannot."

He laughed. "You are rather relaxed for a woman who has been caught by a highwayman—a highwayman who cannot have word going around that his targets are stealing back the things he stole from them. Not only is it bad for my reputation, but it's not good for my business, either."

"Wretched business."

"That feeds me and my men."

That excuse didn't merit a response. Did he wish for sympathy? Then make an honest living! She glared at the man. "And what, pray tell, are you about now? Do you want the horse back?"

"I fear it's not as simple as that."

An ominous feeling chilled her spine. "What do you mean?"

His shoulder lifted in a shrug. "I must make an example."

"Of *us*?"

Theodosia stiffened when he laughed. "Don't worry, my lady. I won't harm a single hair on your head. Your partner, on the other hand—well, I can't say the same about him."

Theodosia glared at the man. "I can't let you do that."

"With all due respect, my lady, you cannot stop me."

He was right. She was one woman facing off against a group of bandits. She could already be considered lucky that they were not harming her. "A highwayman with a conscience," she muttered.

"I'd like to believe so."

"Do you know who I am?" Theodosia asked. "Do you know who the man is that you are after?"

"Titles don't mean much to me."

"Yet you've titled yourself the Black Knight, the infamous highwayman."

"Allow me to correct myself." He grinned. "Titles of the upper echelons of society don't mean anything to me. My own means the world."

"Well," Theodosia said, hoping to Heaven she could buy some time in the wild hope that Field or—and she never thought she'd say this—her brothers might cross her path. On second thought, just her brothers, not Field. This might not end well for him if he showed himself here. "I am someone you should want to know."

"Because your family has money."

"Because I have six big, hellion brothers who all partake in boxing, fencing, and hunting. Three talents they will focus solely on you if you touch even one hair on my head, and by default, Field's."

"You must care for him deeply."

Yes, not that this blackguard deserved to know it. "I don't want his blood on my hands."

"But it would be on mine, not yours, would it not?"

"If you use me to catch him, it's the same thing. Also, I was the one who insisted that we steal back his horse." Amongst other things.

And Field hated the sight of blood. If he fainted, he would be defenseless. She couldn't have that. Wouldn't have that. She needed to escape this. She needed to find Field and keep him away.

"There is no use arguing this point. We shall be taking the carriage now and you with it."

"Theodosia!" came a bellow, followed by the oncoming sound of galloping hooves hitting the ground.

Theodosia whirled.

Field.

He was here—he had chased her. Quite a feat, considering she was the one chasing him. Theodosia didn't understand how this man always found her, but she'd never been so glad, nor so anxious, to see his face.

"Field!"

"Well, look who came to the rescue of his damsel in distress. A true hero."

Field laughed mockingly. "She is no damsel, and I am no hero."

"Well, we can all agree at least that you have been caught."

Theodosia cut a concerned glance toward Field, but the man didn't hesitate to ride straight into the fray, dismount, and stride over to her, placing himself between her and the Black Knight.

"What do you plan to do to us?" he demanded.

"Oh, nothing much. Have my men vent their anger by roughing you up a bit while I take back my horse you stole as well as this carriage."

"You mean to leave us at the side of the road again, this time battered and bruised?" Theodosia demanded. "If you are a man with a conscience, at least don't hurt Field. He'd been shot recently and your man nicked his leg with a knife!"

The Black Knight paused, lifting an arm when his men came to take Field.

Theodosia saw her chance and argued on. "What if he dies from your men venting their frustrations? Do you really want an earl's death on your head? Do you really believe the wrath of his peers will not bear down on you? You shall be infamous, all right, infamously drawn and quartered, a proverbial blood splat on the pages of history!"

Field slanted an inscrutable look her way, while the Black Knight gave an exaggerated sigh. "You do make some valid, if dramatic points."

"Because I am the only one with sense here."

The man laughed. "Very well, I concede. But mark my words, this is the last time I shall let you off." He motioned on of his men forward. "Tie them both to that tree over yonder, Michael."

"What?" Theodosia exclaimed. What madness was this?

"You didn't think I'd just leave you like last time, did you?" the Black Knight said. "I've learned my lesson well enough."

Theodosia cursed the man.

"Don't you dare put your grubby hands on her!" Field growled when one man grasped her arm.

"Cooperate and all will be well," the Black Knight said.

Theodosia tugged at Field's hand. "Let's do what he says."

Field cursed and dragged his eyes over her body. "Are you hurt?"

She shook her head.

"Thank God."

Don't thank too soon, she thought darkly. The bandits were wasting no time dragging Theodosia and Field to a towering oak. The rough bark dug into Theodosia's back as she was forced against the tree. Field was pressed beside her, their shoulders touching, a silent reassurance in this ridiculous situation.

The men worked quickly as they looped coarse rope around them and the tree, binding them tightly enough that escape wouldn't be possible on their own, the rope biting into her flesh. Theodosia could feel the tension in Field's body, which oddly, helped ease her own.

Theodosia couldn't help but wonder how many people had fallen into the same situation as she and Field had. These highwaymen seemed experts with rope.

She glared at the Black Knight. "Ruffian."

"Indeed, my lady," the Black Knight said. "I am a ruffian and more. But be glad I'm a ruffian who doesn't like hurting people. I could harm you, as you and your companion did to my man, but for some reason I'm in a good mood."

"Sir," one of the men said, "should we double tie them?"

The Black Knight considered them before nodding. "Yes, these two have proved far too resourceful. Better to be cautious this time. Focus on their legs this time."

The man nodded and motioned to the other bandits.

"Damn it," Field muttered.

She concurred. "Well, this is certainly new."

"I blame Sandgrove," Field said as the men wound rope around the lower part of their bodies. "If it hadn't been for him, we wouldn't have had to rush to leave the farm and end up caught."

"That's true." But they would have left eventually.

His voice dropped, hopefully remaining unheard by the two men who were fiddling with their knots on the other side of the trunk. "Your brothers are here. In town."

"I know, they came to Louisa's house." She turned her head to look at him. "Where did you see them?"

"At a tavern. I managed to slip out unnoticed."

Her gaze flicked over the Black Knight and his men. "How long do you think we'll be tied here before someone stumbles across us and frees us?"

"Not long, don't worry."

"Oh, I'm not worried. Not anymore."

"Not anymore?"

"I thought they were going to spill your blood today," Theodosia admitted. The thought still made her pulse leap.

"You were worried about me?"

"I can hear the smile in your words, you know." She cleared her throat, suddenly embarrassed. "I was merely worried that you'd faint if they did. However, if I have to be stuck here with anyone, I'm glad that it's you."

"Same," he whispered. "It wouldn't be half as fun or as annoying to be stuck here with anyone else."

They looked at each other, and a slow grin spread from his face to Theodosia's. The highwaymen faded into the background as their heads tilted closer, as though they would meet where their shoulders touched and . . .

The boom of a voice had them both jerking out of the moment.

"What the hell is going on here?"

LUCK WAS DEFINITELY *not* on Field's side.

Six men drew their steeds to a halt and dismounted with a leap, surrounding the highwaymen with grim looks and pistols aimed. Two pistols for each man. So, even though there were seven bandits in this group, twelve pistols were trained on them.

The Black Knight's smile slipped.

This may not end well for Field, but it wasn't going to end well for the highwaymen, either.

Though, quite honestly, given his recent revelations, his own bad ending was never really in doubt. He was on a path bound for misery. And all this was punishment for his sins as part of that deuced heiress list, no doubt. Though all of his friends had found love with the woman on that list, it had to be said.

And Field realized something as the Kings rounded up the bandits—he had held out hope for himself. He had actually held out damnable hope.

Kingsley strode over to them with a gloomy countenance. He motioned with a pistol to the man who had been in charge of securing them to the tree, Michael. "Release my sister. Keep that one tied."

The man nodded and began to undo all his work on the ropes.

"I asked," Kingsley fumed at him, "what the hell is going on here?"

Field glanced at Theodosia as they were being untied. She gave him a small shake of the head, whispering a quick, "Let me deal with my brothers," before looking back at Kingsley. "It seems rather obvious, does it not Seth? We've been held up by highwaymen."

Field didn't dare move as the ropes fell from his body and one of the pups came to drag Theodosia away, while the bandit, Michael, retied him to the tree. The gang had changed but he was still outnumbered, and he was smart enough to know that if he wanted any future with the woman he loved, he would take whatever they issued without a word of complaint.

The pup he recognized as Joshua King laughed in Kingsley's direction. "Well, you did ask, dear brother."

Field sighed. At least one King seemed to be in a good mood. His gaze tracked over the Kings. Kingsley's face resembled pure thunder. The one standing next to Joshua like an ice sculpture had to be the low-voiced Broden. And other two, obviously the twins Caleb and Biorn, appeared serious and ready for anything. They must have ended their search for the treacherous servants and joined their brothers nearly as soon as he'd left the tavern. How conveniently timed. One brother was missing—the youngest one, Francis, if he was not mistaken.

And then there was Sandgrove.

Field pretended not to see him.

Theodosia stepped up to her brother. "Seth."

"Not a word from you," Kingsley growled as his glare raked Field from head to toe when Michael stepped aside with a nod at his revised handiwork. "I shall deal with you later."

"You will deal with me now!"

"Before you two settle into an argument," Joshua pointed at the Black Knight and his band, "what do we do with these thieves?"

"Do we have more rope?" Kingsley asked the other brothers.

One of the twins tucked one pistol away but kept the other trained on the brigands as he quickly checked all the gear of the highwaymen. He tossed all the rope they had on the ground. "We have enough."

Kingsley nodded. "You lot, on the ground," he directed at the bandits. Then he said to Biorn and Caleb, "Tie their hands and feet together, and then bind them together as a group. Make sure the knots are tight."

Field had to hand it to Theodosia's kin—the Kings knew how to settle a matter swiftly. They had subdued the Black Knight and his men in a matter of minutes.

"What about the earl?" Theodosia demanded. "You've made your point, Seth. Untie him."

"No."

And they harbored serious grudges.

"You cannot simply leave him there!" Theodosia exclaimed, and Field could practically see her bristling.

"Why not?" Kingsley asked. "Has he not been doing whatever the hell he wants all this time just like the rest of these brigands?"

"That's not the same and you know it, Seth." Her words shot daggers at her brother.

Field wanted to reassure her that it was fine, but he wasn't all that certain he wouldn't make matters worse if he opened his mouth.

"I'm not debating this with you, Theo."

"If he stays, I stay!"

Field's shocked gaze flew to Theodosia. Her declaration was no small thing. But this was one of her greatest traits. She would never willingly leave a comrade behind. God, he loved her.

"You'd have us leave you here?" Joshua burst out. "With *him?*"

Field held his breath.

"Well, it's certainly better than leaving with you!"

And exhaled it on a bark of laughter.

"What the devil are you laughing at?" Joshua demanded, glaring daggers his way.

Instead of answering that explosive question, Field's gaze dropped to the man's waistcoat. "That's a fine garment. Who is your tailor?"

"What the devil are you going on about?" the pup grumbled.

"Don't answer him," Sandgrove interjected, breaking his silence and striding over. "The only thing that spews from his mouth is insults."

"On the contrary," Field said. "His waistcoat is top notch. It's a John Baily, is it not?"

"How did you know that?" Joshua asked.

If Field could shrug, he would. "I would recognize his stitch-work anywhere."

"Well, you're a dandy one, aren't you?"

"There you go insulting me again. I just love waistcoats. I believe one should always judge a man by his waistcoats."

"That's enough." Kingsley turned to Theodosia. "We're returning to London, and you will be wed as soon as the banns can be read."

"*What banns?*" Theodosia's shocked exclamation mimicked the thud of Field's heart. "What you do you mean by that?" she demanded.

Field cleared his throat. "Yes, what do you mean by that?"

"Sandgrove asked for your hand in marriage. I saw no reason not to accept."

"Seth! That's preposterous!"

"Yes," Field's growl instantly followed. "What she said. What the devil do you mean by wedding her to that fool?"

"I'd love to know that, too!" Theodosia exclaimed.

"I mean just what I said," Kingsley said. "As for you," his gaze burned into Field. Had he been tied to a stake, he'd have been in trouble. "This is a *family* matter. You will stay away from my sister, or we will deal with you as we see fit."

"We should deal with him now," Broden's low, icy drawl came.

Joshua nodded. "I'd love to beat him to the dirt right now, too, but leaving the earl tied a tree with highwaymen to boot is much too appealing an opportunity to let pass."

Damn blackguard.

"Joshua! Broden!" Theodosia admonished. To Kingsley, she hissed, "You can't leave him here."

"Oh, we can, and we mean to do just that," Joshua said.

"What if something happens to him?"

"That is not my problem." Kingsley glared at her. "I suggest you concern yourself with your *fiancé.*"

The words dealt a punch to Field's gut.

Fiancé. And it wasn't him. Bloody hell! Could they even do that? Though wasn't that what he'd wanted to do with Selena? Marry her off to Warrick? But damn it! Then shouldn't they be marrying her off to Field? Why the hell should they involve Sandgrove in this?

He glanced at Theodosia, who was fuming at Sandgrove. Would she allow this to happen?

"Are you merely going to stand there and say nothing?" she demanded of Sandgrove.

"I was the one who proposed the solution," he replied smoothly.

"Solution?" Theodosia retorted. "What utter nonsense!"

Yes, what utter nonsense. She couldn't marry that fool. He had atrocious taste in waistcoats. He had an annoying presence. He . . . he . . .

He wasn't *him*.

Field couldn't let it end like this. He struggled against the rope. "Let me go, you blackguards. Theodosia! Don't you dare marry that fool!"

He lost sight of her as all six men blocked his view of her.

"Why are you doing this, Seth?" her voice scolded from among their ranks.

"Because you are our sister and we refused to see you ruined." Kingsley turned to him. "Be grateful that we are *only* leaving you here, Saville. You'd best not show yourself before my face again. Then I will be obliged to act on what I've learned about you and my sister since my return, rumors or not."

"Oh, I assure you, what you've heard is most likely *not* rumors."

"Field! You are not helping."

Joshua laughed mirthlessly, while the others cracked their knuckles, their faces stormy. "I see you and my sister have moved onto a first name basis. How troubling."

"If you can see it, then why separate us?" Field growled, not even caring that he sounded like a lovestruck fool. This was utterly absurd. Marrying her off to Sandgrove?

"The mere fact that you said that tells me you are in need of separating," Kingsley said. "I don't trust you, Saville. From everything I've heard, and now seen, you are the worst possible match for our sister. She deserves better."

"And Sandgrove is better?"

"Sandgrove didn't have a hand in that atrocious list. Sandgrove didn't cause rumors to taint her name. Sandgrove didn't put her in danger. You did."

Field gritted his teeth. He couldn't bloody argue. But whether he was a good match or not wasn't up for them to decide. And it certainly didn't mean that Sandgrove was any better.

"This is ridiculous," Theodosia's voice blistered forth. "You cannot marry me off just like that."

"I shall make you a good husband, Theodosia," Sandgrove said, setting Field off on a wild curse chase.

"You'll make a terrible husband," Field growled.

"I'll make a better one than you."

"What a deuced joke, you are. Just like your waistcoats," Field taunted. "Be a good husband to *Theo*? Not you, not with her."

"That's enough," Kingsley spoke up. "We'll discuss this after we return to London." He motioned to the others. "Biorn, Caleb, notify the constable that we caught the highwaymen and tell him their whereabouts. He and his men should also have found the servants who betrayed us by now."

Field watched on in horror as the pups nodded and set off. "You're really going to leave me here with them?"

"Are you anything different," Joshua said, "taking what does not belong to you?"

Why not just call him a damn criminal to his face? As a weed, or even a lout, did he deserve to be ranked up there with highwaymen?

What are you even thinking, man? He must have truly hit an all-time low.

Field struggled against his bonds as Kingsley and the others led Theodosia back to Lady's Louisa's borrowed carriage. They allowed him not even the smallest sight of her. He only caught a brief glimpse of the ice sculpture following her inside while the others returned to their horses. Within a few moments they were gone.

"Bloody hell!"

They had taken her and left him here just like that. It wasn't until they left his sight that the magnitude of what happened sank into his bones.

The Black Knight chuckled. "If I'd known you had so many troubles, I'd have left you alone."

"I don't need your pity."

"True." The highwayman sighed. "Perhaps I deserve yours. I must admit, meeting you truly has been my greatest misfortune."

Christ, that sounded like something Theodosia might have said to him at some point in time. "Chasing after me has been your greatest misfortune, highwayman, not meeting me."

"A fair point." Another chuckle. "You must feel the same about me."

"I do not."

"You don't?"

Field just shook his head. How could he regret meeting the man? Granted, the circumstances were unfortunate, but he would not have discovered his feelings for Theodosia had they not embarked on this wild adventure.

Then again, perhaps that was a misfortune. He wouldn't be feeling so rotten now had he not discovered them. Or perhaps he would have. He just wouldn't have known *why* he was feeling this way.

He glared at the cloud of dust in the distance, stirred up by hooves and carriage wheels as they went. They'd taken her away from him, and they'd left him there. They'd bloody left him there. Those blackguards.

I'll get her back.

Chapter Nineteen

Noon, the next day

"MAMA!" THEODOSIA BURST into her home with a determination that would rival any army general. "Mama!"

She rushed straight to the purple drawing room where her mother and aunt usually took tea this time of day. She needed her mother to back her against the madness that had overcome her sons!

"Theodosia, dear," the marchioness said, setting down her cup. "Whatever is the matter?"

"Your sons! That is what's the matter! They have kidnapped me!"

Seth, Broden, and Joshua appeared behind her as three looming forms. She had not been left alone since they retrieved her from Ashford. Broden had scarcely let her out of his sight, and she could hardly breathe from the suffocation of these rascals.

"What do you mean kidnapped? We are your brothers," Joshua protested.

She whirled on them. "When you take someone against their will, it is called kidnapping."

"Are you telling us that you wanted to stay tied to a tree with that blackguard?" Joshua sniped back.

Yes! "I am saying I wanted to go to Brighton. Yet here I am back in London."

Joshua arched a brow. "Isn't that because you are all but betrothed?"

"See?" Theodosia said to her mother. "They are unreasonable hellions!"

"What do they mean tied up to a tree?" her aunt murmured, setting down her cup as well. "And what blackguard?"

"That's not what's important here, Rose," the marchioness said. "What is this about being betrothed?"

Good question! "Your sons wish to tie me to Sandgrove!" Theodosia exploded.

"Sandgrove?" Her mother's brows furrowed. "As in the Earl of Sandgrove?"

"Yes, Lady Kingsley," Sandgrove's voice drawled from behind them as he stepped up from behind Joshua. "Your humble neighbor." He nodded at her aunt. "Lady Rose."

"Sandgrove," her aunt said in greeting.

Speak of the devil and he shall appear.

Theodosia cast the man her most menacing look. She had thought him a kind of friend. At the very least a good acquaintance. But going along with her brothers despite her wishes was the worst sort of betrayal in her eyes. She could not—would not—forgive him. As for marriage, they had better believe she would carve out all their hearts and cause a hundred scandals before she was dragged off to any altar.

She and Field might disagree on a lot of things, but they did agree on some things, including the fact that Sandgrove would make a terrible husband!

Her mother rose to her feet. "This is quite the surprise."

"You don't say," Theodosia said, "which is why I won't have it!"

"It's done," Seth said.

Joshua nodded. "Biddable sisters listen to their family."

"Biddable? When have I ever been biddable?" She glanced at

Sandgrove. "And this is the sort of wife you want? An unbridled, untamed, and unrestrained one? A woman with a fiery temper that will not back down no matter what?"

"If it's you, Theo . . ."

"Do *not* call me that. You have lost every right to call me anything but *my lady*."

He simply remained silent.

Hah! So this was the face of a man who had the backing of her brothers. He need not even utter a word? What a marvelous display of pomposity.

She turned to Seth. "How dare you do this to me?"

"How dare I? That's awfully bold of you to question since you've dared a lot more than we have," Seth said.

"You tied the Earl of Saville to a tree and left in him there with bandits! What sort of person does that?"

Seth sighed. "He will survive."

"Survive? Are you sure? I told you he was shot and fought off highwaymen, yet you still left him there! How could you do that to a fellow peer who has nothing but try to protect me since I was robbed? Is this the sort of men all of you are?"

Seth hesitated.

Good! She'd been shouting and cursing at them since they'd found her in Ashford until her throat hurt, yet this was the first time she'd seen any of them pause to consider her words. Why must men be so obstinate at the worst times?

"We heard you about the duel and the knife wound," Broden finally spoke. "The earl looked fine, though."

Joshua nodded. "Fine enough to glare daggers at us. Be glad we didn't beat him."

"And that makes it all right?" Theodosia demanded. "You left a wounded man tied to a tree with the very highwaymen who were hunting him down and wanted to do him harm."

Her mother and aunt looked at each other, before the marchioness clapped her hands. "I think we might require more tea. Come on, let's cool down. Nothing will be resolved with tempers this high."

"I'd rather not be in the same room with these *sons* of yours. I think I shall go lie down for a bit."

"Wait, Theodosia, dear. Let us settle this matter first." Her mother's smile turned sweet—too sweet. "Unless it is your wish to wed Sandgrove?"

Theodosia's lips tightened into a thin line. That, she refused to do! She plopped down onto a sofa and crossed her arms over her chest, refusing to look at those heathens who shared the same parents as her.

The marchioness also lowered back to her seat. As did her aunt, who asked. "Where are the twins?"

"They still had matters to deal with in Ashford, but they should be back soon," Seth answered, settling into a chair along with the other men. "The constable and I have been keeping each other abreast of developments. He sent word that the maid and the driver that betrayed Theodosia to the highwaymen were apprehended. The courts will decide their fate."

"How did you know to find me in Ashford anyway?" Theodosia had been wondering this for quite some time, but she had been too angry to ask. It couldn't have been Sandgrove. He didn't know. So just how . . .

Seth shrugged. "Between all that Sandgrove told us, word that a highwayman was searching for a man and woman and had even had a sketch drawn up of them, and the constable who had a man in the band, it wasn't that hard to guess you'd go to Lady Louisa, as she'd be your nearest safe haven."

The Black Knight had a sketch drawn up? *You devil.*

"Well, that's quite the adventure you had, dear." Her mother cast Theodosia a look of worry. "And I take it the matter of the betrothal has something to do with this matter?"

Seth nodded. "Sandgrove proposed an alliance to stave off any rumors."

Theodosia snorted. "I don't need his help to stave off anything. Mama, I will not marry Sandgrove."

The marchioness cast a glance at Sandgrove. "What of you, my lord? Are you dead set on wedding my daughter?"

He inclined his head. "I am, my lady."

Theodosia cast him a look of contempt. "Even though I am protesting so greatly?"

"Many matches have started with protests, and many have ended in affection."

Don't make me cast up my accounts. "Be that as it may, I shan't marry you."

"It's for the best." He spoke as though her protest meant nothing. "I recommend we announce the engagement the day after tomorrow at the Greenland ball."

"You can announce it all you want," Theodosia shot back. "I still won't marry you."

Seth sighed. "This is for your benefit, Theodosia. Sketches of you and Saville—the likeness is really quite good—are already being shared around towns and villages. How long do you think it will be before wild tales reach London, even wilder than the truth? We need to get ahead of any rumors that might arise from your little country adventure. I won't have you ruined because of this."

No, only engaged. As if that weren't worse! She cast an imploring look at her mother and aunt.

"I will try my best to make you happy," Sandgrove said.

What was the man still doing here? Was this not a family matter? "You are the last man on earth who could ever make me happy, *sir.*" There was only one man. A man she had never thought she would ever like, let alone love. But she did. She had fallen deeply for that hellion, Saville.

Was Field all right?

Worry still nagged at her heart. He would be fine, would he not? The man was as wily and resourceful as they came. If anyone one could escape such a predicament as being tied to tree with hostile criminals close at hand, it would be him.

He would be *fine.*

Yet guilt still clawed at her. She'd pushed him away in Ashford, but he'd come to her rescue even after that. And yet she couldn't do anything for him now. She hadn't even told him, or given him *any* indication of her affections. Provided he managed to escape both his bonds and the highwaymen, would he even return to London after Seth's talk about betrothing her to Sandgrove?

Field did loathe that man, though. He wouldn't just stand by and allow such a travesty to occur, would he? Her being married to a man with atrocious taste in waistcoats. She couldn't allow it either. So she would do what she could in the meantime while she hoped that Field would chase her down one last time. And this time, she'd be willingly caught.

All she had to do was stand strong.

Not give an inch.

Cause a thousand scandals if she must.

Or, if pushed into a corner with no way out, tell her brothers the truth. That she'd been ruined already. Would Sandgrove want a wife who was no longer chaste? But if she did that, God only knew what her brothers would do to Field then. She would hold onto that card for now.

"Well," the marchioness said. "This *is* all rather sudden."

Her aunt nodded. "I agree. Theo must be exhausted after all that's happened to her. We shouldn't make any decisions too rashly."

Her mother nodded. "Yes, I think it best if we all rest and think matters over."

Thank you, Mama. "I agree," Theodosia said. "Best we *all* think matters over."

Sandgrove nodded and rose to his feet. "Then I shall take my leave and await word about the Greenland ball."

So the man could catch a hint.

Seth nodded, rising. "I'll call on you later today."

Theodosia snorted. To draw up the betrothal agreement? Go right ahead, Seth. Let us see if things go your way. Urgh! *This* was why she hadn't wanted to be in London upon their return. She loved them dearly—in her heart, she really did—but they could be so infuriatingly overbearing at times. And usually, they always got their way.

Not this time, brother.

This time, I will have the last say.

SAVILLE FELL BACK onto his bed and shut his eyes. He had traveled back to London in record time, yet it felt like a damn lifetime had passed.

He had wanted nothing more than to burst into the King's residence upon his return. But he was dead tired, looked like hell, and smelled of sweat and dust. He needed to look his best when he faced Theodosia again.

At least those blackguards had had the foresight to leave his horse with the constable. The authorities had come eventually, but he'd still been tied to a damn tree for hours with that lunatic Black Knight. And, little as he liked it, he was certain the Black Knight so pitied him now that he and Dream would be safe from him from this point on.

Thank all the stars in the heavens that debacle was over and done with. Now he just needed to find out about Theodosia. Had those heathens truly betrothed her to Sandgrove?

Did it end like this?

No.

Theodosia would never marry that dandy. This Field was sure about. Just as he was sure she could never thrive as a country wife in a life that would never do her vibrancy justice. She deserved so much more, so much better.

She deserved much better than *him*.

Field groaned.

What was even the point of barging into her home when she didn't want him anyway? He couldn't allow her defense of him beneath that large oak tree to cloud his senses. But damn it, how was he supposed to practice patience when he missed her like hell?

He wanted her as his wife.

He wanted . . .

A family.

How did I sire a son like you? What a waste you are.

Field pressed both palms of his hand against his temples.

There was that phrase again.

A waste . . .

Damn his father to everlasting hell. He had put that word into his head just to haunt him.

Because weeds were wastes too, weren't they? They grew where they were unwanted, and he was most certainly unwanted by the King brothers. Even Theodosia didn't seem to want him for anything more than what they had become to each other on their mission—and the mission was over.

But she didn't think he was a waste. He knew she didn't.

His eyes shot open and he drew his hands away from his face to inspect them. They were good hands. At least as far as hands went. They had picked apples for Theodosia. Lifted her onto a horse. They had even carried her to the door of Mr. and Mr. Bell.

They weren't wasteful.

Her touch obliterated that one word.

God, Field.

You must really have lost your mind.

Nevertheless, mind lost or not, these hands had suddenly become a bit more precious. Weed, waste, or whatnot, he would still try to win her heart. Because he loved her. And because he loved her, he could no more walk away than he could stop breathing.

A knock sounded on his door.

Field glanced over when Warrick entered. "I heard you were home."

"And you're still living in my house, I see." Field shut his eyes again. "In sin."

"Come now, your sister and I are already married."

Yes, yes. "In your hearts, I know." Field lifted an eyelid to eye his friend. "Just when are you going to marry for real?"

"We plan to elope."

"Of course you do. Why do I even bother asking these things?"

"We were planning to leave tomorrow, but judging by the look of you, we might have to postpone our plans."

"Please don't do so on my account," Field muttered. "I'd rather have you marry than worry about my state."

Warrick sat down on the bed. "What happened for you to get into this state? I've never seen you this unkempt before."

"Ah, well, it's a tale so incredible that it belongs in the category of fiction."

"But it's not."

"It's not." Field sighed, looking over to his friend. "But the end of the story is that I have once again failed spectacularly."

"Or perhaps you just haven't succeeded yet," Warrick countered.

Field scowled. "Wise blackguard, what did I do to deserve such sage words?"

"You are my friend and future brother-in-law."

Field scoffed. "Don't remind me of either."

"Stop fussing over shite." Warrick slapped a paper over his chest.

"What's this?" Field asked, his eyes dropping to a familiar set of sheets.

"The latest gossip rags. Don't you enjoy reading them?"

Field sighed. "I'm not in the mood to read them today."

"Not in the mood? Now I know something terrible must have befallen you."

"Go to hell."

Warrick chuckled. "I would, but then I won't be able to urge you to read your beloved columns."

"What's so damn important about them anyway?"

"Lady Theodosia," Warrick said, almost like an announcement. "The very one you chased after a few days ago."

Field shot upright, grasping for the paper that flitted to his lap and scanning it rapidly for her name. "What about her?"

"She is attending the Greenland ball, and everyone can expect an announcement to be made by her brother. Know anything about that?"

Bloody hell. "Just who would announce *that* in the damn papers?"

Warrick shrugged. "Then you do know what announcement they speak of."

"Yes. That damn Sandgrove! Kingsley is thinking about announcing their engagement." He spat the last word out like a curse.

Warrick brow shot up high. "Is that jealousy I hear?"

Field snorted. What did he have to be jealous about really? Sandgrove would never make it to the altar—not with Theodosia. "Merely a violent impulse that momentarily overtook me."

"Ah. So jealousy."

"Who would be jealous about that fool?"

Warrick nodded thoughtfully. "A fool, eh?"

Selena breezed into the room in the wake of his friend's mild taunt. "Ah, there you are." She raised a brow at her brother, coming to a stop before the bed. "Lord, Field, why do you suddenly resemble that portrait of yours?"

"You mean the one you turned into the devil?"

"Well, *I* didn't do that."

"Right, Theodosia did that." Another reminder of her affection for him that he had nearly forgotten about. Should he go to the ball and intercept the announcement? Would it change anything?

"Should I even ask what happened? We expected you back much sooner." Selena settled on Warrick's lap.

"Can you not do that in front of me?" Field growled.

"Can you answer my question?" Selena snapped back.

Field pulled a face. "The Kings," he muttered. "They caught up to us."

"Ah," Warrick murmured.

"Us?" Selena questioned. "You *and* Theodosia?"

Field nodded. "Who the hell else?"

"Well, you used the word 'caught.' That means there was a reason to use the word 'caught.' What happened? I'm surprised my dear friend even tolerated your surly presence."

"She had no choice. We lost the betting book, had to get it back, and in the end were caught by her brothers." He didn't go into all the other details. Field was sure her dear friend would relay everything in time.

"Where is the betting book now?"

"Ashford. With Lady Louisa."

Selena pointed at the papers. "What about the announcement?"

"An engagement to the Earl of Sandgrove." Warrick filled her in.

Selena blinked, and Field probed his sister's expression, hunting for any clue that Theodosia would ever marry that tasteless clout.

"Oh."

"Oh?" Field's hackles immediately rose. "What do you mean *oh*?"

"Her older brother must have engaged her, correct?"

"What does that have to do with anything?" Field asked Selena. "I tried to engage you but that didn't work."

"Theodosia's situation is different from mine. I only had to fight you. She has to fight six brothers. Besides, what does this have to do with you?"

What did it have to do with him?

He was madly in love with the woman, that's what it had to do with him! Damn it, what do you do when the woman you love not only doesn't return your affection, but was also being engaged to another man, *and* her brothers—six damn heathens—did not approve of you either?

"I need a drink."

Warrick nodded. "Good idea."

"Before the two of you start drinking, at least take a damn bath."

"I'll drink while I'm bathing."

"Well, I'm packing. Warrick must have told you of our plans."

Field nodded. "Congratulations on your elopement."

"Well, we shall be leaving in . . ." she paused, looking him over, "a day or so."

Field sighed. He must be the most pitiful person in the world if his own sister was postponing her elopement because of him. "When is this ball?" he asked Selena.

"Tonight."

Tonight? They were going to announce the engagement *tonight*? He would need some fortitude.

"Better bring a bottle."

Chapter Twenty

THEY WERE ACTUALLY doing this—announcing her engagement tonight.

She stepped into the ballroom, her entire family crowding her. Neither her mother nor her aunt had been able to persuade them. No matter. Theodosia was not worried. Her path forward remained clear.

The moment her brother announced her engagement was the moment she denied it.

Publicly.

If Seth wished to take her choice away, she would damn well embarrass the hell out of him for trying to do so. She would make all of her brothers laughingstocks before she ever agreed to such a ridiculous marriage. What did she care?

In truth, she cared far more about Field and the fact that he didn't seem to care for *her* after all. He'd been so attentive, so constant. She'd begun to think his actions showed affection, but had she been mistaken? Now that he wasn't here, it was clear to see how much of a presence he had been in her life these past few weeks—ever since the list.

Her gaze traveled over the sea of people.

No Field.

But then, would he even be able to penetrate the barricade her brothers had seemingly formed around her if he were here?

He'd be blocked the moment he approached her. She wished her mother could be here, but her aunt hadn't been feeling well this afternoon, so she had stayed back to care for her. The marchioness had, however, told her that no matter what she did tonight, she would support Theodosia.

A hand settled on her arm.

Theodosia glanced to see Selena smile at her. Her calm returned a bit at the sight of her friend. And Field's sister. It was if a part of him had just entered her space. "Selena! I've never been so relieved to see your face."

"Theo, are you all right?" her friend asked. She peeked at Theodosia's brothers before she lowered her voice to a whisper. "Do you need help to escape?"

"Escape?" Theodosia shook her head. "I can't. I have a brother to put in his place."

Selena nodded. "The announcement the papers spoke of."

"Yes, the announcement." And she looked forward to seeing those heathens' faces when she went against them.

Her friend's brows drew together, but she didn't say anything. Theodosia wanted to ask about Field, was dying to ask, but she couldn't make her lips form the question. No news was good news, was it not? Or was it bad news? Either way, asking for confirmation would only feel like pouring salt into a wound.

She was reminded of a time she once said to Selena that her brother made her skin crawl. But what now? What if the man who makes your skin crawl is also the only one who sets your heart on fire? Would Selena think her crazy?

"I heard my brother say that the betting book was lost but you retrieved it."

Theodosia's head whipped to Selena. So Field *was* back in London? Her heart thrummed in her chest.

Did he know that her brothers intended to announce her engagement tonight?

Seth had had an oblique bit of gossip about "an announcement" published in the papers—no doubt as a taunt, should Field happen to see it. And the man could not resist a gossip sheet. Field would certainly put together what it was about.

Theodosia cleared her throat. "And just where is Saville tonight? Seems odd that he is not lurking about."

"He's at home," Selena answered softly. "Sleeping off his drink. He and Warrick started earlier today, though that brother of mine truly outdid himself this time."

What?

Field was at home? Sleeping off drink? This meant that blackguard was not going to show his face tonight despite almost certainly knowing about her engagement announcement.

What an infuriating man.

And the most vexing part was that she couldn't blame him at all. She'd done everything she could to make it clear that she had no interest in pursuing any sort of relationship or future with him.

Even after that night.

Especially after that night.

"Oh, *no*. This is not good."

Theodosia glanced at her friend. "What's wrong?"

"Trouble on the staircase."

Theodosia followed her friend's gaze where a commotion at the stairs caught everyone's attention. What in the world? Was that Field?

Theodosia blinked.

Yes. Yes, it was.

But this was a Field she'd never glimpsed before: a beautiful, chaotic disaster stumbling into the ballroom. He appeared frantic, rushed, and half dressed. He wore breeches, boots, a shirt with a purple waistcoat that was riddled with holes. Nothing else.

Holy Heaven.

The man had lost his mind.

He clung to the balustrade of the stairs, a bellow exploding from his lips. "Theodosia!"

Yes, he had lost the entire damn thing.

"Dear Lord, is he still drunk?" Selena muttered beside her.

Theodosia stared at him wide eyed. "Definitely still drunk."

"Theodosia!" He swayed. "You cannot marry another man!"

"This is far worse than any scandal we heiresses have ever caused," Selena said, glancing around.

Theodosia was inclined to agree. His effect on the room was rather dramatic. Every single pair of eyes had turned to that staircase. Shock displayed on the faces of Field's audience, who all stood frozen with their gazes locked on him. Honestly, it was like watching a wheel come off of a careening carriage and it toppling over. One didn't want to look, but neither could one look away.

"Where is Warrick?" Theodosia asked, eyeing her brothers, whose faces had clouded over with fury. "We need to stop this."

"He stepped out for a bit."

"Stepped out for a bit? Why on earth would he do that?"

"I imagine he's relieving his bladder," Selena hissed back.

Oh.

"Theodosia!" Field bellowed again. "How can you marry another man when you already married me? Did you forget about the farm?"

Mary Mother of Christ.

"I want to marry you, Theodosia King," Saville shouted, almost stumbling over a step. "Only Theodosia will do!"

She caught Seth's furious look her way.

Well, there was no undoing this. At least she would not have to marry Sandgrove now. However, Field . . . Her brothers would, reluctantly or not, march them straight to the altar, after which they might just kill her new husband.

This is not how I wanted things to go.

But then, did it really matter?

He had come.

For *her.*

Her brothers suddenly cocooned her and Selena.

"Get out of my way, pup," Field growled as he made it down the stairs and stumbled toward them. Theodosia cast a nervous glance at her friend. She was rather surprised her brothers hadn't dragged her from the ballroom and away from scrutiny.

Did they actually want this confrontation?

"*People* should know their place," Seth growled.

"You never practice what you preach, do you?" Field shot back, slurring slightly. "You barge into other people's homes, causing them to hide under their desks. So why should I know my place if you don't?"

Theodosia's eyes widened in part horror and part fascination. Just how much had he consumed to lose all sense of self-preservation like this?

"Back away, Saville," Seth growled.

"Oh, Lord," Selena groaned. "By tomorrow he's going to be plastered all over the gossip columns he loves so much."

"Did my brother call on yours?" Theodosia whispered.

Selena nodded. "Four of them did. And yes, I made him hide under the desk. Ah, wait, I think I spotted Warrick through a crack!"

"Is he coming over?"

Selena craned her neck, attempting to get another glimpse. "Yes! I see him, he's coming this way."

Field wasn't giving up, though. "Theodosia!" he called out again. "Get out of my way pups."

"Go to hell," Joshua snapped.

"Fine, you can stop me from seeing her, but you can't stop me from saying what I want to say! Theodosia, listen to me." His voice rose. "You said you wanted to marry below your station! Then marry me! I'm below you no matter how you look at it."

Her breath caught. What was he going on about now? Was this still about country wife thing?

"And if that's not enough," his voice rang out again, louder than before, "you can strip me of my title every night."

Oh, Lord.

He was foxed to a lethal point. To the point that whatever it was that he had drunk might just be the cause of his death tonight.

There was only one way to end this. Only one way this didn't end up in a bloodbath. She needed to draw her brothers from the ballroom and trust that Warrick would take care of Field.

Theodosia turned to Selena. "I need your help."

"Anything," Selena said. "What do you want to do?"

Theodosia grabbed her friend's arm. "Run."

SAVILLE STARED AT the paper before him blankly. His temples throbbed. And not just any normal brandy-influenced throb, but the sort of throb that threatened to split his skull in two. And his jaw. He dragged a hand over his cheek where Seth King had punched him.

I deserved it.

The moment he'd opened his eyes this morning, he'd half wished Kingsley had just ended his life and been done with it. That way he wouldn't have to live with the mortifying memories of last night.

Warrick entered the breakfast room, glancing at the papers before settling in and pouring himself a cup of tea.

"I hate to ask, but are you all right?"

"No, I'm not," Field said, nursing his strongly brewed coffee. "I'm in the mood to brood."

"I would say you look like death, but I wager you already know."

"Go to hell."

"Does your memory match the gossip columns?"

"They always exaggerate," Field muttered, then pulled his brows together as other memories, vague shouts and bellows, raided his mind.

"Not even their exaggerations could truly do justice to the scene and scandal you caused last night, old friend."

Field glanced at his friend, who looked as though he had just risen from bed. "That's only because they don't know what's going on this this bloody house."

"That is why they call it *private* life. You aired all *your* laundry in public last night."

Damn it. "Not all."

"Most of it, then. I daresay you ruined Lady Theodosia's reputation in the airing as well. It was quite the spectacle."

"Why the hell didn't you stop me?"

"How was I to know you would pull a stunt like that? I stepped away for one moment and you wreaked all that havoc. It's rather impressive if I may say so myself."

"You should have locked me in my damn room."

"Had I thought for one moment you would actually commit such a bold affront, I would have. You even hid that damn waistcoat beneath a coat until we'd already arrived." Warrick eyed him up and down. "Why are you still wearing the godawful travesty now?"

"Because it's in tatters, like my life."

Warrick chuckled. "I can't deny that. At least you are still alive."

Field scowled at him. "You drank just as much as I did. Why do you look so sprightly?"

"I assure you, I didn't even drink half of what you consumed. And frankly, I'm surprised Kingsley hasn't broken down your door this morning."

"There's still time."

He'd made an utter arse of himself last night. God, if he hadn't woken up today in that tattered waistcoat he would never have believed the gossip columns about his fall from grace. How was Theodosia doing after all that?

His waistcoat alone could have caused a scandal, but no, he had to be foxed and bellowing out scandalous things along with it.

"I am ruined, Warrick."

"Ah, well, all is not necessarily lost," Warrick said with

amusement.

"She will never speak to me again."

"Do you want her to speak to you again?" Warrick asked.

"Don't act as if you don't know I love the damn minx. It's deuced insulting."

Warrick nodded. "Well, it's about time you admitted it."

"What does it even matter? She hates me. Didn't you see her flee the ballroom last night?" Of all the hazy memories he'd retained, that was the clearest. Just the memory of the sight caused a sharp pain in his chest to flare up whenever it surfaced. And it surfaced a lot. No matter how much he tried to suppress it, it was always there taunting him.

His head, his jaw, and his heart all ached.

"She did flee," Warrick murmured in agreement. "But I suspect that had more to do with her fear of you getting slain by her brothers. They looked like they were ready to throttle you."

"Nothing new on that front. They left me tied to a damn tree in Ashford. Blackguards."

"In any case, this scandal won't just disappear. Something will need to be done."

"I can't do anything."

"Of course you can," a woman's voice breezed into the dining room just ahead of the woman herself—the Dowager Marchioness of Kingsley. "You could marry my daughter."

Field shot up from his chair and flinched. He ignored the pain in his head and said, "Lady Kingsley?"

Warrick rose and murmured his greetings.

She arched a brow. "Well?"

Field cleared his throat. "Your daughter doesn't want to marry me."

"Have you asked her yourself if that is true?"

"I haven't."

"Then how do you know?"

Field frowned. How the hell could he *not* know? "I've been the recipient of your daughter's barbs and rejection firsthand many times."

"But you still love her, do you not?" The marchioness smiled. "You don't have to answer that. The entirety London knows you love my daughter. However, my sons are stubborn, and they refuse to listen to any reason where Theodosia is concerned. But do you still want to marry my daughter as fervently as you did last night?"

Field didn't hesitate. "I do." There can be no doubt about that.

Her grin widened. "Good."

An ominous chill spread down his spine at the marchioness's smile. *Good?* Then why did it feel like the exact opposite? Theodosia smiled like that too when she had mischief up her sleeve.

"What about Sandgrove?" He didn't want to ask, but he needed to.

"Oh, him? Seth is still adamant that the betrothal will go on. Sandgrove is in his study right now."

"Your sons will never approve of me as a match for Theodosia."

"We don't need their approval," the marchioness said. "All we need is you and my daughter's willingness."

Field inhaled a breath of hope. "And you are sure Theodosia is willing? Everything up to this point suggests otherwise."

"We women can be complicated beings. Trust me, I know my daughter."

He was too much of a besotted fool not to snatch hold of this chance. But that didn't mean she loved him, so he needed to remain steady. Calm. Patient. "You will go against those heathens?"

"Heathens?" The marchioness suddenly smiled. "Theodosia calls them that as well. My sons must learn that the world does not revolve around their word. I heard that Seth told you last night people should know their place. He should discover his as well."

Impressive woman. He could see where Theodosia inherited her spark. "I hate to ask this, but short of kidnapping your daughter, how do you propose we do this?"

"I have a plan."

Field and Warrick glanced at each other.

"Please don't tell me you are questioning my abilities," she said with an arched brow.

Warrick shook his head furiously.

"No, no." Field followed suit. Question his future mother-in-law? Never. He was already at a loss after last night's debacle. He would take all the help—any help—he could get. "And this plan . . ." Field said slowly. He was almost too scared to ask.

The marchioness tilted her head to the side, looking so much like Theodosia that his heart pinched. "Well, I believe it is your only option, and we don't have much time."

"What is it that you want me to do?"

"Attend a blind matchup gone well."

A what gone what?

Chapter Twenty-One

THEODOSIA PACED BACK and forth before the shut door of the study where Seth and Sandgrove were meeting. They'd been in there for over an hour. Just *what* could be taking so long to discuss?

She refused to believe it was her betrothal. It shouldn't take Seth that long to sell his dearest, most beloved sister off, should it? But she didn't want to think about her brother, any of her brothers. She glared at the five leaning against the wall, watching—or rather *keeping watch*—on her through lidded gazes.

They were like a pack of dogs that refused to leave her side.

None of them, however, were her target.

She couldn't appeal to them, so she would have to appeal to Sandgrove. Would he listen? He hadn't before. But what benefit did he think he could gain from trying to marry a woman so decidedly opposed to being with him? She couldn't fathom it.

Field had once said the two of them separating was a bad idea. Lord, the context wasn't even the same as it was back then, but Theodosia had to agree.

It was a bad idea then. It was an even worse thing now.

She didn't want to be separated from him.

She also wanted to give him a nice, big slap over the head for last night, then an equally nice, big hug. He'd effectively, and scandalously, caused trouble for Seth and the achievement of his goal.

The door opened and two figures stepped out. Theodosia stepped up to them. "A word, Sandgrove."

Seth frowned but said nothing.

Theodosia led the way to the purple drawing room, and after a slight hesitation, he followed her. She'd quickly become fonder than usual of this room since returning to London. It reminded her of Saville's favorite waistcoat. She almost laughed again at the absurd image of last night. Purple was clearly the man's favorite color.

"Lady Theodosia—"

"I want you to stand down." She chose to be blunt.

He blinked. "Stand . . . down?"

"That's right. I want you to tell my brother you shall not marry me," Theodosia clarified so that there could be not even the shadow of a doubt.

"I cannot do that."

"Why not?" Theodosia demanded.

"Because I truly do wish for you to become my wife."

It was her time to blink at him dumbly. "Why? Wasn't this just a hastily devised solution to a problem you and my brothers decided existed?"

"No, it wasn't just that, Theodosia. Do you know how worried I was when I found you at one of my family's farms with Saville of all people?"

"You know very well he would never harm me!"

"But that's not true, is it? He harmed you last night, didn't he?"

"This may come as a shock to you, Sandgrove, but my reputation and myself are two separate things. I care about myself. I don't care about my reputation. Therefore, the only thing that Saville harmed last night were the delicate sensibilities of you and my brothers. *I* remain perfectly fine."

"Be that as it may, the man has had a terrible influence on you. Can you imagine the depth of my distress when I woke up to find you gone from the farm? To find that you had gone off with *him*? The old Theodosia would never have done anything so reckless. Not even to speak of the fact, which I have been trying very hard to ignore, that you shared a bedchamber with him."

"And why didn't you tell my brothers that?"

"Because then I'd have been complicit in Saville's death, would I not? You know as well as I that they would not have spared him if I did."

Did he expect her to thank him? She snorted. "So you *are* in possession of a conscience."

"Of course. I am not an evil man, despite what you may feel about me at the moment."

Hah! "What I feel? How shall I put it plainly so that you may understand? I don't wish to marry you. Not today. Not tomorrow. Not *ever*." She thought about it, and then ended her declaration with, "*My lord*."

He sighed. "Lady Theodosia, I am aware that you cannot see this now, but this is for the best."

"For whom? Certainly not for me." And the fact that he could not see this confirmed again for Theodosia that she was right. This man was not her match. But with her brothers' backing, he would never back down. This much was as clear as the rain pitter-pattering against the window. "I can see now that you are determined to follow the direction of my brothers."

He shook his head. "I am following the direction of my heart."

"Your heart, sir? How is this the first time I hear about this heart of yours? We are hardly even friends. I don't accept your heart, and I certainly shall never give you mine."

It already belonged to someone else.

But she wouldn't tell him that. She suspected that, if anything, it would only make him more determined to thwart Field. And her brothers might keep a tighter watch on her than they already did. She needed to break free from them.

But how?

Her brothers had her cornered, surrounded in the most insufferable, infuriating way.

That didn't quell her determination, though. It merely strengthened it.

"Theodosia, there you are." Her mother strode into the room with a bright smile. "Oh, dear. Please don't tell me I've interrupted your conversation."

"An interruption I find most welcome."

"I see," her mother said thoughtfully. "Well, Lord Sandgrove, if I might steal my daughter from you, I wish to cheer her up. The whole house has succumbed to a gloom that not even I can stomach."

He inclined his head. "Of course. That is to be expected given the events of last night. Anything to improve the ladies' moods."

Dear Lord, the man was obtuse. How had she never seen this before?

Theodosia glared at Sandgrove's back as he left the room. "Just what are you up to, Mama?"

The marchioness smiled. "Why do you believe I am up to anything?"

"That smile right there. And why else would you also smile in so syrupy a way at my future scandal?"

Her mother laughed. "Future scandal? I daresay we can prevent that, can we not?"

"And just how are we going to manage that?" she asked skeptically.

"Why, by causing another, I suppose."

Theodosia arched a brow. She hadn't seen that spark of mischief in her mother's eyes for a very long time. It ignited her own spark. Whatever her mother was thinking of doing, Theo was ready.

"Are you going to help me run away?"

Her mother nodded. "Yes. Unfortunately, we don't have much time. You leave as you are."

"I don't mind leaving with nothing but the clothes on my

back. However, I have rather more than that. I have six tails."

"Oh, they are about to be occupied."

Theodosia glanced at the door. She wanted to ask how, but then, this was her mother. She would find out all the details later. There was just one point of concern.

She glanced back at her mother. "Where will I go?"

"I already have everything planned out. You do not need to worry. Just follow me to my room. And when I give the signal, you shall sneak down the servants' stairs and a maid will take your place by my side."

Heaven above, had her mother always been this crafty?

"What then?"

"Millie will point you to a waiting carriage. The rest you will see for yourself and decide what you want to do."

THERE HAD BEEN a time in Field's life when he believed being a waste was better than being a father who abused his son.

He had never possessed a good personality. At least, he didn't think so. Though he could scarcely recall how he'd been before his father started using his fists as a method to teach him lessons at the age of nine. But for as long as he could remember, he'd always been mildly irritable, impatient, and quick to lose his temper. And it seemed to him those traits had only worsened with time. There even came a point where Field had wondered if, in spite of everything, he was like his father. Would he one day lay a hand on his own son?

But he had discarded that idea almost instantly.

He wasn't his father.

And even though he had never quite believed he could fall in love, and despite the emotion being so starkly contrasted with his irritable personality . . .

Hope truly did spring eternal in a man's breast.

Perhaps those bad traits would somehow become good or at least lessen—he certainly felt different after these past few days with Theodosia—but in that moment, Field's impatience had him irritably, *restlessly* tapping his foot on the carriage floor.

"Are you sure you are all right?" Selena asked.

"No, I am not." Field glanced at the two people sitting across from him. "And just what are you doing in *my* carriage? Shouldn't you be in your own?"

"We are here to keep you company," Selena said.

"I don't need your company. All you are doing is making my head throb even more with all your not-so-discreet touching."

"I told you we should have given him space, love," Warrick said.

"Space, what space? When you were confessing your love, did he give us any space?"

"I was tied to a damn chair," Field growled. "I couldn't have left even if I'd damn well wanted to. And I did!"

"There seems to be a pattern forming here, dear brother," Selena said. "Being tied to chairs and now trees."

"Chair, tree. Singular."

Selena shrugged. "Now you are going to be tied to a person in matrimony. I certainly see a pattern."

Field cursed.

"Besides, if you are as fine as you say you are, why is your knee jerking back and forth?"

Field froze, slapping his hand on his knee to keep it from starting to twitch again. Damn it. When had he ever been this nervous in all his life?

Hope had sprung up like a seedling in springtime when Theodosia's mother had shown up at his house. A part of him, however, couldn't yet quite believe that the minx would open the door to this carriage and step inside.

And if she did . . .

What the hell did he say? Christ, last night had already been deuced embarrassing. And nothing could cover the swelling on the left side of his face. He looked like a mess. Felt a mess. Was a mess.

He could only hope she would be able to look beyond all that.

And not laugh outright when he confessed how he felt.

"So, brother," Selena said. "You never did tell us what happened on the farm, or even how you came to be living on a farm for a few days."

"Don't bloody remind me about it."

"About the farm or about you shouting at all of London how you had lived on one with my friend?"

Field dragged a hand through his hair, still damp from his rushed bath.

"What else did he say again, Warrick?" she asked sweetly. "Something about Theo already having married him on the farm? Is that a reference to something else, perhaps?"

Field groaned. He was never going to live this down.

"Don't tease him, love. The man has been through a great deal already."

"Very well, very well. I suppose I can wait until Theo spills all their adventures."

Theodosia . . .

Theo.

Field peeked through the carriage window.

"How many times have you peered through the window now? It won't make her come faster, you know."

He did know. He just couldn't help himself.

"Does love always feel like shite?" Field muttered, trying and failing miserably to express this feeling inside.

Selena shrugged. "Only when you do things that cause shite."

Field glared at his sister. "Aren't you supposed to be on your way to Gretna already? Do me a favor, loving sister, and elope already."

"We'd already have eloped if not for your untimely return."

"I don't remember stopping you or Warrick."

"That is true, yet it's also false. And you should thank us. If it hadn't been for Warrick's ministrations and interventions, I might not have a brother anymore."

"Speak some sense, woman."

"I believe," Warrick drawled, "that your sister is saying that your sorry state upon your return spoke louder than any of your words could have."

"I should be insulted by that, yet I can't even muster up the urge. Your concern, however, is truly touching. As are your words. And let's not forget you almost got rid of your brother all by yourself." Field suddenly glanced at his sister, a new thought occurring to him. "Did she say anything to you about me at the ball?"

Selena hesitated.

"What? What did she say?"

"Nothing, really. She seemed to be looking forward to the night. In a way."

"Meaning the announcement?"

Selena shrugged. "I couldn't rightly say. I didn't ask either."

It couldn't be that she wanted to marry Sandgrove. No. If she did, why would her mother arrange all this? Knowing Theodosia, in all likelihood she'd have had a spectacular scandal planned. One he must have foiled with his arrival.

He would have loved to have seen what she'd come up with, and if her brothers had caused trouble, he would have loved to have distracted them so that she could do what she had to do. That, however had never come to pass. And in any case, Field was rather skeptical that he would have attended the ball had he been sober.

Though he probably would not have been able to hold out. Since what a man did when he was drunk, while exaggerated, he at least thought of while he was sober.

Field peeked through the window again, his eyes tracking up and down the street. And then she appeared across the street, such a beautiful sight that Field's breath caught.

She came.

He whipped back and plastered himself against the seat.

"What's wrong?" Selena asked.

"She came."

"You mean, Theodosia?"

"Yes, I mean Theodosia, who else?" He glanced at Warrick. "What do I do?"

"What do you mean what do you do? You are already here, man. Just stay put."

"Should I go and greet her?"

"Let her come to you. That way, at least if someone sees, they won't have seen you."

Right. Excellent point.

"Dear Lord, Field. I never thought I'd ever see my brother in such a state."

Damn it, why the hell wasn't she here yet? Patience, man. Only a damn second had passed. But then, perhaps she had gotten in the wrong carriage, since Selena and Warrick's was right before his. Wait, did she even know he was here? She must have gotten in the wrong carriage. He whipped open the door and half rose to look.

Sure enough!

Field cursed. What rotten plot was this? "Damn it, she set off in your damn carriage!"

Selena burst out laughing.

He glared at Warrick. "Stay put, you say?" Field rapped on the roof. "After that damn carriage!"

Chapter Twenty-Two

THEODOSIA ENTERED THE carriage her mother had prepared for her with a touch of confusion. She was half surprised her brothers hadn't chased after her yet. But then, she didn't doubt her mother's capabilities. The marchioness clearly had a plan. However, this reminded her of the time she had first set off for Brighton. But back then, she had Nancy to accompany her.

Now she had no one.

The carriage rocked forward and she rested her head back on the seat. She wondered where her mother planned for her to go. Should she stop by the Savage residence?

No.

That would be the first place her brothers and that snake Sandgrove would storm if they discovered her gone and her mother failed to hold them back.

She missed the rogue.

She missed him so much.

Theodosia frowned when shouts came from the outside. Could it be . . . Her heart froze up. Surely not? Had she been caught this soon? If Seth caught her now, there was no telling what they'd do. And she refused, absolutely, irrevocably refused to marry Sandgrove. She would ruin the entire family name if that was what it took for them to see reason!

Perhaps it's not them. Her brothers weren't the only ones who could shout like madmen.

The carriage slowed to a halt again, and Theodosia's heart sank.

You tried, Mama.

Theodosia braced herself. She didn't want to be dragged back home. She would fight tooth and nail. They'd have to carry her home if they wanted her to return.

The door of the carriage was wrenched open and she leveled a frosty glare at the person who appeared there, then blinked, her face clearing.

"*Field?* What are you doing a here?" A delicious sense of familiarity skittered down to her toes.

He let out a shaky breath. "You are always running away from me."

Theodosia blinked at him some more, afraid that he might change into Seth at any moment and this would all turn out to be a dream. "You always chase me."

He nodded. "This time, I have permission to chase you, too."

Her brows knit. "Permission?"

"Yes, by some miracle, I have been selected as a blind matchup for you."

Theodosia didn't know what to make of *that*. "I beg your pardon? Blind matchup?" Could it be? "My mother . . ." *This* was the plan her mother had set up?

He nodded. "Is there space for one more? Unless I am another blind matchup you are keen to escape from."

"What nonsense!" Theodosia grabbed Field by his jacket and pulled him into the carriage, grinning. "Get in here before someone sees you!"

The carriage shot forward again the moment the door shut. Theodosia stared at the man before her. She'd never been able to see him properly the night before, but up close she could see that stubble coated his jaw. He must not have shaven for a few days. His right cheek was a bit discolored.

"One of my brothers did this, I'm sure," Theodosia said quietly, reaching out to gently trail over the bruise. "I'm sure it was Seth. I'm sorry he hit you."

"I deserved it."

"Whether you did or you didn't, it still doesn't excuse his actions."

He shrugged, rubbing his bruised cheek. "I'm not so sensitive that I cannot take a blow from that temperamental beast."

Theodosia bit back a smile. *It takes one to recognize one, rogue.* "Just what is going on here? You mentioned a blind matchup? Has my mother set this up?"

He nodded. "You mother called on me this morning to arrange a blind matchup." His gaze searched hers. "You're smiling, but I cannot tell if you are happy because I'm your matchup or *happy* that I'm your matchup."

She arched a quizzical brow. "Is there a difference?"

"A big one."

"I'm *happy* you are my matchup." Her grin widened. "Also that my mother went so far to set this in motion."

"I was just shocked," he admitted. "I never believed she would choose me as a match for her daughter. After all, I'm just a—"

She leaned over to place a finger over his mouth. "If you are going to say anything about a weed I shall add another bruise to your jaw."

The corner of his lips lifted against her finger. "If I ever went on about it, it was only because you were the one who said it. If anyone else had insulted me, I would not have cared one whit about it. But from you it bothered me like hell."

Her heart pinched. "Well, I've come to learn that weeds aren't all that bad." He arched a brow at her. "You don't believe me? Well, some would argue that weeds capture and trap dewdrops to keep the soil moist."

"Are you romanticizing weeds now?"

"No." Theodosia smiled, leaning back into the cushions. "I'm merely trying to state there are good sides to every bad and a bad side to every good."

"Then I can take it that you have seen some good in me despite all the bad?" He leaned forward to rest his elbows on his leg.

"Well, yes. I'm not all good either. Just look around—how many scandals have I caused now?"

"Sweet little scandals. Hardly even noticeable."

"Only you would say that." They stared at each other, and Theodosia's heart thumped at the emotion that filled the depth of Field's gaze. "Well, are you so mesmerized by me that you're not going to tell me what is going on here? This blind matchup? In a carriage? My mother must have shared her plan with you."

"Yes," he said straightforwardly. "I am mesmerized."

Her heart seized. *My Field.*

Now she was the one mesmerized. "My mother arranged this, and she can be a force. You are here of your own free will, are you not?"

"How can you bloody ask me that?"

The sour note in his question made her laugh, and a sudden urge to tease him filled her to the brim. "Are you even sober at the moment?"

That earned her a hot look, but a blotch of red appeared on his cheeks. "I've never been more sober in my life." His voice came out raspy. "So tell me, princess, how do these matchups work?"

Princess. Very well, "I ask questions, you answer them."

He nodded slowly. "Can I ask questions?"

"Possibly, depending on the quality of your answers."

He took on a thoughtful expression. "What if you don't like my answers?"

Theodosia grinned at him. "Then you ask no questions and I shoo you away."

"Ruthless."

"Yes, ruthless. I've always loathed every second of each matchup. This is the first one where I find a thrill of anticipation crawling its way up my spine."

"A thrill of anticipation, you say?"

She nodded.

"Then, have you shooed many gentlemen away?"

"A great many. Every single one."

"Except me."

"Well, *that* still remains to be seen," she quipped playfully. "Usually, we would start with tea, but we don't have that at the moment."

Dark eyes probed her. "Just drink in the sight of me."

"Are you sure? It's pretty haggard."

His eyes narrowed. "Then quench your thirst on this haggard sight, because it belongs to you, and only you."

Lord. Where had this delightful rogue come from? "Well, even though we start with tea, I've never poured a cup for a matchup since the start. The suitors always pour. So, Field Savage, *you* had best 'pour' over the sight of me first."

He grinned, and her heart stuttered once more. Field Savage with such a bright grin. Utterly *savage.* "I'd love to. It's such a beautiful sight. Beyond beautiful."

Theodosia melted. Where was this man a few weeks ago? "Do you wish to marry me, my lord?"

His grin slipped. "I beg your pardon?"

"It's the next step in my matchup ceremonies—my first question."

"You ask this question to all the men you have blind matchups with?" he asked in astonishment. "The concept is already somewhat unnerving, but to ask this outright? It's damn dangerous!"

"And yet, it's quite effective. Also rather informative and quite entertaining to watch the men's reactions." She placed a contemplative finger on her lips. "Every single one has said no."

"Are they damn fools?"

"Fools, yes. Self-tormentors, no."

"Self-tormentors?" He suddenly laughed. "For you, I would gladly endure this self-torment for all eternity."

"Be serious."

"I bloody am." However, his eyes were filled with laughter.

Hah! This man. "Are you saying that you would marry me?"

"In the next heartbeat." His gaze bore into hers. "How would you respond to that?"

"I shall remind you that you would be accepting a wife who is loud, outspoken, and stubborn to the bone, who hates dancing, loves brawling, and has no filter when it comes to insulting the opposite sex."

"A perfect complement to a husband who is blusterous, hot-tempered, stubborn to the bone, who can do without dancing, is not scared of brawling with a woman, and has no filter when it comes to matters he is passionate about."

"I'm not sure," she murmured softly. "It sounds as if we are much too alike."

"Opposites do not always attract." He shifted forward in his seat, drawing closer to her. "I find that the more common the tempers, the more exciting the match. At least, I have confirmed this for myself."

"That exciting, is it?"

"Yes, princess. Without you, I might stay a weed all my life that never captures any damn dewdrop. Only you can give a weed that power. Only *you* can turn a weed into a desirable vegetation."

"Field . . ."

He shook his head. "I need to say this. I can't promise I'll be the best man, but I can promise that I'll catch as many dewdrops for you as I can, weed or not." He pulled a face. "Bloody hell, that sounds ridiculous." He captured her cheek in his. "My point is this: I love you, Theodosia King."

Her hand clutched at her chest. "You love me."

"I love you, Theo. With all my bloody heart."

She swallowed, heat spreading through her body. "Field Savage, I didn't realize you had such a romantic side to you."

"I don't," he said gruffly. "It's just the truth."

"But wouldn't you know, you hellion, you infuriating Earl of Saville," she launched herself onto his lap, looping her arms around his neck, "I find myself loving you in return."

He laughed, and while it wasn't the first time, she had never seen him laugh like *this* before—carefree, unreserved. It was pure joy.

Theodosia couldn't look away.

⫸⫷

FIELD HAD ALWAYS been a man to be overcome with emotions of many sorts. Anger. Annoyance. Envy. Resentment. Longing. Even at times greed. These he was all intimately familiar with. Many of them had clung to him like second skin. But never in his life had he been a man to be overcome by sentiments of love.

Never *this*.

He didn't quite know what to do this rush of *feelings* that threatened to choke him. If he opened his mouth to speak now, a croak would probably be the only sound that emerged from his throat. That was how tightly this love was clamped around his heart, his chest, the very bones of his body.

"I still can't believe you are here," she said after a moment. "That you love me. That *I* love *you*."

"You cannot take it back. Ever."

"I won't. Ever."

His heart, damn it. It wouldn't survive it. Survive her. Field suddenly chuckled. "I still cannot believe you got into the wrong carriage."

"That is hardly my fault. I got into the first carriage. Wait, if you were in the other carriage, whose carriage is *this*?"

"Selena and Warrick's."

"Selena and Warrick are here, too? How? Why?"

Field circled his arms around her. "First, kiss me." Those beautiful eyes gazed into his and he suddenly recalled the careless remarks on that heiress list. "Wait, Theo."

She pressed her temple against his. "Yes?"

"Your eyes."

She pulled back, narrowing them slightly. "What about them?"

"They are . . . piercing. Beautiful."

She cocked her head. "Not Satan's eyes?"

He deserved that. "No, princess. The first time we met, your gaze unnerved me so much . . . the challenge them, the unapologetic mettle. But that was my flaw, not yours. I was a complete blackguard. I was an utter fool back then, and with the list as well."

She framed his face in her hands. "I already know that. I forgave you the moment I vented my spleen on your portrait and snipped your waistcoats."

"You forgave me? Just like that?"

She nodded. "Because I knew you were not a complete blackguard. And now you are the man that I want to spend my life with."

Field couldn't hold back. He captured her lips with his. Their first kiss and been all heat and enticement laced with gin. This time, Christ, this time was so damn sweet, he could scarcely keep from pressing her down into the seat and losing all control.

His tongue traced over the seam of her lips, welcoming their parting and sweeping inside to claim all she offered, her fingers playing with the tufts of his hair. His skin broke out in gooseflesh.

So good.

He longed for this touch, *her* touch, like nothing else in his life.

He had wanted to do this countless times after the night they'd shared at the farm, and now he finally had the woman of his heart, his life, his *dreams*, in his arms.

The sweetness . . .

It stripped him raw.

No moment could surpass this.

Damn it, he wanted to do more than kiss. He wanted to devour her. Kiss every inch of her skin, and do it sober. He wanted to use all his faculties, all attention directed toward making her come undone in his arms again. He'd almost lost this—lost her—and he wanted to make sure she knew now how much he valued her.

Which reminded him . . .

He pulled away from her lips, the sudden question on his mind demanding an answer. "What about Sandgrove? Your mother said he met with your brother this morning."

"That man . . . I even asked him to distance himself from the betrothal, but he refused."

Field scoffed, then dragged his lips along her jaw. "Sandgrove proved *and* reaffirmed that the one thing I believe about a gentleman remains true." He smiled at her.

"Oh? Does it have anything to do with tailoring?"

"A man ought to be judged by his waistcoats."

"You really must have been a peacock on your last life. Speaking of waistcoats, last night. . ."

"Don't even start with that. I'm utterly ashamed of myself."

She lightly nudged the tip of her nose against his. "Just so we are clear, you are ashamed of the tattered waistcoat, not anything else?"

"It was a fine waistcoat before it was snipped to shreds."

She laughed, poking his chest. "You're still not wearing one now, though."

"I've sent word to my tailor to commission two wardrobes' worth of them. I shall keep extra ones hiding in the event that scissors should be taken to any of them."

She nodded. "That might happen, I agree."

"I shall also send last night's one for repairs."

Her brow furrowed at that. "But it's ruined. Completely."

"I daresay it is ruined." He tightened his arms around her, securing her closer against him. "But have you not shown me that nothing is beyond repair? And besides," Field smirked, "it has sentimental value."

The minx had the nerve to dart her eyes heavenward at that last bit. "If you say so." He pinched her chin and pulled her face back toward his. When her gaze met his again, a perceptible smile was on her lips. "I know, I know. When you find something precious, never let go. So then, let us never let go."

God. He kissed the corner of her lips. "Is that a promise?"

"Yes." Her lips found his to brush across. "It's a promise." Then she pulled away just enough to grab his cheeks between her fingers and pinch. "So are you going to confess where we going, or are you being secretive for a reason?"

"No secret." Field allowed her to squeeze his face without protest. "We are going straight to Gretna Green."

Her hands went slack, and her eyes widened to saucers. "We are *eloping?*"

"You can stop the carriage at any time, princess." His hands trailed down her back. "I don't mind going into hiding until your brothers' tempers cool."

"Well, I do. And I do so delight in a countryside adventure."

Field buried his head in her shoulder. "Thank God."

"But wait. Was this part of Mama's plan?"

Field smiled, then nodded his head. "That woman is as devious as they come. I wished I could be there to see how she handles those heathen brothers of yours."

"You do realize, Field, you just called your future mother-in-law devious."

"Don't all men call their mothers-in-law devious? I meant crafty. Definitely crafty."

"Not untrue." She laughed, then pulled him in for a long, long kiss. Field didn't protest, neither did he restrain himself. He reached out bunch up her skirts, his hand trailing up her leg, but stilled, reeling back to look at her. "You are wearing a gown."

"What else would I be wearing? Those godawful Turkish trousers?"

"Don't put it like that. They've grown on me."

"*Really?*" Amusement spilled into her tone. "Unfortunately, my brothers ripped them to pieces."

His hands ran up her legs. "I'll purchase you all the trousers you want."

"No need," she grasped his wandering hands. "Mama is already on it."

"Like I said. Devious." Field nuzzled against her skin. "I would say, 'your poor brothers,' but I wouldn't mean it."

"Let's not talk about those heathens. You said Selena and Warrick are in the carriage behind us? Are they eloping too?" Her eyes widened. "A double elopement?" Her eyes widened even more. "A best friend elopement!"

"I hadn't thought about it like that. Can we divert this runaway marriage?"

"No!" Palms framed his face again. "Let us just stay the course."

"Very well, but only if we can stay on it forever."

"My heart could wish for nothing else."

Epilogue

Thistle and Crown Tavern, Gretna Green

H E WAS MARRIED.
Married.
Him.
Field Savage, Earl of Saville.

And he was married to the woman of the dreams he never knew he had. How does a man's luck become suddenly so supremely magnificent? The barman set four pints of ale on the bar before him, and Field nodded his thanks, pushing a few coins at the man. The deep oak-furnished tavern was lively with the hum of conversation and the clinking of tankards, the air thick with the mingling scents of freshly baked bread and hearty stews.

Normally, the latter would be enough to arouse his appetite.

But Field wasn't hungry for stew.

The only reason he hadn't dragged his wife straight to their lodgings upstairs and ravaged her was that she and Selena wished to enjoy a few pints of ale, claiming they were in need of some fun after being cooped up in a carriage for far too long. He could think of so many *other* things that would be more fun, but what's a man to do when his wife wants to have a beer or two in celebration? He and Warrick could do nothing but surrender to their request.

Field smiled. When last had he been *this* happy?

He grasped two tankards per hand and was about to return to their table when someone patted his shoulder. "Need some help, brother?"

Field glanced at Selena and arched a brow. "I believe I can manage."

Her face split into a wide grin. "You also managed to win a woman's heart with that surly temper of yours."

He scowled at her.

"See." Her grin widened another notch. "A miracle."

"Did you come here to help me or insult me?"

She chuckled. "A bit of both."

"Save it for another day, my wife is waiting for me."

A hand on his arm stopped him. "Wait, Field." Her gaze suddenly turned serious. "Thank you."

Field paused, eyeing her with suspicion. Selena thanking him meant only one thing. "What do you want? Go ask Warrick. You're his . . . wife now."

Her eyes narrowed. "You wanted to say problem, didn't you? I'm his problem now?"

"I would never call you a problem," Field said nonchalantly. "How can you even accuse your beloved brother of this?"

She snorted, but a small wistful smile returned to her lips, almost. "How indeed. In any case, what I want to say is that as we're both moving into the next stage of our lives, I've been thinking more than a bit about past stages. I know you shielded me from our father when we were young, and I've never properly thanked you for that."

Field stilled, his heart dropping to his boots. This was the one topic he had determined never to talk about with her, the one burden he never wanted her to share. Or at least it always had been. But he'd spoken of it with Theo, and it hadn't driven her away, hadn't made her pity him. Perhaps, it might be all right to bend that resolve. Just a little.

He set the tankards back on the bar slowly, and turned to

Selena. "You know about what, exactly?"

Her eyes softened. "I don't mean to bring it up to make you uncomfortable, Field. Only I wanted to tell you that I know the man was not the best, and you had it hard as his heir. I also know you tried your best to protect both me and Mama from his temper, though it came at a cost to yourself."

He nodded, not saying anything for a while. "Mother leaving—"

She cut him off with a wave of her hand, the other reaching for one of the beers to take a sip. "Don't even mention it. I have always been at peace with the matter." She smiled at him. "Because I had you. But if you had tried to send me away at any time, I'd have clung to your neck for dear life."

"Well." Field cleared his throat, attempting to dislodge the emotion that threatened to choke him. "I would never have sent you away. No need to get all sentimental about it."

She punched his arm. "Who is getting sentimental?" She cleared her throat, too. "In any event, the past is in the past. And above all, we are all happy now. That is all that counts."

Field honestly didn't know how to respond to Selena's admissions. Over the years, there had been times that he'd lost all words in fits of utter vexation, but he had never been this speechless at anything before. He didn't rightly know what to do with this tightness in his chest. But she was right. The past was in the past. They *were* happy now. Truly. And they deserved to be.

He grabbed a tankard and downed the ale in one go.

"Are you all right?" Selena asked uncertainly and then narrowed her gaze once more. "I haven't broken you, have I?"

Field scoffed, wiping his mouth with the back of his sleeve. "It will take a bit more than that. In any event, you do not need to thank me. You are my most favorite sister."

"I'm your only one."

The corners of his lips inched upward. "Exactly."

"What are the two of you doing here drinking alone?" a soft, but firm voice interjected, and Field turned to find Theodosia sauntering up to them, Warrick following on her heels. "Have you forgotten about your partners?"

Field grinned at his wife.

His *wife*.

"I could never forget you," Field murmured, pulling her into his arms. "You are rather unforgettable."

She beamed at him.

Warrick placed an arm around Selena's shoulders, his gaze flicking between Field and Selena, but he didn't say a word. He just smiled. But that smile said more than the lengthiest of conversations.

Field suddenly chuckled, then burst into low laughter. Happiness seeped into his bones.

This was his family.

He would protect them with his life and love them every day of it.

The End

About the Author

Tanya Wilde is an Award-Winning author that developed a passion for reading when she had nothing better to do than lurk in the library during her lunch breaks. Her blazing love affair with pen and paper soon followed after she devoured all their historical romance books! In 2020, she won the Romance Writers Organization of South Africa (ROSA) Imbali Award for Excellence in Romance Writing for Not Quite a Rogue.

When she's not meddling in the lives of her characters or pondering names for her imaginary big, white greyhound, she's off on adventures with her partner in crime.

Wilde lives in a small town at the foot of the Outeniqua Mountains, South Africa.

Website – www.authortanyawilde.com
Instagram – instagram.com/tanyawilde
Facebook – facebook.com/groups/843373666456177
BookBub – bookbub.com/authors/tanya-wilde